Wixumlee
Is My
Salvation

Georgia Ann Mullen

Georgia A Mullen

First published by Dog Ear Publishing
4010 W. 86th Street, Ste H
Indianapolis, IN 46268
www.dogearpublishing.net

ISBN: 978-160844-472-4

This book is printed on acid-free paper.

Printed in the United States of America

To my grandson, Elijah

Other books
by Georgia Ann Mullen

A Shocking & Unnatural Incident

Historical fiction about three young women whose lives reflect
the issues leading up to the First Woman's Rights Convention
in Seneca Falls, New York in 1848

Temperance · Abolition · Female sovereignty

Book One in the Canal Tales Series

Praise for
A Shocking & Unnatural Incident

The pace of the book is quick, but becomes almost frenetic as we near the end. Indeed, events happen so quickly that the story grabbed me and dragged me to the final pages almost faster than I could read. The ending was...shocking...

I was impressed with Mullen's ability to make the characters accessible. Yes, these people are multiple generations in our past, but they seemed quite real. Mullen's perspective on women's lives more than a century and a half ago and use of events associated with the first public women's rights conference completely fascinated me...

— Historical fiction reviewer Lonnie Holder
on Amazon.com

This morning, sometime around 1:30, I finished A Shocking & Unnatural Incident. *Indeed shocking! Wonderful! Moving! A stay-with-it read. Tess moves the story forward with a zeal matched by her intelligence and desperate desire to get away from her circumstances. She is surrounded by well-drawn people who, in different ways, both advance and impede her efforts. Wow!*
Written in a brisk style, the adventures of Tess, Beany and Lucy pull the reader into the era. This was an age when women were locked in insane asylums for speaking out. And Tess speaks out. Shocking? Yes. Unnatural? Yes. Don't miss this great, page-turning read.

— Historical fiction author Blonnie Bunn Wyche
The Anchor - P. Moore, Proprietor
Cecilia's Harvest, A Novel of the Revolution

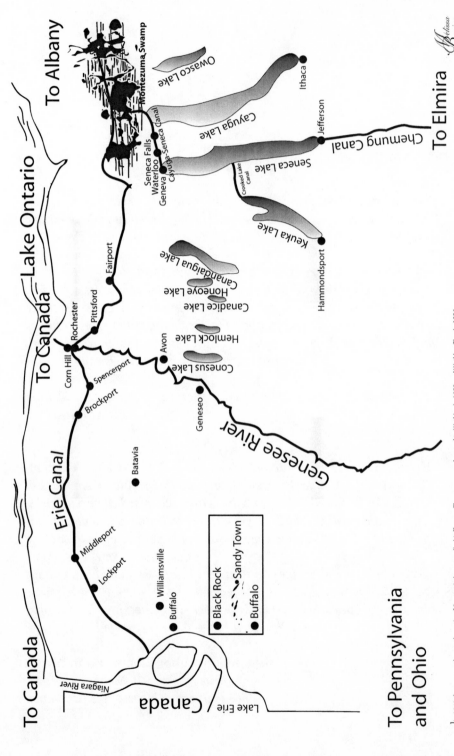

To Albany

To Canada

Lake Ontario

To Canada

To Canada

Lake Erie

Canada

Niagara River

Erie Canal

To Pennsylvania and Ohio

To Elmira

Chemung Canal

Montezuma Swamp

Owasco Lake

Cayuga Lake

Ithaca

Jefferson

Seneca Lake

Crooked Lake Canal

Keuka Lake

Hammondsport

Cayuga-Seneca Canal

Seneca Falls

Waterloo

Geneva

Fairport

Pittsford

Rochester

Corn Hill

Spencerport

Brockport

Avon

Canandaigua Lake

Honeoye Lake

Canadice Lake

Hemlock Lake

Conesus Lake

Geneseo

Genesee River

Batavia

Middleport

Lockport

Williamsville

Buffalo

Black Rock

Sandy Town

Buffalo

[1] In 1848 the town at the southern tip of Seneca Lake was called Jefferson. The name was changed to Watkins in 1852 and Watkins Glen in 1926.

Black Rock Pork

I shipped aboard of a lumber boat
Her name was Charles O'Rourke.
And the very first thing that they rolled on board
Was a barrel of Black Rock Pork.

They fried a chunk for breakfast,
And a chunk for luncheon, too.
It didn't taste so goody-good,
And it was hard to chew.

From Buffalo to old New York,
They fed it to dear old me.
They boiled the barrel and the rest of the pork,
And we had it all for tea.

About three days out, we struck a rock
Of Lackawanna coal.
It gave the boat quite a shock,
And stove in quite a hole.

So I hollered at the driver
Who was off a-treadin' dirt;
He jumped aboard and stopped the leak
With his crumby undershirt.

Now the cook upon this canal boat
Stood six feet in her socks;
She had a bosom like a box-car,
And her breath would open the locks.

Now the cook is in the poor-house,
And the crew is all in jail,
And I'm the only canaller
That is left to tell the tale.

from *Canal Water and Whiskey*
by Marvin A. Rapp

GLOSSARY

Canal Terms Used in This Book

aqueduct A structure that carries a canal across another body of water. The Rochester Aqueduct spanned the Genesee River for more than 800 feet and was the world's largest.

Black Rock In 1851 Black Rock was a vigorous Erie Canal town located about two miles north of its rival Buffalo. The town was named after a large, triangular shelf of dark limestone that once protruded two hundred feet from shore and rose four to five feet above the water. The huge rock was sheltered from river current and was an ideal place to dock boats and the oar-propelled ferry that crossed the water to Canada. In the early 1820s the dark limestone was blasted away during construction of the Erie Canal bed that ran parallel to the shore and advanced by way of the Buffalo River to Buffalo Harbor. The City of Buffalo annexed the town of Black Rock in 1854.

Canal Street The seediest street in Buffalo, crowded with saloons, blacklegged gamblers and the crookedest crooks.

canawler Standard pronunciation for the name given to a person who worked on a canal (or canawl). Of possible Dutch or Irish derivation.

cuttin' didoes Get into mischief.

Commercial Slip A remnant of Little Buffalo Creek, the Slip flowed into the Buffalo River just before the larger stream entered Lake Erie. The Commercial Slip formed one boundary of Buffalo's infamous Canal District and was a crowded, bustling center of commerce.

Erie Canal Harbor For much of the 19th century, Buffalo's Erie Canal Harbor served as the "portal to the west" for passengers and goods moving from the East Coast across the Great Lakes. Buffalo's Canal Street was a stone's throw from the canal terminus.

foofoos Foreigners or immigrant workers.

hoggee A mule driver, usually young boys, who earned low wages.

mule The sterile offspring of a male donkey and a female horse; sometimes called a long-eared robin.

packet A canal passenger boat that traveled about four miles an hour and was horse-drawn.

rhino Ready money, cash. A person with lots of cash was rhino fat.

runners/scalpers Agents or young boys hired to secure passengers or cargo.

Sandy Town A stretch of sand between Buffalo and Black Rock where the space between the Erie Canal and Lake Erie widened.

snubbing post A sturdy post along the canal berm used to tie up canal boats.

soaplocks A haircut popular with young men that was short in the back and long on the sides.

towpath A path along the canal trod by mules or horses towing boats.

Author's Note

In 1851 the town of Black Rock was a vibrant Erie Canal port. Thirty years earlier it had fought to be named the Erie Canal terminus but lost that honor to its rival, the city of Buffalo, two miles south. Because of its strategic position across the Niagara River from Canada, Black Rock was an important crossing place for slaves escaping via the Underground Railroad.

Rochester's first waterfall in a series of three was a bit closer to the aqueduct that carried the Erie Canal over the Genesee River than is portrayed in this story.

All characters in this book are fictional except for Harriet Tubman, Elizabeth Cady Stanton, Amelia Bloomer, Henry Stanton, Frederick Douglass and Gerrit Smith. The western New York towns and cities mentioned are genuine locations. Sandy Town was the name given to a stretch of sand between Lake Erie and the Erie Canal. Some aspects of this story have been inspired by old canal tales.

CHAPTER ONE

"Ride the *Dark Shadow*! Best rates! Best ride!"

I stand in the center of towpath tumult hawking tickets, keeping Beany in the corner of my eye.

Cargo boats bang against docks. Crates crash onto decks. Canawlers curse. Gulls scream. Wild-eyed sailors itch to fight. Fearful foreigners fumble for coins and each other, falling off packets stuffed with foofoo paraphernalia. The grinding racket of water on wood, wood on metal, metal on rock, fist on face shreds the few nerves I have left.

This is Black Rock, a town still furious Buffalo stole the terminus title—end of the Erie Canal. If Black Rock throws this much terror, what's Buffalo like?

"Now, what's wrong with this little gal?" The tall, blond woman stops in the middle of the teeming towpath. Travelers dragging heavy satchels ooze around her then bear down on packets thumping against the dock. She peers at the scrawny colored girl slumped against a snubbing post.

I step in front of Beany. "Nothin's wrong—Ride the *Dark Shadow*! Best ride on the Erie!"

The woman steps around me, bends down and squints at Beany. "Sure there is. What's wrong, darlin'? You sad about something?"

I block her again. "Leave her alone!—*Dark Shadow* here! Fastest packet on the Erie! Get your tickets now!" I keep one eye on the large woman and the other on the line of bewildered foofoos stumbling over their own feet.

"Tess Riley! Stop your jawing and sell my tickets!" Captain Cross' shout from the packet deck chills my heart. "Ain't paying you to stand and gab, girl."

"Let me look at you, honey." The big blonde ignores the captain and ogles Beany. "What's that you're holding?" When she reaches out to touch the blue stone knife in Beany's hand, I yank the kid off the ground and push her behind me.

"Dang it, lady, I said leave her alone!"

Beany's hands, light as bird wings, touch against my back.

The woman rears back and stares at me with bright, sharp eyes. I feel Beany's forehead touch my back.

"Look, lady, can't you see I'm working here?"

The woman crosses her arms and gold bracelets clang together like cow bells. "I need to see that child."

I shake my head. "No. No you don't. She ain't your business." I set my hands on my hips, but my knees are shaking. "So if you're not buying a ticket to Albany, get out of my way."

"I'm not in your way!" The big woman's voice curdles from honey to vinegar and her eyes, pale yellow like a mongrel dog's, glare menacingly.

I reach back and wrap my arm around Beany's skinny shoulders, pulling her in tight. Boatmen glance our way and snicker.

"I don't want trouble, lady."

"Well, I'll give you a lifetime of trouble if you try to keep me from that child."

One hand—long, painted fingernails filed to a point—stretches toward Beany. A heavy red ring clings to her middle finger like a bug. Her jewel green dress shimmers in the September sunlight, and I feel a pang of pain for the purple bird that croaked giving up feathers for her fussy hat. I'd peg her for one of those do-gooders bent on cleaning up the gutter scum, but she doesn't look like the churchy type. I don't like her fancy clothes or her bossy voice. And it ain't wasted on me that even strangers give her wide berth, careful not to jostle her on the towpath.

"Get a move on, Tess!" the captain shouts. "Fill this boat!"

I swallow hard and try to keep my voice steady. "You're holding up my business, lady. I'm trying to make a sale here. I don't sell, we don't eat."

The woman's face softens and her hand drops slowly. "Well, look at you. Of course, you're hungry." Her voice turns sugary again. "Come on, I'll feed you. Feed you both." She starts down the towpath. When I don't follow, she turns sharply. "I said, come on! You gonna turn down a free meal?"

My stomach growls. "Captain won't want me leaving the landing. He's paying me to scrounge passengers."

"Girl, don't talk silly. You're just a ten-cent scalper. He'll find someone else before you take five steps off this rowdy path." When I don't move, she scowls. "Well, okay, okay, what boat is that? *Dark Shadow*, you say? Captain Cross is it?" Without even looking at the boat or its captain, she waves her hand and smiles, showing large, white teeth. "Captain Cross is a friend of mine. I'll take care of him, no worry. You'll keep your job — if scalpin' potash and foofoos is all you want in life."

She laughs — not a polite lady twitter, but a string of harsh, boisterous barks. Then she frowns just as quickly and waves impatiently for us to follow. I'm stunned when Beany slides out from under my arm and shuffles after the large, loud woman.

She doesn't set us down with bowls of mush on the back step. She doesn't even settle us with a plate of scraps in her kitchen corner. The woman called Wixumlee pulls out our chairs herself and seats us in front of a large picture window trimmed with lacey white curtains and pots of blazing red geraniums. The Black Pole ain't like any tavern I've ever known.

The establishment's paying customers nod, smile and don't seem put out that two grimy girls — one black, one white — are sitting at the best table — sticking out like horse flies on tea cakes. We've been on our own for a few weeks now after fighting off slave catchers in Seneca Falls. What's left of our clothes is torn and stained with blood and my attempts to wash them out in brown canal water. Our feet are bare, our heads plastered with greasy hair. I don't care that mine sticks to my head like a flattened cap, but Beany was always proud of her clean, shiny ringlets. Now her dark curls are matted with straw and horse shit from sleeping in the canal stable. And Beany doesn't care.

My brother Cooper's job cleaning the mule barn allows us to sleep inside at night, but the owner doesn't want us hanging around during the day. Says we look dangerous. So Beany stays with me, while I scalp passengers for the *Dark Shadow* and cargo for any other captain who'll give me a chance.

Scalpin's tough 'cause I scare off the customers. My face is tattooed with scabs from cuts left by the slave catchers' fists and boots. My nose turns at an odd angle and has a horny bump on top. Coop says it will stay that way, 'cause he doesn't have the heart to sock me once more to straighten it out. We're filthy and hungry, but some-how we've managed to survive one week in Black Rock, the can-tankerous canal port crouched north of the Buffalo Harbor. I hate Black Rock but hope Coop doesn't take us down to Buffalo. He always said Buffalo was the meanest.

Beany sits still as death next to me at a round oak table big enough to host a wedding. One hand rests on the tabletop, the other clutches her mama's blue stone knife. She never puts down that knife — the knife her mama used to stab herself. Not even when she sleeps. I push away memory of August laying limp on a bed of wild daisies and glance around the dining room, taking in the Black Pole's rosey walls, gold-flowered carpet, painted china plates and vases of fresh flowers. Late summer sunlight sneaks in through the lace curtains, throwing streaks on the faces of diners plunging forks into overflowing plates. A colored boy comes out and fills our water glasses. He smiles at Beany and gives me a wary look. I stare at the tabletop, conscious of my scarred face and crooked nose.

"My Ma will bring the food out shortly," he says. Not a blink later, a tall woman trots to our table, smiling like a kid on Christmas, and places a large platter of good-smelling food in front of us.

"Lucky for you gals, it's Polish night." She grins at Beany and I catch a flicker of light behind the kid's tortured eyes. But when the cheerful woman turns, I gasp! Her right eye is covered in a startling eye patch, and visions of the one-eyed slaver I fought on the tow-path streak through my mind. Fear kicks at me and I start to sweat. I don't want to look, but I can't look away.

The woman stares back at me happily, and I notice something odd about her patch. While the one-eyed slaver's patch was solid blood red, this patch is the same shade of brown as the woman's skin, and not round, but cut to fit her eye socket. Strangest of all, someone has sewn the brown fabric with different colored threads to make it look like a wide open, bright, happy eye. Except the col-ored part is bright blue and clashes with her real eye's rich brown. The good eye's lashes aren't as thick or long as the patch eye, either.

"Oh, you looking at my gob," she titters. "Well, truth is, I always want blue eyes, and when I get old enough to sew, I stitch myself up a winner, don't I? Only problem, it don't blink. Wide open all the time, even when I sleep. Mama says, 'Take that thing off at night, Savannah. I walk in your room and just about die seeing that big blue gob wide awake, staring back at me while the whole world's snoring.' But I like my big blue gob."

"Savannah, come on back, honey," a voice croons from the kitchen. "Let those girls eat."

"Bye now." A grown woman, Savannah skips from the dining room.

"Don't mind Savannah." Wixumlee strolls to the table. "She's just an egg short of a dozen. Well, maybe two eggs." She laughs, gently this time. "But she is a happy soul."

Wixumlee pierces two large flat pancakes with a long-handled fork and drops them on Beany's plate then gives me two.

"These are made from potatoes. Here, try some warm applesauce with them. And this here's a cabbage roll. Big, juicy meatball inside. Real good." She plops one on each plate. "You want milk or cider?"

"Cider, thanks." I haven't seen this much food since I sat in on a mill girls' supper at my home back in Seneca Falls. The mill girls downed mounds of meat and piles of potatoes that Beany and her mama cooked in our hot boarding house kitchen.

Beany, motionless, stares at her plate.

"You want milk, honey?" Wixumlee asks.

"She'll drink either."

The blond woman watches Beany.

"Uh, you gotta know, lady. We don't have money."

"Shush! I know you don't have a nut to crack. You're my guests."

I wait a few seconds, inhaling the hearty food smells, then shrug, pick up my fork and lop off a chunk of meatball. Soft, fragrant cabbage hangs in strips, and I stuff the hunk into my mouth. Chewing, I reach to chop Beany's meat. Nudge her with my elbow.

"Eat up now, girl." I pick up a potato pancake with my fingers and bite off half, then the other half. It's salty and I taste onions. August always cooked with onions. My throat starts to sting and I bite my upper lip.

"Get going now. This lady's treating us to a meal. Be nice and eat it." I almost add, "like your mama says." I feel a rock hard lump rise in my throat. I try to swallow, cough, and the food flops back onto my plate.

I flinch. "Sorry, ma'am. Food's good. I just choked. Eatin' too fast, I guess."

Wixumlee glances from Beany to me. Taps her long, pointed fingernails on the tabletop. "You ain't fooling me, girl. I heard that sob. What's going on with you two? Why you crying and what's wrong with this little gal?"

"Nothin'." My chest tightens. "Nothin's wrong with her. She'll eat."

"Yeah, she looks like she'll eat. All skin and bone that she is."

"She's just shy." Something tells me to grab Beany and run, but the power of this large woman — and the fact we're starving — holds me in my seat. I take another bite, wipe my mouth with my hand and look toward the front door. I'm just about to push back my chair, when Wixumlee lifts Beany into her arms and heads for the kitchen, calling over her shoulder, "Bring your plates, girl. Talbot! Bring that platter back to the kitchen. Mariana! Clear the table."

I jump up, knock over my chair and bump into the colored boy hurrying into the dining room. Customers calmly cram food into their faces, as if kidnapping happens every day at this saloon.

I race into the kitchen. Wixumlee is already sitting at a table cradling Beany in her lap, feeding her bits of pancake with her fingers.

"What you think you're doing?" I'm shaking and pacing in front of Wixumlee's chair, reaching out now and then like I might grab Beany back. I want to grab her. I want to.

"Shhhhh." The woman holds a finger to her lips. "Settle yourself, girl. Why you waving your arms around like that? Sit down. This child's got to eat."

"She's not your child, lady." I say it with as much force as I can muster.

"Shhhhh." Wixumlee rocks Beany gently. "This child needs food. I can give her body food. But what do I give her soul?" She runs a finger along the top of the knife sticking out of Beany's hand. Looks at me with questioning eyes.

I get gutsy and kick the table leg. "Her soul's just fine. I'm taking care of her. Me and my brother. So just give her back!"

"You're not taking too good a care of her if she's weak like this." A calm voice. No anger. No threat.

"We got food. She won't eat it." Drops of sweat slide down my forehead into my eyes.

"She should stay here."

My heart slams against my chest. "No! I'm not leaving her here with you!"

"Then you stay, too."

I kick the table again. "No! I'm taking Beany with me."

"Beany? Beany? Is that your name, darlin'? Who gave you that name? Some funny person, huh? Some funny person named you Beany."

"Shut up!" I yank my hair with both hands, afraid of what horror this evil woman's words will set off in my shattered friend.

"Don't use that tone with Wixumlee!"

I whirl and face a woman shorter than the big blonde, but by no means small. She's my height and large-boned with jet black hair that might fall to her waist if it wasn't tied in a thick loop behind her head. Her dark eyes spark with anger. A long black skirt covered with yellow flowers swirls around her ankles and her solid black shirt is open at the neck. That neck, long and a bit thick, is strung with multicolored beads. Her fingers, gripping wide hips, are banded by large gold rings flashing blue and red stones. A small, black bag swings heavily from a cord tied to her belt, the shape of something inside suggesting a weapon.

"Wixumlee is my salvation! Be smart, girl. She can also be yours."

My armpits slip with sweat. "I don't need her help," I croak.

"But that child does. Leave her here."

"No! Never!" I take a wobbly step toward the threatening woman, but she doesn't retreat.

"Quiet! Both of you. This child needs peace. Look how she eats. Look, Mariana." Beany calmly chews each piece of pancake, each bit of meat Wixumlee places in her birdlike mouth.

I'm glad she's eating, but I have to get her out of this kitchen. I must! I don't like these women. Neither one. But I can't take on both of them and manage Beany, too. Panic pounds my head. Sobs thicken my throat.

Wixumlee looks up at me. "Sit down, girl. Eat. See how peaceful your Beany is? Now you eat some supper." Wixumlee glances at the table. "Mariana, get her another plate. Go on, girl, get some warm food off the stove. You're weak. Can hardly stand. Mariana, get her some food."

The beaded and ringed Mariana fills a plate and sets it down with a thump.

"Pull up a chair." Wixumlee smiles. "You're Tess, right? This here's Beany, and you're Tess."

"Yeah." The smell of onions, potatoes and cabbage makes my mouth water.

"What's your family name? What did that captain call you?"

"Riley."

"Sit, Tess Riley." Mariana pushes a chair into the back of my legs. "Pride feeds fools."

I drop into the chair. Hunger slices through my belly.

"Go on. Fork, fingers, I don't care. Just get it down." She croons to Beany, but impatience creeps into Wixumlee's voice.

I stare at Mariana's craggy face, then at Wixumlee humming over the top of Beany's head. I don't trust these two. I'll eat, but I'm taking Beany with me when I leave. God's my witness.

CHAPTER TWO

"What do you mean, you left her there? You left her with strangers?" Cooper kicks a stall door, sending a weary mule skittering into a corner. "What the hell's wrong with you?"

"I didn't want to. Cripes, Coop, you know I didn't want to leave Beany there." My whining sounds pitiful to my own ears. "They took her. And they had a gun! The bossy one, that Wixumlee, she carried Beany out a side door and the other one with all the beads and rings—the spooky one—she pulled a gun out of a bag tied around her waist. Pointed it at me! Told me to get the hell out of there or she'd give me a third eye smack in the middle of my forehead. What was I gonna do?"

Coop looks at me like I'm a stranger. He sighs. "Was Beany scared? Did she cry?"

I shake my head. "She didn't do nothin'. Beany's too far gone, Coop. Her body's barely alive and her soul's dead. I don't think she even knows what's going on." I wipe my runny nose on my shirt sleeve. "And now I think that Wixumlee woman put a hex on her."

Beany has not said one word or given any sign of wanting to live since we pried her off her mama's bloody body on the towpath in Seneca Falls three weeks ago. Always thin, she's turned into a walking skeleton, barely swallowing a few drops of water and gagging on the tiny scraps Coop and I force down her throat when we get too desperate, too scared.

"I can't believe she just went with that white woman." Cooper kicks the stall again and the mule brays. "Beany's scared of white folk. You know how August taught her. And after those slave catchers fought us. I don't get it! You say she followed that woman off the towpath?"

"Yeah! I didn't want to go. Even when she said free food, I just stood there. But Beany walked right after her and that fuddled me. All she's done for weeks is sit in a puddle of pain, pining for August. I know she's starvin'. Maybe she finally wanted to eat, I don't know. I went, too. I wasn't gonna leave her alone with that woman. But it was a mistake. I should have dragged her away. But I didn't know it would turn out like this. I never thought they'd steal her!"

Coop pulls me to his chest, and I sob into his shoulder. My big, tough brother. Eight years on the canal, first as a hoggee walking behind the long-eared mules, then a seasoned canawler loading freighters, sliding up and down the length of the Erie. A rebel and a warrior. A brawler with a soft spot. He was the one who came up with the plan to bust August and Beany out of jail when the all-talk abolitionists hid behind their law books.

"I know you didn't leave her on purpose. I'm not mad at you."

"What we gonna do?" I bury my head, embarrassed by the snotty sounds my busted nose makes when I wail.

I'm mortified by how soft I've gotten since August—died. Stabbed herself. Killed herself to escape slave catchers. The sight of her laying in a bloody mess on the towpath with her knife in her chest, and Beany clutching her mama and covering that ragged hole with her little fingers—that horror killed something in me, too. Riding west on the Erie Canal, all I did was hold Beany, listen to her hum her mama's kitchen song, and watch her drift farther and farther away. As she drifted, I drifted someplace, too.

Once we got to Black Rock, I had to care for Beany and find food. We shouldn't have been so hard up with our friend Lucy Manning giving us travel money, but I lost that loot. The whole dang bag. Lost it to a hoodlum on the dock.

Like an idiot, I let Beany hold the ruby-colored bag, afraid to pull it from the kid's bloody hands. Beany clutched it from Seneca Falls to Black Rock, where a skinny punk in shaggy soaplocks jumped into our boat and snatched it before I could do anything about it. Why'd he do that? What'd he expect to get off a bloody black girl anyway?

Coop was madder than a sweat bee. Said there was scum like that all up and down the Erie, making their living stealing off passengers. Swooping down as soon as a boat docks. Catching travelers off guard. Maybe it's true, but I can't help thinking Coop's making excuses for me. He never asked me why I didn't chase that kid, clobber him, and take the money back.

I hate myself for losing that red bag full of Lucy's college money. Coins it took her years to save working a mean little job sewing gloves and writing stories for *The Lily*, Amelia Bloomer's temperance and women's rights newspaper. Her college dream is dead 'cause she showed up on the towpath and gave her money-stuffed, velvet bag to Beany. A sacrifice I made worthless by losing it. Didn't fight for it. Was too chicken to chase a skinny thief not much older or bigger than Beany.

When he dropped us in Black Rock, Coop's Captain Beale gave us some money and orders not to steal. "Lay low. Best to hop a Lake Erie steamer for Canada," he said.

But Coop said no to Canada. "I know the Erie Canal and New York state. We're staying here."

I wish I had the gumption to argue with him. In Canada, nobody would know Coop killed Constable Parker and I wouldn't have to worry about defending my brother. My stomach tilts at the thought of another bloody battle—fist flying, boots kicking—broken teeth, busted ribs. The nastiness, the meanness I'd perfected in Seneca Falls is dead—along with August. I've turned chicken, pure and simple, afraid to get hurt again.

I pull away from Coop and collapse onto the stable floor. Now I've gone and lost poor helpless, motherless, starving, silent Beany. If I had a smidge of courage, I'd jump at the challenge to get her back. Not long ago I chased adventure, connived to escape dreary Seneca Falls. Well, I succeeded, all right. By events I regret and can't change. One of the few people who'd ever been kind to me is dead. There's a price on Coop's head. Beany's a lost soul, and now I've gone and lost her body, too.

I want to be home again in Seneca Falls. I miss Ma. I miss Miz Bloomer and Lucy and printing *The Lily*. I miss Miz Stanton and running around in the fields with her bratty boys.

I escaped on the Erie, just like I wanted, but found agony not adventure. I'm chasing up and down the towpath with a dozen other runners scalpin' passengers and I hate it. Competition is tough and there isn't an ounce of nerve in me. I'd have been a hell-raisin' scalper a year ago. Even a month ago. Nobody would have tricked coins away from the foofoos better than me or gotten a load of lumber away from my boat. My mind wanders to Beany when it should be thinking up ways to boost my business.

Now Beany's lost. Stolen.

What's happened to me? Where's that cocky attitude that landed me a job at *The Lily*? It was me who whipped my weight in wildcats, me who chased those young toughs who shamed Miz Bloomer and Miz Stanton just because they wore comfortable clothes. I have to get that fight back in me! I have to go back to Wixumlee's place, face her and that spooky Mariana and get Beany back!

But I'm scared. I shiver beside Cooper, flopped down in the straw paging through some scrap newspaper dated 1848. The year Miz Stanton held her big woman's rights convention. Cripes, when was that? More than three years ago.

I wonder if Coop's as befuddled as I am. "We gotta get Beany back," I whisper.

He doesn't move, but answers, "We'll get her."

"How?"

"We need a plan. Isn't that what I always tell you? You always need a plan. But first, I want to learn about this Wixumlee and that woman with the pistol. We need information, Tess. Can't go in blind."

"Okay, so, let's snoop around. Ask some questions."

"Yeah, strike up some conversations. If these women are as flashy as you say, there'll be lots of gossip." Coop rolls onto his stomach. "When we know the enemy, we'll strike."

CHAPTER THREE

"Ever eat at that place at the top of Ferry Street, the Black Pole?" I lean against a snubbing post, chatting up a couple of lazy locals sitting on overturned buckets under a wide-spreading maple at water's edge.

"Once or twice," the older guy mumbles into his pipe. "Strange place. Pretty inside, but still a saloon. Always busy. People going in, coming out."

Yeah, lace curtains and flowers. What did Wixumlee hope to disguise with those?

"Good food there," the younger one says. I admire the way he flips his knife into a rotten log near his feet. "Weird sometimes, but always good."

"I'd eat there more if I had the money," the first guy says, tapping out some ash. "Always serve something different, they do. Try to please the foreigners, I guess. I don't think they serve breakfast, though. Odd, ain't it?" he asks his buddy. "Tavern like that don't serve breakfast?"

The younger one shrugs, reaches behind his back and scratches his shoulder with the tip of his knife.

"You hungry?" the old gent asks me.

"No, I ate." A lie. "I was in there yesterday, though. That big, blond lady offered me a free meal."

"Blond? Oh, yeah, that one." He chuckles and pokes his friend and they snicker. "Yeah, she does that now and then."

I watch the old man. "Met the cook, too. Mari...Mari...?"

"Mariana. Yeah, the Polish gypsy."

"The what!" I jerk up straight.

"Polish gypsy." He moves his butt around on the bucket, trying to get comfortable. "Loaded down with beads and rings? That one?

Yeah, she's a character. Half the town's scared of her. Thinks she's a witch."

"Thinks she'll steal their kids," the younger one smirks.

My heart slams against my chest. I laugh nervously. "You're just cuttin' didoes, right?"

The old guy hacks a couple times and spits out something green. He looks me over carefully, eying the scabs on my face. "You ain't scared of gettin' nabbed, are you? Big gal like you. I expect you can handle yourself in a fight." He studies my bent nose.

"'Course I can. She don't scare me. But you're not serious about her stealing kids, are you? I mean, people'd have the sheriff after her fast if they even thought she was doing stuff like that. Wouldn't they?"

"Hell, Wixumlee's got the sheriff in her pocket."

My throat goes dry and my legs wobble. I slide down the snubbing post.

"She's got at least half the police, too," the young one says, eying me on the ground. "I know that for a fact. My sister's husband's one. He says most constables dance to her tune. 'Course the police ain't worth squat in Black Rock. Buffalo neither."

"Is he on the take? Your sister's husband?" the old man asks.

"Prob'ly."

"Why would Wixumlee need the sheriff in her pocket?" I try to control the quiver in my voice. "What's she doing that's illegal? Besides stealing kids."

The old man laughs. "Hey, we're just joshing you, gal. Those two don't steal kids. Do they?" He nudges the younger guy who smirks and shrugs.

My palms sweat. "What does she do? Besides own that saloon?"

"Oh, well, Wixumlee's into a lot of stuff. Why you want to know?"

"Just wondering." I play with the dirt. "Sounds like an interesting lady."

"Well, it ain't no secret around here what Wixumlee does. You need money, she lends it. But you gotta pay her back a tad more, of course. And she runs that poor man's hotel on the lake—at Sandy Town."

"Sandy Town?"

The old one spits twice. "Between here and Buffalo. A spot of land between the lake and the canal. Just a collection of shacks, but she's making money off 'em. The angry Erie's been coughing up sunken ships for decades and piling 'em on the sand. Every few years a bad storm comes up and ol' Erie swallows 'em back again. That's the great lake I'm talking about, girly, not this little ribbon of slime canawlers think is God's gift to transportation." Both men laugh.

I grin. "Where's the *hotel* come in?"

"Well, it's remarkable, really. Wixumlee took some of those old broken boats and turned them into cheap rents for all these foofoos Europe's spittin' up like the whole continent's been poisoned. Boats from the East are bringing 'em in by the thousands. On packets. On cargos. They'll ride with hogs and even skunks if we took to hauling 'em." He snorts. "So hurried are they to get to the wonderful West."

"Wixumlee's fixed those old boats up fine. I saw 'em," the younger one says. "She scrubbed 'em down. Painted 'em. Fixed the furniture. 'Course, none of the good stuff that washes ashore stays in those rents. Anything washes up that's valuable she hauls out fast and sells faster."

"How does she get the goods so quick?" I remember stories Coop told me about ships lost in Lake Erie storms. The Erie's merciless, striking fast and with a wickedness usually credited to humans.

"How?" The young guy shakes his head. "She's got a crew down there watching for it. Big husky guys nobody's gonna mess with. That's how she gets first crack at everything. Hell, I hear she gets wind of a ship going down at sea—and she's got snitches everywhere—she sends her crew out in a tug or in a dozen rowboats to buy the cargo dirt cheap off the drowning captain. He don't want to go broke just 'cause his ship's sinkin', does he? 'Course he sells! Then they load it on the tug and—poof!—it disappears! She's got a buyer lined up before that barge hits land."

"Yeah, that's what she did with that load of coffee beans, remember? Sunk right to the bottom last spring," the old one says. "Lucky for her not in deep water, but those beans still got wet. Hell, she sent divers down. Divers! They hauled the boxes up, and damned if she didn't set up drying coffee beans right on shore. Dried 'em up, bagged 'em up and sold 'em up in New York City. Those big city fools thought they were getting Buffalo's Best

Roasted when they were just swillin' down salvage!" He roars like he'd made some profit in the deal.

Police in her pocket. Thugs on shore. Wixumlee's a bad egg. And now she's kidnapped Beany. What'll she do? Sell Beany, too? I can't wait for Coop's plan. Beany needs rescuing now. I struggle to stand, take two deep breaths, wave to the lazy locals, and head toward Ferry Street and the Black Pole.

I lean against a lamppost across the street from the tavern, working up the nerve to go inside. No customers walk in or out. The old canal coot was right, Wixumlee doesn't serve breakfast. Her place looks closed up tight. Dark. I wonder what's going on behind those walls. What's Beany doing? Or what are they doing to her? The alley on one side of the tavern prob'ly leads to the kitchen in back.

I swallow the fear scratching at my throat and laugh at myself for being chicken. That Mariana won't shoot me. She pointed her gun at me, but it was just show. And Wixumlee may be big but she's too gussy, too fussy to be good in a fight. I'll just walk in, push past them all and take Beany back.

I pull myself off the lamppost, suck in a bellyfull of air and cross the street. My bare feet pad silently down the alley's brick path. I slow up at the back of the building and watch where I step, but no garbage or dog crap threatens to trip me up, like behind most canal town buildings. It doesn't stink either. In fact, the bricks are swept clean and look damp, like they've been swabbed down. Hmmm, Wixumlee's a clean crook. A tidy kidnapper.

"What you doing back here?"

I dash behind a wagon.

"Yeah, I see you. What you want? Looking for trouble? I'll find you some. Go on, git!"

I hunker down, knees shaking like birch trees in a winter wind.

The gypsy Mariana stands on the back step holding her broom like a weapon. "You got no business here."

"I want to see Beany!" I mean it as a yell, but it comes out a whimper.

"Beany ain't here!"

I jump out from behind the wagon. "What'd you do with her?" I run toward the step, but Mariana hops back and slams the door. I pound furiously. "Open up! You tell me where she is, you kidnapping gypsy!"

But the solid door stays shut. I pound until splinters slice my fists. When the window curtain sways, I beat on the glass. I pick up a rock but remember what the locals said about Wixumlee's burly bodyguards and paid police. The shrinky, scared Tess inside me cries *stop* and I hate myself for listening.

"Idiot!" Coop punches the stable wall. "Didn't I say we need a plan?" He kicks the wall. Kicks it again. "Stupid! Now they know we're coming."

I eye him warily. This isn't the playful, joking brother who teased me in Seneca Falls. This is a brother toughened by hard years on the Erie Canal. The cusser. The fighter. The ball bustin' brawler. The brother who thinks he killed the constable bustin' August out of jail. I know this temper is a small showing of the fury Coop can spend. He scares me, but I deserve his anger. I am an idiot. I am stupid. I flubbed a feeble rescue attempt. Went in with no plan, no backup.

Cooper flops onto a rickety chair and stares at me murderously. I wish he'd swat me. Collapsed on the dirty stable floor, I try to stifle the sobs that threaten to strangle me. Tears skate down my cheeks and my broken nose honks. Coop reaches for an old cotton sack. He digs inside, pulls out something brown and throws it at me.

I pick the small, thin, hard hunk of what might have been a pork chop off the stable floor.

"Eat it."

I put the meat to my lips and don't even ask where he found it. I was too torn up with worry to scalp that afternoon, earned no money and had nothing to contribute to a decent supper. The stable owner's wife sometimes leaves a plate of scraps on her kitchen step, but not tonight.

I spit out a tasteless bite, throw the meat into a corner and roll onto my belly, humiliated by my sissy sobs ricocheting off the stable walls.

After a minute Coop stoops down and touches my head. "Hey, don't kick yourself too hard, Tessie. At least you found out something. Beany's not there."

Those three words are as searing as three prongs of a branding iron. Beany's. Not. There. The words scorch my heart. I don't deserve Coop's sympathy. Confronting Mariana was a lame-brained thing to do.

"We should go to the police," Coop says.

"No! Wixumlee pays off the police. They won't help us. They're crooked. They'll protect her."

"Even when it comes to stealing kids?"

I sit up and grip my knees to my chest. "We can't go to the police even if they aren't in her pocket. They prob'ly know about Parker getting killed. A lawman gets killed, they send that news all over the country. I know from working at *The Lily*. Somebody's looking for us for sure."

"They don't know we did it—I did it."

"Well, somebody back home will put it together. I'm gone. You're gone."

"I've been gone a long time. Who'd suspect me?"

"Somebody will remember seeing you. Or Lucy Manning will talk."

"She won't."

"Somebody will suspect her."

Coop snorts. "Who'd think a rich kid broke a runaway slave out of jail? Besides, her old man will protect her."

"He's a lawyer. A law-abiding citizen."

Cooper laughs. "Come on, Tess. He won't set the dogs on his kid to get at you and me. What does he care about us? You said Abner Manning can't stand Constable Parker. And what does he care about August anyway? Do you think anybody in Seneca Falls, except Ma, misses August? Do you think anybody cares about those slave catchers? They were just trash looking for booze money. Nobody's missing them."

Cooper flops down next to me on the straw. "Anyway, Captain Beale hid those bodies real good in the swamp. They won't float." He pokes my knee. "I think we should go to the police."

"No! I don't trust them. This Wixumlee's bad, Coop. She's rich and she's bad." And nobody cares if a little colored girl gets stolen anyway. The police don't care. Nobody cares but me and my brother.

We lie in the dirty straw, hungry and miserable.

"We should check out this Sandy Town," Coop says. "I was there once. And I've been thinking about scouting out a job down that way."

My heart sinks. "In Buffalo? Why?"

"I know the town real good. There's lots more work there 'cause of the lake. The granaries are always busy. Lots of factories. There's the loading docks. Steamers are running back and forth to Canada and from one big lake to the next all day long. All that cargo has to be loaded and unloaded. I can get a job there easy."

"So you're gonna leave me here?" My voice cracks. Whiner. Since escaping from Seneca Falls I hardly recognize myself.

"Hell no! You're coming with me."

I sit up fast. "I won't leave Beany! I can't believe you'd leave Beany."

Coop studies my face. "Tess, Beany ain't here. That woman said so."

"She's lying. She just said that to get rid of me. Get me to give up. You already gave up!"

Coop's eyes flash. "No, I haven't! We're not giving up. We just need more information before we go knocking down doors. Then the police will really be after us."

We sit silently. Coop's stomach growls.

"Let's hike to Sandy Town," he says. "It was a garbage dump when I was there. If Wixumlee's turned it into some kind of low-class Buffalo hotel, people will be talking about her. The more we know—like where she holes up in that town—the easier it'll be to find where she's stashed Beany."

Stashed her? I'm pretty sure she's sold her. Sold her south. To some wretched plantation.

CHAPTER FOUR

A high-pitched screech starches the hair on the back of my neck. I follow the noise across the sand to the shoreline. A woman has stripped a little boy down to his skin and is pouring Lake Erie right over him. He shrieks and dances. The mama holds his arm and lathers him with soap. Every now and then he jerks away and dances wild in the water 'til she catches him back. He has a gay time 'til she attacks his face. Then his playful yelps turn angry and he holds out his chubby arms to a blond man in a brilliantly colored shirt to come rescue him.

"This place used to smell like rotten fish." Coop glances up and down the beach, grinning. "Now all I smell is paint and supper. Lordy, Tess, if Wixumlee's cleaned this place so good, she can't be all bad."

I scowl. Beany's missing—lost—stolen—I know who snatched her and Cooper's complimenting the kidnapper on her housekeeping.

"All the broken glass, tin cans, dead fish, driftwood and seaweed are gone. The sand's raked clean. She's turned those old broken hulls and captain's cabins into little houses."

I wince at the wonder in his voice then scan the settlement. The cabins are tiny, the nearest one not more than ten feet on a side. The foofoo mama carries her towel-wrapped son through its front door, followed by his papa. Then, out she comes with another little kid. A short, round, older woman with a red and yellow scarf tied under her chin carries a third child. Those two get the same soap and water treatment.

"Hey, that's what we should do, Tess. Take a bath."

"Why? Only got the same dirty clothes to put back on."

"We ain't been cleaned in weeks. It'll feel good."

"Yeah, maybe, but I'm not stripping down in front of these foofoos."

I shield my eyes against the shards of light bouncing off the water. The bright sand, too, hurts my eyes. It's hard to pick out the little shacks stuck here and there in the sand. They're painted faded red, dusty gray, washed-out white and blend secretively into their surroundings, almost as if on purpose.

The foofoos, though, blaze like fireworks. Many of the men wear long, embroidered shirts with bright sashes over balloon-legged pants tucked into black boots reaching to their knees. On the plain, hot sand, they stick out like clowns in church. All of the women cover their heads with scarves, from somber black to gaily colored. Some of their dresses are flowered and beaded, others painfully plain. Many of the newcomers are yellow-haired. Some set trunks in front of their cabins to use as tables. Others seem to be traveling with one tattered satchel. A few with just the clothes on their backs.

"You two looking for a place to sleep?"

We spin and face a thick-chested colored man, shirt sleeves rolled up to reveal inky snakes crawling up his arms. He cradles a rifle.

"Huh? Us?" I step behind Cooper.

"Yeah. You. Want a cabin?"

Coop is as tall as the tattooed guy, but not as meaty. "No, just looking around."

"Move on then." He shifts his rifle slightly. "I don't like lookers. Payers, yeah, lookers — get lost."

I scan the beach in awe. How'd I miss them? Beefy brutes shoul-dering rifles rest on rocks — as confident as mountain lions — or pace the edges of Sandy Town. Wixumlee's henchmen.

"Come on, Coop." I tug his arm.

"I ain't in no rush." Coop, unmovable, locks eyes with Snake-man. "No problem in looking."

"Ain't a problem if you like getting busted up."

"I been busted up. I come out okay."

"Coop, let's go." My brother's canawler-brawler mood is kick-ing in, and I want no part of it. Snakeman reminds me of Big Slaver and Big Slaver reminds me of One-Eye and One-Eye reminds me of Savannah and Savannah reminds me of losing Beany. "I'm hungry. There any place to eat around here?"

Snakeman answers without taking his eyes off Coop. "Well, I could send you over to the Black Pole."

The name licks me like a whip and I muffle a yelp. "In Black Rock?

"That's a long hike for supper." Coop's voice is dangerously steady.

Snakeman chuckles. "Not Black Rock. The *new* Black Pole just opened on Canal Street. At Commercial Slip."

From Coop's stories, I know Commercial Slip — a narrow band of water connecting the canal to the lake — is the heart of Erie Canal Harbor — or the Buffalo Harbor, depending on whether you're a scabby sailor or cantankerous canawler. Buffalo's Canal Street, a tobacco spit away, is the most dangerous street in Buffalo. So Coop tells me.

It's a moment before Cooper asks, "Same owner?"

Snakeman grins widely. "The one and only Wixumlee." I hear pride in his voice — and a protective tone that makes my belly quiver.

"I ate there. In Black Rock once. Good food."

"The best." Suddenly he relaxes. Takes a step to the side, releasing Cooper from the stand-off. "If you got a few coins you can join these foofoos. They'll be heading out that way tonight." He waves his hand at the freshly bathed family sunning themselves outside their cabin. "Know why they're going tonight?"

We shake our heads.

"It's Polish night!" Snakeman laughs, turns his broad back on us without fear, and struts down the beach.

Polish night *again*. Good food, bad ending. Bad memories, but I nudge Cooper. "We should go."

"Yeah. Uh, huh." He looks at me like I'm loony.

"I want to get my hands around that Wixumlee's throat!"

Coop scoffs. "You gonna get past her bodyguards?" He nods at Snakeman prowling the beach. I hang my head. No bodyguards threatened me at the Black Pole in Black Rock, and I still ran like a smacked puppy. One gun-toting gypsy was enough to scare me off.

But I persist. "Let's walk down there, Coop." I'm scared but have a funny feeling — or pathetic wish — that we'll see Beany.

"Walk down to the Slip?"

"Yeah. Please."

He cocks his head. "Maybe. If you take a bath."

"Come on, our clothes — ."

"I'll get us clean ones. And soap. I know a safe spot down around the bend. No one will see us. We'll take a bath, dress up clean, then hike to the new Black Pole."

It's an easy deal. "Okay. If you find me a pair of pants, a shirt and a pair of shoes *that fit*, I'll take a bath."

"Done." Coop leads me around the bend away from Sandy Town and Snakeman.

I button my fly. Bend my knees. Stretch my legs. Walk around.

"Like 'em?"

"Like 'em? Tarnation, Cooper, these are the best pants I've ever worn!" They're soft, roomy, comfortable.

"Knew you'd like 'em. Got a pair for me, too." He pats his thighs. "I heard the gold rush miners out in California like 'em 'cause they wear like iron. Real sturdy denim cloth."

I know Coop stole everything we're wearing — pants, shirts, shoes — from someone's clothesline.

We stand in the curve of a lonely cove Coop claims he found a few years back when one of his many Erie Canal trips terminated in Buffalo. Hidden by a dense stand of staghorn sumac and prickly blackberry vines, the cove's entrance is guarded by a colossal apple tree. Wild grape vines stretch up from the ground all the way to the tree's top, then wrap themselves in lacey patterns up and around, then back to the ground again, forming a shadowy room within the fragrant boughs. If someone nosy doesn't pull the vines apart and visit the secret room first, the quiet cove and shadowy cave stuck in the cliff behind it remain hidden and secure.

Coop says he spent a few nights in that cave healing up after a fight. He takes me to the entrance, and I see it's narrow and deep — just tall enough to walk through and wide enough for two people to lay down in. Not a soul's come by the cove the whole time we're here washing and dressing. Although small boats can land, the beach, covered with rocks, rotting fish and large, mangled heaps of driftwood, looks unfriendly.

Now Coop and I are clean and dressed well enough to swallow a meal at the Black Pole, but we still don't have money.

It's already dusk. "Let's go anyway, Coop. Just to look around." Maybe some food will fall right out of Ma's heaven.

"And if we see something, then what?"

"We'll pin those women down and beat the blazes out of them 'til they say where Beany is!"

"Yeah," Coop snorts, "there's a plan."

We hunch under a streetlamp on the lip of Buffalo's Commercial Slip watching Europe's castoffs file in and out of the new Black Pole restaurant. Foofoo families go in tired and uneasy and come out laughing and patting their bellies.

I hear a series of short, harsh barks near the front door and recognize Wixumlee's cackle, but she doesn't come outside. Good smells float out the door each time it opens, and my stomach groans.

"Coop, let's try the alley. Maybe they threw out some scraps." I figure back alleys cough up most of my brother's contributions to our meager meals. We cross the street, passing whole families smelling of garlic and onions. Most of the men blow whiskey breath.

To my disappointment, the rear of the tavern is as clean as the one in Black Rock. No boxes spilling rotten vegetables block the alley. No mangy dogs pace the yard grumbling over knobby bones. No cats hiss over scraps of fish. It doesn't even smell like pee. And it's dead quiet. Curses and screams float from all points along the heaving Buffalo harbor, but this back alley behind the Black Pole is church quiet.

I'm spooked. "Nothin' here for us, Cooper. Let's try someplace else."

We turn to leave but that young colored kid who filled my water glass two days ago in Black Rock steps out the back door and squats down on the step. I squeeze Coop's arm and we melt into the shadows. The boy wipes his face and neck with a towel and leans against the door jam. He looks ready to fall asleep.

"That kid works here. His ma's one loony lady."

"Maybe he knows where Beany is." Coop leans closer to me. "Want to snatch him?"

Thrill shoots through my veins, followed by a deadening dread. I gauge the kid's size. He's short and kind of skinny. The old Tess could take him half asleep, but fear claims the new Tess. Fighting it, I manage to squeak out, "Yea—yeah."

We shift our weight to spring but stop dead at the dull clip-clop of horses' hooves. An oversize farm wagon, its bed piled with hay bales, pulls up to the Black Pole's back door. Two old men sit hunched on the front seat.

"Hey, boy," the driver calls softly. The kid lifts his head. "I come for the night delivery."

Without a word the boy goes inside. Both men climb down and stand beside the wagon. One reaches under the wagon's belly and I hear the sound of wood sliding. Softly. Smoothly.

In less than a minute the back door opens and people file out—what looks like two men, two women and two little kids. They're fully dressed—over-dressed for the warm night—the men wearing caps, the women and children in bonnets and shawls. They're dark-skinned. Colored people. They move straight to the farm wagon, followed by two large men with rifles.

The first black man in line stops. One of the old men points to the side of the wagon, then tugs at the colored man's arm. The horses don't raise a hoof. No one even whispers. Then one of the rifle thugs comes up and nudges the first guy in line and he bends down and disappears into the side of the wagon.

A woman crawls in next, followed by the two little girls, the second woman and the last man. Again, I hear wood slide. The two old men struggle up onto the wagon seat and the driver turns the horses up the side alley toward Canal Street. The riflemen return to the tavern and the black boy sits back down on the stoop. Me and Coop slide from the shadows and inch along the alleyway toward the front of the tavern. The colored kid doesn't raise his head and already looks asleep.

The farm wagon stops in front of the saloon, and I hear Wixumlee's barking laugh.

"Hey, honey, don't worry, we'll give you a ride home. Give you all a ride. Just hop aboard the Black Pole Express, darlin'. These gents will drive you back to Sandy Town. They're just two old codgers, but together they can steer a horse." Wixumlee cackles again and begins guiding—pushing—six or seven drunken foofoos, young men mostly, toward the wagon. Her two thugs have stashed their rifles and help lift and shove the boozers onto the hay bales. The drunken men collapse in a pool of grunts and sighs, sending a cloud of liquored breath into the warm air.

"Okay, boys. Take 'em home." Wixumlee waves and the old driver snaps the reins over the horses' backs.

"Giddap!" Heavy hooves, suddenly loud on the brick road, signal a speedy departure.

"What's going on, Cooper?" I feel sick. My heart beats in spurts, slows, then surges ahead. "Looks to me like they're stealing people!" The men, women and kids were forced into the wagon at gunpoint.

"And covering it up by giving drunks a lift home." He frowns. "You think one of them is Beany?"

"No! Too big. She's thin as a twig. They must have moved her out earlier. Maybe even the first night they snatched her." The memory twists in my heart like a rusty knife.

"Well, if they moved her like that, where'd they take her?"

"Let's find out. Let's follow that wagon, see where it goes after they dump those drunks at Sandy Town."

"Wagon's moving too fast now — got too much of a head start. And it could go in any direction after Sandy Town."

We can't follow on foot. I wipe clammy hands on my new denim pants. "Coop, this is an awful thing happening! Wixumlee's capturing colored people and selling them down south."

He frowns but doesn't look at me. "You don't know that." But his voice is a low growl. He's thinking about it.

"What else could she be doing? Little kids got into that wagon, Cooper. She's stealing whole families."

Someone is singing behind the Black Pole. We creep back along the brick walk, and I pick out a dirty little canal ditty Coop whispered to me back home. The kind that made Ma cover her ears and cross herself. Coop smiles, recognizing it, too.

The singer is enjoying his tune, a rhyming song about a canal boat cook who falls in love with a frog with six-foot legs. The singer chuckles every now and then. His voice cracks on a few high notes, and I know the balladeer is the water boy who went inside to bring out the *delivery*.

"It's the water boy. He's still there." I punch Coop's arm, suddenly brave. "Let's snatch him!"

My brother rummages on the ground and comes up with a chunk of brick. I shudder. But I want this guy. Want what he knows. If he's helping stuff colored folk into the bottom of farm wagons, he knows what happened to Beany. My anger swells. He's going against his own people! His ma's people. What kind of place is this — run by a loud, white woman with blacks and gypsies under her command, dealing in slaves?

Coop whispers instructions in my ear. I walk straight toward the singer.

He's looking off across the back alley, but catches me coming up in the corner of his eye. He leans forward, ready to jump. "What you—?"

Conk! Cooper catches him as he falls.

It's easy getting the kid off the waterfront. Coop slings him over his shoulder, and I pour the last of a bottle of rum I find in the gutter over his head and shoulders.

"Just my buddy," Coop says to the one or two folks who show interest. "Just my buddy, drank a little too much rum. Taking him home." But most of the rabble cluttering up the Slip that time of night can't care less.

We find a wobbly wheelbarrow, dump the kid in, and tote him past rowdy canawlers and feisty sailors. We make a wide berth around Sandy Town and find the quiet path that veers toward the vine-draped apple tree guarding the cove.

The kid doesn't stir as we pull him into the narrow cave, drag him across small rocks and twigs and lay him atop some creature's smelly nest. We don't care. We have no sympathy for him. He's a major player in the gang that snatched Beany. His ma—that loopy, one-eyed Savannah—might be one slice short of a full loaf, but her kid is no dummy. He knows what's going on and he's gonna talk.

CHAPTER FIVE

The conk doesn't kill the kid. He comes to in the early morning, curled on his side and stares glassy-eyed at Cooper, but closes his eyes quick when he sees me.

Coop pokes him with his boot. "Quit fakin'."

I want to smash my shoe into his face. "Scared, Talbot?" The sound of the familiar old sneer in my voice makes me bolder. "You hope someone's looking for you, don't you, Talbot? That's your name, right? That's what they call you at the Black Pole." I want him to tell us everything he knows right now.

"Yes, my name's Talbot." He opens his eyes but doesn't move another muscle. Acts like he's hog-tied. Doesn't look at me.

"I only got one question for you, Talbot, and if you're smart you'll answer it."

His eyes swing warily to my face.

"Where's Beany?"

"Safe."

I ram my shoe into his forehead. "That's not good enough." I drop to my knees, ready to jump on his chest and pound him.

Coop puts his hand on my shoulder and pushes me back. He leans down close to Talbot's head. "Beany's my friend, too, buddy. I want her back."

"I don't know if you'll ever get her back."

With a howl, I lunge. Land my balled fist into the boy's stomach and again into his face. He rolls into a ball, covering his head with his skinny arms.

"Stop it, Tess!" Cooper pulls me off. He grabs Talbot's shirt collar and sits him up against the cave wall, banging his head on the low slope of rocky ceiling.

"Look, kid, your boss stole Beany."

In the dim cave, Talbot's eyes shine teary with pain. Or, I hope, fear. "Didn't steal—Beany's happy."

"No she isn't!" I pound my fists on the ground and kick at the cave wall. "She's not anyway near happy. She can't be happy."

"Grandma's nursing her back to health."

"Where? Where's she got her? Tell us." Coop pushes his face close to Talbot's.

The kid looks down at the cave floor. "I can't tell you." He flinches, expecting blows. "Grandma swears everyone to secrecy. No one ever snitches. Never. Snitches are severely punished."

Coop leans back. "Wait a minute. Grandma? Who the heck's your grandma?"

Talbot looks up, surprised. "Wixumlee."

Coop and I laugh.

"Don't give us that crap, kid," Cooper hisses. "Wixumlee's a white woman."

"No. No, she's not." Talbot doesn't seem surprised at Cooper's remark. "She looks white, but she's got colored blood and that makes her a black woman. Don't ever call her a white woman. She'll tear you to pieces. She's colored, like me. Why do you think the tavern's called the Black Pole? *Black* for my grandma and *Pole* for Mariana. Pole as in Polish. You know, Polish night. Polish food. They're partners. Have been in business..."

"*Shut up!*" Coop and I both yell. He does, and Coop and I stare at him, at each other, and back to him. Talbot's as loony as his mama.

"Look, kid, we ain't stupid. Wixumlee's got yellow hair and her skin's lighter than mine." I hold up a bare arm, not really visible in the dark cave.

Talbot looks at it anyway. "So?"

"So, she's white. Don't mess with us."

"I'm not messin'. Actually, her hair is lighter than it looks. She darkens it with some concoction Mariana mixes for her. Washes her hair with it once a month. She..."

"Shut your jabber mouth!" Cooper pushes away from Talbot and leans against the opposite wall.

With a little more breathing room, Talbot relaxes. "She was called an octoroon in the Quarter."

"What quarter?

"The French Quarter. In New Orleans. That's where she's from. Well, actually, she's from a lot of places, but that's where she landed after she ran away from the plantation. Well, after a bit of traveling around — ." Talbot stops, hunches over, grabs his knees. His nose bleeds onto his pants from my punch.

"Go on, kid." Coop smiles. "You're starting to get interesting. What's an octo-roon?"

"Someone with one-eighth black blood. The rest of the eighths are something else. White, I guess," Talbot mumbles. Suddenly he doesn't seem so keen on jabbering.

"Thanks for the arithmetic lesson," Coop grumbles. "Keep talking."

Talbot shrugs. "So, she ran from the plantation, traveled around, made some money. Now she has a couple nice taverns. That's all."

"And she carts people away at night in the bottom of a farm wagon," Coop whispers, leaning away from the cave wall. Talbot's eyes grow large. He presses his scraped forehead into his knees.

"Yeah, kid, we saw it." Coop reaches over and jerks the boy's head up by his hair. Blood smears in the gash over one eyebrow. Prob'ly from my kick. "What does she do? Sell them?"

"Sell! Sell them!" Talbot looks shocked. "Of course not! Those people — ." He stops.

"What?" I lean in menacingly."Those people *what*?"

"She's not selling them, for cripes' sake. And that's all I'm gonna say. You can't make me say more. I never will! Never!"

"Okay, kid." Coop shrugs. "It don't matter. Now that we got you, we'll trade."

"Yeah, we'll trade," I echo. "You for Beany." That was our plan and Talbot's odd look pleases me. "What's the matter? Afraid granny won't want you back?"

"She's taken a real shine to Beany," he says softly. "Everybody has."

I find some old rope, and we leave Talbot bound hand and foot in the cave behind the cove hidden by the apple tree. We walk to the top of Commercial Slip, steal a pencil and paper off the general store counter, write a short note, and walk to the Black Pole. One of Wixumlee's thugs — another unusually tall guy — guards the front entrance on Canal Street, giving customers the once over before allowing some to pass through the doorway. Others he turns away.

We sneak around to the back of the tavern and see Snakeman guarding the kitchen door, then steal back to the Slip. With the promise of a nickel we don't have, we convince a street scamp to hand our note to the thug at the front door.

When he reads it, his head jerks up, and his long, black curls dance around his eyes like loopy hair on a rag doll. He reaches for the street kid, but the boy dashes away. The thug runs his thumb and forefinger over his black mustache, looks up and down the street, then takes the note inside.

Within five minutes an open carriage pulls in front of the tavern. Wixumlee, wearing a flashy yellow dress covered with sequins, like she's going to a ball—and looking madder than a sweat bee—lopes through the front door and climbs inside. The loopy-haired thug follows, holding the hand of a pretty young colored girl dressed in a purple and white flowered frock. Her hair is dark brown and falls in long, shiny ringlets to her shoulders. There's an ornament in her hair—a puffed up ribbon or a flower. The girl is thin and moves slowly, but she doesn't hesitate getting into the carriage and plunking herself down next to Wixumlee.

Beany? Beany! I hardly recognize her. But I'm so happy—so relieved she's alive. I take two steps forward, but Coop yanks me back. "Wait."

The black-haired bodyguard climbs into the carriage, his hand stuck inside his open jacket. The driver slaps the reins and they set off toward Commercial Slip. Wixumlee swallows her scowl and leans back into her seat, casting serene eyes from side to side. Like she's royalty, the boss of Buffalo surveying her subjects. Me and Coop run down back alleys and up side streets, getting glimpses of Beany as she rides in a slow circuit around the waterfront. She doesn't smile, but still looks like a princess.

Me and Coop are out of breath by the time the carriage returns to the Black Pole. The thug takes Wixumlee and Beany inside, but comes back out quickly. He waves over the same street scamp, grabs him roughly by an ear and hands him a note. He bends down to whisper something, then the kid takes off at a dead run. Me and Coop make chase and corner him near the harbor. I grab the note and read aloud.

I'd invite you for a healthy meal at the Black Pole—Lord knows you need one—but you'd be stupid to accept. Why trust me? I trust you, sure — you're just hungry kids. But me — I'm considered a criminal in some circles. You shouldn't trust me.

I want my grandson back, but I can't give Beany back, not yet — she's too sick. You want her healthy, don't you? So, you can keep my grandson for a week. In that week I'll fatten Beany up — I've already cleaned her up — and do my best to salve her bleeding soul.

In the meantime, feed my grandson! If he loses weight, if there's a mark on his body — especially his beautiful face — I will send my men to hunt you down and chop you up for cannibal stew on African night!

Wixumlee

"Cannibal stew! Cooper!"

He laughs. Grabs and crumbles the note. Throws it on the ground.

"She's joking!"

I pick the note up and smooth it out.

"Look." I point to a postscript that tells us to come to the back of the tavern in ten minutes to pick up a basket of food.

Our note had been much shorter.

We got Talbot. Give us Beany or he dies.

CHAPTER SIX

We argued a bit about whether to trust Wixumlee's offer of food. I thought it was a trick to nab us and beat the blazes out of us 'til we told her where Talbot was. Coop said he could sneak behind the Black Pole quicker than a fox and grab the basket and that's just what he did.

"So, how's that make you feel, huh, Talbot? Your granny dumped you on us. Ain't even gonna try to get you back."

I pull food out of the large basket and think how pretty Beany looked in her purple and white dress. The last time I saw a dress with those colors, it was on August's lifeless body. August. One of the kindest, most secretive women I'd known—a woman dead by her own hand. Funny how Beany'd dolled herself up in her mama's colors. No, not funny. Not at all.

"Your grandma doesn't want you, Talbot." It makes me feel better to dig the hurt into him.

"That's not true."

"Yeah, it is."

"She just exchanged me for a week. That's what you said, right?" He aims his question at Cooper. "To give herself a chance to nurse Beany."

Coop ignores him. The basket of food smells much more deserving of his attention.

"Uh, huh. You go ahead and think that." I unroll some butcher paper and find three huge sandwiches. Beef. "Hey, Coop, think we should trust this stuff?"

Coop licks his lips but stops his reach for the meat. "Yeah, why not?"

"Maybe she's trying to poison us."

"Then feed it to him, first. Here, kid, have a sandwich."

Talbot grabs it and bites down like a starved man. We watch him carefully for sign of sickness.

"You know, some poisons take a while to kick in," Coop says rubbing his stomach. I take some paper off a bowl of potato salad and smell onions and horseradish. My mouth waters.

"Eat this." I point a spoonful of salad at Talbot's mouth. He opens wide and I drop it in. The kid's eyes turn toward heaven. We watch his jaw grind. He swallows and takes another bite of sandwich.

"I can't wait." Coop sinks his teeth into beef sheltered top and bottom by dark rye bread. I chomp into my sandwich, and we take turns spooning the potato salad. We share an apple, some grapes, three little smooth orange things Talbot calls apricots, and three bottles of cider.

"Where does Wixumlee get this stuff? These *apricots*?" I lean against the cave wall, my stomach full for the first time in weeks.

"New York city. Special order. That's where Mariana gets ingredients for her special dishes. New York and the roadside."

"The road?" I stop glugging down cider.

"She picks a lot of wild things out in the fields. Chicory, chamomile, wild mustard. You should taste her dandelion wine."

"I don't drink spirits." I poke among the potatoes, looking for weeds Mariana slipped into the salad.

Cooper burps. Talbot burps. So just for the heck of it, I burp. Talbot laughs and stretches out on the cave floor.

"So, what we gonna do for the next week?"

I hoot. "You're gonna lay here tied up, that's what."

The boy jerks straight up. "Why?"

"Look, stupid. You think we're gonna let you parade around and give your granny a chance to snatch you back? Then we'd never get Beany."

"You'll get Beany. Grandma said you could keep me for a week."

"Thanks, grandma."

"And after a week — after she's had time to make Beany better — she'll give her back."

"Why should we trust her?" Coop stretches his legs.

"She gave her word." When Coop snorts, Talbot adds "and she's an honorable person!"

We laugh.

"Look, kid, we saw colored people marched out of the Black Pole at night — guns in their backs — and stuffed into the bottom of a wagon." Coop pauses, but Talbot doesn't peep.

"Then we saw you try to fake it by piling those drunken foofoos on top," I continue, "and hauling them back to Sandy Town, like you were just giving them a ride home, that's all, and that you didn't have a whole stolen family stuffed somehow beneath the hay!"

Talbot roots through the food basket and doesn't answer.

"And what'd you do with 'em, huh? Where'd you take 'em? Who'd you sell 'em to?"

"Sell?" Talbot shakes his head. "You got it wrong."

"Then explain it to us," Cooper says, pushing Talbot away from the basket. "So we get it right."

But Talbot only lays back and shuts his eyes. I want to beat it out of him, but remember Wixumlee's warning. I've already marked his face pretty bad. There's a wide shoe print on his forehead. Maybe it'll fade in a week.

I sigh. A week. Another week without Beany. I see her settling down in that fancy frock on the carriage seat. She looked good. Clean. Some strength in her step. She looked good enough that she might not want to go back to pacing the towpath, while I hawk for packets and cargos. Sleeping in a stable. I feel a darkness creep into the cave and cover me, a suffocating blanket. I want Beany back. But will Beany want me? I have a sick feeling that the goose everyone waits for has laid the golden egg right in Beany's lap. She just might be better off with Wixumlee than with me. Might?

"Coop." I nudge my dozing brother with my foot. "Cooper."

"Huh?" He slides down the cave wall and curls up across the entrance. "Watch Talbot, Tess. I gotta get some sleep."

"Wait!" I lay down on the ground next to him and whisper in his ear. "What do you think of Beany? How'd she look to you?"

Cooper sighs. "I think she looks like she's got it made." His breathing slows.

"Yeah. Yeah, she does." I press closer to Cooper. I can't let Talbot hear. "What — what if Wixumlee won't give her back, like she promised."

Cooper opens one eye. "You're smarter than that."

I stare at the ground, refusing to admit what I know Coop's thinking.

He opens his other eye. "Okay, I'll say it. Isn't it more likely Beany won't want to leave that fancy lady? She won't want to come back to us?"

"Shut up, Coop!" I fight the lump in my throat. "'Course she will. She'll want to come back."

"Come on, Tess. You saw Beany. She didn't look like a hostage. She looked like she wanted to be there. All primped and prissy and wearing nearly the same dress August died in!"

So Coop noticed that, too.

"Hush up!" I punch him and shift my eyes at Talbot.

"Wixumlee can give Beany everything—anything!" he continues, ignoring me. "A white dress with purple flowers, just for askin'. A bath every day. Good food. A clean bed. And to top it off, Wixumlee's colored, according to him." He jerks his head at Talbot, who pretends to sleep. "She's just what Beany needs. A strong black woman to look up to."

The golden egg. The *real* golden egg. Much as I hate it, I can't call Beany greedy. It's not unreasonable to replace her dead mama with a woman not afraid of nothin'. Gold on the outside, gold on the inside. Not unreasonable at all. But unacceptable.

"Do you think Beany knows Wixumlee's colored? I mean, we didn't know, 'til Talbot told us."

Coop shrugs. "She knows. If she didn't know when she walked off the towpath with her, she knows now. None of those folks are white, except for that gun-toting gypsy. They might be coffee-colored, but they're still black folk. Beany knows."

"So, you mean we should leave her there?" My throat is thick with sharp, cutting sobs. "You're giving up on her." Before he can answer, I turn my back on him.

He gets up on one elbow and leans over me. "What can we offer Beany? Huh, Tessie? What can you and me give Beany that rich colored woman can't?"

If I open my mouth to answer, I'll throw up. Instead, I gnaw my lower lip. When I taste blood, I gnaw the upper one. Coop falls asleep, his long body blocking the cave's entrance.

After a while, Talbot opens his eyes. "You know, I have to admit, when you said Grandma was leaving me with you for a week, I was excited."

I frown at his smiling face. "Shut pan, fool!"

"No, really. You got me out of that tavern, away from all those women."

Oh, how I want to smack him.

"Now I'll see the side of Buffalo Grandma keeps hidden. I don't get out much and I'm already thirteen."

"Cripes, Talbot, the Black Pole's on Canal Street. On the Slip. Right in the heart of the harbor! Not a livelier spot in the whole dang city. All of Buffalo walks through that waterfront one time or another. Just open your eyes and look! Or don't you even look out the window?"

"Well, Grandma works me pretty hard. At both taverns. We divide our time between the two. Monday, Tuesday and Wednesday in Black Rock. Thursday through Sunday in Buffalo. Grandma likes to be here for the weekend. In case the sailors and canawlers take to busting up her new place."

"Is that what her thugs are for? Or do they just rifle people into wagons and scare off kids trying to get their friend back?"

Talbot lowers his eyelids.

"And why do you only talk about your grandma? What about your ma? Doesn't she have anything to say about you? Sounds like your grandma runs the whole dang show."

Talbot sighs. "That's true. Grandma does run the show. But that's 'cause my ma's not right."

"No kiddin'. Your granny said she's two eggs short of a dozen." Talbot glances up. "Yeah, that's what your granny said." I want to hurt him.

"Sometimes Grandma talks mean." His voice thickens. "She says she's just joking or being honest." In the quiet of the cave I hear him swallow hard. "She loves my ma. Loves her to pieces." And then in a rush of words, "My ma's the reason she—never mind." And with one hushed sob he rolls over to face the wall.

I study his back. At thirteen, he's still a kid, short and skinny, but with naturally broad shoulders. He needs to get out of that kitchen and do some man's work. I wonder if he's ever been east on the Erie Canal, or if he's been stuck down here at the butt end in Buffalo all his life.

"Hey, Talbot." I nudge him with my boot. "This being Sunday, is Wixumlee going back to Black Rock tonight?"

"No," he mumbles. "It's late afternoon. She's long gone."

CHAPTER SEVEN

The next morning Cooper says he's going down to the Buffalo docks to hunt up a granary job.

"You stay here and watch Talbot."

"But then I can't scalp the towpath. How am I supposed to earn money, if I have to watch this kid?" For some reason, Talbot looks younger and smaller than he did when we snatched him.

"Tie him up and go."

"I can't do that!"

"We left him when we saw Beany on the Slip, didn't we? Just go! Run the path a couple hours. Hustle some change. Stop your whining."

Talbot whimpers like a wet puppy, but we bind him hand and food, stuff him in the back of the dark cave and leave. Coop heads toward the lake; me to the canal. I'm glad to be out but have a nagging fear that if something happens to Talbot, however small, Wixumlee will never give Beany back. It isn't a fear. It's a certainty. Thugs guard her. She packs her pockets with police. A gun-toting gypsy is her constant companion. What power do Coop and I have? None. We lose Talbot, we lose Beany.

Cooper gets his granary job and I find a canal captain willing to let me hawk his cargo, so we leave Talbot on Tuesday, too. When I ask the captain if he knows a Wixumlee, his face darkens.

"Why you mixed up with Wixumlee?"

"I'm not. I—I just met her. On the path."

"And then what?"

"What?"

"And then what happened?"

"I don't know. Nothin'."

He glares and I think he might fire me just for mentioning the woman.

"Stay away from that one."

He turns his back and I hustle away. The captain's advice is good, but comes too late.

When I return to the cave hours later, Talbot is in agony from laying on his side, ankles tied, hands bound behind his back. I notice his raw wrists, but heck, he's a prisoner and wouldn't be if his grandma didn't steal Beany.

"You trying to get out of these ropes?"

"No." His voice is small, wounded.

"Then why are your wrists bleeding?"

"I don't know."

"You trying to get us in trouble with your granny? Get her thinking we hurt you?"

"You are hurting me. Keeping me tied up in this dark, wet place all day."

"It ain't wet and it ain't all day."

"It is for me. You're out in the sunshine. It's hot out there, but it gets cold in here. I'm miserable and —."

"Shut up! Beany's a prisoner, too." But Beany isn't tied up, laying in smelly clothes, face down in the dirt, for hours at a time. Not even for a minute. She sits on fancy sofas, her flouncy skirts spread like pretty tablecloths. Will she trade places with Talbot? Will she go back to a filthy face, ragged clothes, sleeping on a stable floor?

On Wednesday Cooper tugs the ropes tight around Talbot's bloody wrists. He winces and whines, but we have no choice. I can't stay. I need money to survive. The weather's still warm, but winter often blasts in as early as October in this western end of New York. The canal boats will soon stop running and what will I do after that? Do they hire girls at the granary?

When I return late Wednesday afternoon Talbot is limp and silent. Both me and Cooper bring food back every night, so it ain't our fault the kid's dwindling. We offered him back to his granny. Fair exchange, him for Beany.

I leave the cave Thursday morning in good spirits. Wixumlee's coming back to Buffalo today, and we're more than halfway to Sunday — when we get Beany back. I hawk a fistful of packet tickets and connive like a pro to get my captain a load of lumber for a new house going up near Seneca Falls.

But as soon as the lumberman says Seneca Falls, my heart aches for Ma. Is she doing all the housework herself and the cooking, too, now that August's gone? The sudden picture of Beany's mama peeling potatoes at the kitchen table sends violent chills across my shoulders. I squeeze my eyes shut and behind my lids the cook's stabbed breast squirts thick, red blood. I see August's wilted body laying in the daisies as we slide past on Captain Beale's cargo, the two mangled slave catchers oozing red glue onto the tarp beside me. I leave the lumberman standing there, run behind a tree and puke.

My mood brightens some when I hand my captain a fistful of money and he cuts me a share. I decide to treat Talbot to something sweet and head back to the cave carrying a large, cream-filled pastry shaped like a horn with powdered sugar on top.

Pushing my way through the vine-draped apple tree, I hear noise coming from inside the cave. Inhuman sounds. Growls. Then human cries, sharp and snapped off at the end. Talbot! I fight through the vines then gasp and jump back. A large, black and white dog stalks toward me, head low, ears flat, teeth bared. He lunges, knocking me onto my back. The dog stands over me, baring red gums and black-rimmed fangs. I hold my breath, expecting teeth in my throat at any second. Growls and cries fight their way out of the cave. How many dogs are there?

"Help!

"Talbot!" I instantly regret shouting. The big dog snarls and levels me with mean, yellow eyes. *Talbot*. It's only a thought this time.

"Help! Tess!"

I don't know what to do—stare the dog down or look away.

"Tess! Dog!" Suddenly the snarls change to the nasty, wet gnashes of a dog in full attack.

"Aaahhh! Oowww! Tess!"

Flat on my back, I feel around for a rock or stick, but the ground offers only pebbles.

"Tess!" Talbot screams in agony. "Help!"

He's being slaughtered, laying there with feet bound, arms tied behind his back while the animal chews him alive.

Suddenly the vines part and a large rock strikes the black and white dog's neck. It yelps but recovers quickly and lunges at me. I glimpse Cooper bursting through the vine-green curtain swinging a hefty tree branch. He catches the dog upside the head, knocks it off balance and proceeds to pound it to death with the club. He flips open his pocketknife and runs straight into the cave. Screams, snarls, curses and howls—both human and animal—assault me outside. I crawl to the mouth of the cave, praying for the noise and pain to stop.

Then silence. Either Coop killed the dog. Or—.

"Cooper?" I barely whisper his name. "Coop?"

Silence.

My throat feels swollen, as if I'd been screaming. My body throbs, and I feel blood running down my arms, but they're clean.

"Talbot?"

A great aching sadness washes over me and I start to cry. Then I hear dragging, grunts, and Coop's boots appear. He backs out, pulling a large, red dog. He hauls it off to the side, frowns at me, crawls back into the cave. I hear mumbling, rope snapping. Coop's boots reappear as he pulls Talbot into the sunshine.

"Oh, Lordy, no!" I bite down on my fist. Talbot's pants are blood-soaked. Ragged bites mark the back of his neck, his head, his hands. His shirt is shredded. He must have tried to protect his face and chest by turning his back to the gnashing dog.

Cooper picks up Talbot, and I follow them down to the cove. Coop sets the boy on the ground then takes off his own shirt. "Wet this."

I soak it then twist water out of the cloth. "What we gonna do?"

"Clean him."

"There's too much blood."

"Gimme that." He snatches the wet shirt and gently wipes the blood and dirt off Talbot's head and neck. Tries to wipe the wounds on his back, but they're too deep to touch. "He needs a doctor." Talbot doesn't make a sound. He barely looks alive. "We'll take him back."

"To Wixumlee? No! We can't! Not like this. She'll never give Beany back, she sees how chewed up he is."

"The bites are deep." Coop looks straight at me for the first time. His jaw is stiff, his eyes hard. He's angry. At me. He's disgusted with me. I didn't help. I didn't fight. "He needs to get sewed up."

"No, Cooper." I blubber like a baby. "She'll take Talbot and keep Beany. And who knows what she'll do to us."

Coop turns on me. "Get the wheelbarrow!" When I hesitate, glancing at Talbot's pained face, he grabs a fistful of my hair and shakes me. "Now!"

I push the rusty wheelbarrow over to Cooper. He lays his shirt at the bottom, sinks Talbot gently into its depth, and speaks soothingly when the boy's torn back touched the hard metal. Closer to town, Coop snatches a blanket off a clothesline and covers him, as much against inquiring eyes as against the evening chill.

We walk slowly to the new Black Pole.

CHAPTER EIGHT

Every time Mariana walks past us, sitting on a bench in a corner of her kitchen, she shakes a fist and cusses. I shrink into the protective curve of Coop's arm, scared to death of the angry gypsy and the black-haired guard standing over us with a rifle. I glance at the greasy kitchen rag wrapped around my brother's bleeding hand. Talbot isn't the only one the red dog chewed. But I'm the only one unmarked.

Things have settled down some since we wheeled Talbot, bloody and moaning, to the Black Pole's back door and pounded. Wixumlee herself answered and screeched to high heaven. She picked Talbot out of the wheelbarrow like an infant and carried him into the kitchen.

"Lay him face down," Coop called from the doorway. "His back's bit up bad."

When Wixumlee fumbled with the boy, Coop ran inside and helped turn him over.

"Come on, Coop. Let's go!" I hung on the doorjam ready to run.

"Quin! Larkin!"

"She's calling her thugs!"

Coop took a step toward the door, but it was too late. A large, tan-colored man with a dark mustache and looping black hair—the man who'd taken our ransom note—grabbed me from behind and pushed me into the kitchen. A second guy—Snakeman—dashed in from the dining room and pointed a rifle at Cooper. Since getting tangled up with Wixumlee, I've seen more guns than I've seen in my entire life.

One of these rifle-toters—the loopy-haired Larkin—stands over us now, his raisin black eyes roving from the tops of our bent heads to the kitchen table, where a doctor pushes at a needle and thread, closing up Talbot's many open wounds.

Wixumlee sits in a chair holding Talbot's fingertips, while Mariana bathes his raw, red wrists with some concoction she's mixed from the jars above the sink. The gypsy has already cleaned the vicious bites on his head and back with the strange-smelling liquid and is humming a soothing tune, slipping in foofoo words, as she pours and pours the mixture over first one marred wrist then the other. She and Wixumlee take turns peeking at the doctor's stitching and shouting angrily at me and Cooper, before switching back to soothing Talbot.

"That should do it." The doctor stands up straight and stretches.

Wixumlee mumbles something and jerks her head at Cooper.

The doctor grunts. "Where you hurt, boy?" Coop holds out his crudely bandaged hand. The doctor unrolls the rag. "Ah, dog got you, too, huh? It's a bad one."

Coop nods. He'd done all the wheeling from the cave to the Slip, gripping the rough wheelbarrow handles without complaint.

The doctor turns Cooper's hand over, back and forth. "Have to clean it first."

Mariana comes over with her bowl of smelly water and washes Coop's bloody hand, maybe not as gently, but as thoroughly as she'd cleaned Talbot. The blood gone, I can see a mean puncture in the meaty part of Coop's hand at the base of his left thumb.

"It's bleeding, so that's good," the doc says. "I can't stitch a puncture, so you better keep an eye on it." He pours some whiskey from a bottle over the holes, then pours on some purple, stinking stuff from a smaller bottle and wraps Coop's hand in a clean, white bandage.

"You're good with herbs, Mariana," the doctor says. "Keep an eye on this boy's hand, okay?" The gypsy ignores the compliment and throws us dagger looks.

"And how about you?" The doctor turns to me. "Where are you hurt?"

I shrug. "Nowhere."

"You sure?"

"Yeah."

"These boys got bit bad. You're not hurt?"

"No." It's barely a whisper.

Mariana snorts and mumbles foofoo talk.

"No, you won't find mean dog bites on that one, doctor." Wixumlee's snarl curls around my heart and squeezes. "Not one little nip. Amazing, isn't it?"

"Tess." My name is the first word Talbot speaks since being laid on the kitchen table.

"Yeah, Talbot?" I stand, but Larkin's large hand lands on my head, pushing me down.

"He's asking for her," Coop says, flexing the fingers of his sore hand. "Let her up."

"She don't get up, 'til Wixumlee says she gets up." Larkin's loose black curls bounce around his eyebrows. I watch the muscles in his upper arms ripple as he shifts his rifle from one hand to the other.

"Tess." Talbot moans with the effort of turning his head to look back at us. "Grandma — ."

"Oh, okay. Get her up here," Wixumlee snaps, jerking her head around. "Let her up, Larkin. But watch that boy."

Wixumlee scrapes her chair aside to make room. I slip past Larkin and squeeze in between her and Mariana. They step away, so as not to touch me.

"Yeah, Talbot?" I wince at the black crisscross stitching on his neck and back.

"Thanks for helping me, Tess."

I stare at him.

"For keeping that other dog off me."

I'm silent, motionless.

"I know he had you cornered out there."

I peek at Mariana, then at Wixumlee.

"I guess we're lucky Coop came along when he did, huh?" A weak smile traces Talbot's lips.

My face burns with shame, but I don't correct him. "Yeah — hey — you're gonna be okay, Talbot."

"He's gonna be okay *now*," Mariana snarls. "Now that he's home instead of tied up, cold, wet and starved in a dark cave!" The conditions of Talbot's confinement came out in Cooper's story of the dog attack.

"No, no. I ate good — they fed me good."

Wixumlee kisses Talbot's head, somehow finding a spot that isn't raked raw.

"They treated me good, Grandma."

Wixumlee's face loses its haughty twist and turns mushy. Her eyes flood.

"I'm just glad you're safe at home now, honey. Just glad you're safe. I'm sorry it happened, Talbot. I never thought you'd get hurt. It was stupid of me to think they'd take care of you." She nails me with an angry glare.

"They did okay by me, Grandma. Where's Mama?"

"You'll see her soon enough, baby. You know this is not the right time." Wixumlee pushes clumsily at her yellow hair. "You know how she'll get."

"Can we see Beany?" Coop's question stuns me. Wixumlee freezes in her chair. I spin around, afraid Larkin will pound him with the rifle butt. My heart hammers out the seconds 'til he — or she — attacks.

Slowly, Wixumlee turns. "No. No, you cannot see Beany."

"Come on, lady, you got Talbot." There's pain in Coop's eyes, but his voice is strong.

Wixumlee exchanges looks with Larkin. The guard's jaw is rigid, his shoulder muscles tense. I hold my breath. Please, Coop, don't make trouble. You're crazy if you think you can take Larkin with a dog-bit hand. I send these messages through my tearing eyes and pray he understands.

"You're in no position to make demands, boy. Besides, the child's asleep."

Cooper laughs and shakes his head. How can he laugh? He shifts on the bench and Larkin moves, too. They lock eyes. I start to sweat. Coop will expect me to help him fight, but I don't want any part of a bruiser Larkin's size. I don't want to fight anybody, ever.

"Grandma, let them see Beany. The week's up and you promised."

"No, Talbot, the week is not up." The words are firm. Wixumlee pats Talbot's leg gently then barks, "Move away, girl! Away from my grandson."

I slide back onto the bench beside Cooper. Wixumlee rises from her chair and faces us with arms folded stiffly across her chest, as if she is afraid her fists might fly.

"The week is not up until Sunday. And the deal was that you'd get Beany back if I got Talbot back undamaged."

She takes a step toward us. When a hand flies out, I flinch, but she only waves it behind her.

"Look at him! Is that boy undamaged?"

No one says a word.

"Quin! Does Talbot look undamaged to you?"

Snakeman, posed to strike beside the kitchen door, shakes his head. My shoe mark is faintly visible on Talbot's forehead, but it is the least of his injuries.

"Grandma, you promised."

"I promised? Did they keep their part of the bargain? Or did they let your head get almost chewed off by a wild dog?"

Wixumlee's gleaming yellow eyes illuminate the pale skin beneath her light eyebrows.

"Escort them to the door, Larkin. Their business is finished here. Forever!"

"No, please." I clasp my hands together. "Let us see Beany. Just see her, please. We'll do anything you want."

"Shut up, Tess." Coop shoves me past Larkin, the men passing nose to nose, eyeball to eyeball. "We'll get Beany back, lady. Don't even think of selling her off."

Wixumlee's mouth pops open.

"Yeah, we know your business. And don't think we'll keep quiet about it."

"Cooper! Shush!" I hiss into his ear.

"What are you talking about?"

"Grandma, never mind." Talbot strains to see behind him.

"What did you see?" Wixumlee advances on us.

"I'll tell you later, Grandma. Let them go! Please!" His voice cracks with the pain of moving and Wixumlee rushes back to him.

Cooper sneers at Larkin and steps into the alley, pulling me behind him. The door slams shut.

I hurry to follow him down the alley leading to Canal Street. "Coop, we can't leave Beany there."

He turns on me.

"Shut up! What are *you* gonna do—rescue her by whining? Damn sissy! *'Oh, please, let us see her,'*" he squeals, wringing his hands. "What the hell's wrong with you? You gotta be strong with these people. Where's your spirit? What the hell happened to you, Tess?"

He stomps toward the waterfront. I tag meekly behind, confused and afraid of everything and everybody.

I roll over in the straw inside a Buffalo stable on Erie Street Coop's convinced the owner to share, now that we've abandoned the cave. I'm heartsick, unable to sleep. Coop's words ring true. I'm a crybaby. A whiner. A damn sissy. I can't stand up to anybody. The only person I've pushed around since the bloody battle on the towpath is Talbot, a skinny kid younger than me and half my size.

I'm scared to death of fighting. Of getting hit. Of getting killed. I never expected August to get killed. I expected Coop's canawler buddies to hop off the boat and beat off the slave catchers. We'd all hop back on the boat and off we'd go. Maybe the slavers would get hurt—even killed—but not August. She shouldn't have died and not by her own hand. Not by plunging her own blue stone knife into her own chest.

I should have saved August. But I didn't. I'm weak. Useless. I didn't save August. I lost Beany. And should the need arise, I couldn't even save myself.

CHAPTER NINE

Despite his sore hand, Cooper works Friday at the granary loading sacks of flour onto cargo ships docked in the Buffalo harbor. I try to hawk cargo, but my heart isn't in it. We were supposed to get Beany back on Sunday. Supposed to, if I hadn't messed up and left Talbot to get almost eaten alive. Coop won't talk about Sunday and Beany. He says not to worry, we'll get her back. He's bone tired from loading flour sacks sunrise to sunset and growls at me to shut pan when I try to push him to plot Beany's rescue.

Hoping to catch sight of Beany, I walk past the Black Pole several times Saturday afternoon and finally summon meager courage to press my nose against a window. I can't see anything inside and when I pull back bump into something hard. Turning, I find my nose pressed against Larkin's rock-hard chest. Heart thumping, too scared to run, I stand motionless staring up at him. I see a hard-faced man about Coop's age with the same strong man's body. His rippling muscles, dark eyes, stony manner and devotion to Wixum-lee scare me to death.

Larkin takes a step back, looks me up and down and smirks. He studies my broken nose and the scabs that healed roughly over the gashes on my cheeks and chin. I lock onto his large, almond-shaped eyes for only a second before staring down at my feet. My arms hang at my sides like two hanks of ham and I want to disappear into a bottomless smokehouse.

"Git!" Larkin's hiss and raised fist send me racing down the street. I knock over a crate of potatoes and the shopkeeper's curses chase me down the Slip. I glance back over my shoulder and see Larkin bent over, laughing.

Feeling like a fool, I slip behind a horse's rump to catch my breath and slow my pounding heart. Looking back at the tavern, I see a carriage pull in front of the Black Pole. Larkin snaps to attention. When the front door opens, Wixumlee and Quin walk out and climb into the coach. Then Larkin draws a young girl in a bright blue dress through the doorway. Beany. He lifts her into the carriage and Wixumlee settles her on the seat. Larkin climbs aboard, Wixumlee signals the driver, and they take off in the direction of Sandy Town.

I lope after them, my feet stinging with each slap on the cobblestones, panting with exertion, 'til I'm able to hop on the back of a farm wagon that takes me to within sight of Wixumlee's carriage parked near her little foofoo village.

Slipping off the wagon, I see Wixumlee hand Quin some papers. With Larkin standing tall in the carriage, rifle across his chest, Quin walks across the sand to the first tiny cottage and pounds on the door like he owns the place. A small man with black hair and a droopy mustache steps outside, closing the door behind him. He barely reaches Quin's shoulder but balls his fists, spreads his feet and readies himself for action. His eyes dart from Quin to the carriage, then bounce off Wixumlee's soldiers patrolling Sandy Town's borders.

Quin thrusts a piece of paper at the man and talks and waves his hand toward the Slip. The fellow listens with his dark head cocked to one side, but I can tell he has no idea what the tattooed man is jabbering about. He shakes his head and turns to go inside.

Quin grabs his arm and quick as a lick, a thin, shiny knife falls into the little guy's hand and he swipes at Quin's belly. Quin jumps back and looks at Wixumlee, standing hands on hips in the carriage. He raises his arms as if asking, "Now what?"

Wixumlee stamps her foot and instead of sending big, bad Larkin to help him, climbs down and wobbles through the sand in her fancy, high-heeled shoes.

The brassy woman snatches the paper from the knife-wielding foreigner and begins talking loudly. I catch words like "food" and "eat" and "vino." She pretends to spoon food into her mouth, points toward Commercial Slip, shouts "Eat! Eat!" and waves wildly toward town. She repeats her directions, instructions, whatever she's doing, mixing in fork and mouth motions, until the little man smiles, nods and waves his hand as if to say, "Okay, I get it."

Wixumlee raises her arms in victory, turns her back on the little foofoo, then she and Quin make the rounds of the other cottages.

Like a small circus act, they go through their dog and pony show until every family, and especially every man, has a piece of her paper and what I figure are directions to the Black Pole.

Through it all, Beany sits silently — and it seems to me, unseeing, unhearing. She pays no attention to Larkin, braced above her, clutching his rifle. He turns slowly to survey the beach, the road, and the colorfully dressed Poles, Germans and Italians, but Beany barely blinks. Every now and then Larkin glances down at her dark, wavy hair, as shiny as a freshly brushed horse's mane. Something hanging on a silver chain around her neck also glitters. As if remembering, Beany reaches up, strokes it, caresses it. Larkin looks away and his chest heaves a sigh.

Quin walks Wixumlee back to the carriage, and a paper falls from his back pocket. When the group heads back to town, I snatch it up and try to figure out the message. I see the road marked from Buffalo's Black Pole to Sandy Town and hand-drawn pictures of food — full plates of sausages, bowls of potatoes and beans, pies, cakes and loaves of bread. Big mugs of foaming beer and bottles with "vino" written on them cover half the page.

There are also drawings of coins and paper money with big, thick Xs drawn through them and the words "Free Food and Drink" printed in big letters at the top of the page. Well, that's the hardest idea for Wixumlee to get across. *Free* food. In the few times I've been to Sandy Town, I've never heard one word of English spoken by any foreigner camped here.

I walk slowly back to town. Why is Wixumlee offering these folks free food? If they all show up she'll lose any profit she makes from the paying folks — if she even has room for paying folks.

Cooper jogs down the road from the harbor. "Tess!" He looks weary but smiles. "I just saw Beany."

"Yeah, me too."

"You get to fussing with Wixumlee?" He frowns.

"No. They didn't see me. But look at this."

He takes the paper.

"Wixumlee and one of her goons just spent a half hour passing these out. Trying to get these foofoos up to the Black Pole for free food."

"Free? Hey, maybe we can get in on that." He grins like a hungry lion.

"Yeah, like she'd feed us. But Coop, why's she trying to get these people to her tavern?"

Coop scratches his head and cocks an eyebrow.

"Yeah, that's what I'm thinking, too."

"It's only a guess."

"What we saw last week wasn't a one-time thing, Cooper. See these bottles and mugs of beer? She wants those guys liquored up. Then she can use them to disguise her kidnap wagon. She must run it regular as a stagecoach."

"Maybe. You don't know anything for sure." Coop folds the paper and puts it in his pocket.

"Come on, Cooper! It's the first thing you thought when I showed you that handbill!"

Wixumlee's still carting off coloreds, but at least Beany's okay. Wixumlee's taken pity on her and she's escaped whatever fate befell the others shipped off in the bottom of farm wagons.

CHAPTER TEN

Cooper tells me about a guy at the granary who wants to share a room with us for the winter. Coop expects me to chip in my share of the rent. That's fair, but I tell him I don't like sharing sleep space with a stranger. Coop doesn't know much about the fellow outside work, but he needs cheap rent like we do and we can all help each other out. So Coop says he'll bring the guy around to the stable so we can get acquainted. Now here he is, banging around the barn, shouting at the mules, acting like the top dog.

"Tess. Here's the guy I told you about. Nicky Pappo." Exhausted from tossing fifty-pound flour sacks all day, Coop collapses in the straw and closes his eyes.

I concentrate on petting a flea-bitten stable cat, and Pappo, ropey arms draped across the top of a stall, ignores me, too. Suddenly, he shakes the stall door violently, spooking the weary horse inside.

"Don't do that! That's an old horse, don't bother him!" I pick up the scabby cat protectively. Pappo rattles the wooden door again then faces me.

"Who the heck beat the tar out of you?"

Surprised by Pappo's southern accent, I scoot against the stable wall.

"Who busted your nose?"

"None of your business." I press my forehead into the cat's gnarly neck.

"You in a fight? You a fighter? Huh? Or a loser? Looks like somebody took a peeling knife to your face."

"Shut up!" I know Nicky Pappo less than a minute and already hate him.

Pappo's lashless eyes glare. He has a scarred, bald head and his smooth, shiny arms dangle over the stall door like water moccasins caught on a cliff. Pappo stares 'til I drop my head, then pulls himself off the door and squats in front of me. Reluctantly, I raise my head. His face is creased with dirty flour and sweat. I feel the heat coming off him.

"Cooper?" I barely squeak.

Coop opens his eyes. "Leave her alone, Nicky. I brought you here to make friends. Where you guys want to eat?"

"Well, I kind of want to try that new place on the Slip where all the foofoos go." Pappo smiles wickedly, his nose inches from mine.

"The Black Pole?" Coop raises up on his elbows.

"Yeah, that's the place." Pappo's words slip across his tongue in single file, none in any hurry to overtake the others.

"Me and Tess can't go there."

"Why not?"

"Had a run-in with the owner."

"She *say* you can't go there?" Bouncing on his toes, Pappo talks to Cooper but stares at me. I want to push him over.

"Well, she never really *said* we couldn't."

"Then that's where we'll go." Pappo sets a dirty hand on my head and tips it back. My palms sweat. "I can fix that nose, girly. One sock and it'll be straight as a ruler."

Cooper laughs. "Yeah, I want to do that, too. Sure is awful looking at that crooked beak."

"I'll fix it quick." Pappo knocks his knuckles against the stable wall.

"No!" I reach up to swat Pappo's hand off my head then let my arm fall back onto the straw.

Pappo snorts. "Chick, chick, chick. Here chick, chick, chick." He pushes me over and shouts, "Let's eat!"

I'm as mad at Coop as I am at Nicky. When we were little, my brother would sometimes let his friends push me around, and it always made me savage as a meat ax. He said it toughened me up. Pappo didn't hurt me—just made me feel like a sissy. I put up tougher fights when I was five.

But what's Coop doing hanging around this creepy guy anyway? Acting like pals, joking and sharing stories like they've known each other half their lives. Like Larkin, Pappo looks about Coop's age, but other than that, I can't figure why my brother would get tangled up with this troublemaker.

He's a bad egg, I know it, the stink coming off him like out from under the wall of an outhouse. The thought of sharing a room with Pappo sickens me. What should have been a nice end to a miserable week—a hearty supper at a good tavern, any tavern but this one— turns sour. As we approach the Black Pole, my spirits sink further. Larkin guards the front door.

"Coop, let's not go here." My voice quivers as we cross the street. He puts an arm around my shoulder. I know my brother wants another chance at Larkin. If he could ever find him without that rifle.

"Aw, what's the matter, you scared?" Pappo flings his arm around my neck, too, and I pull away from his sticky armpit.

"He won't let us in, Coop." I try to wriggle out of Pappo's grasp.

"Yeah, he will." Pappo squeezes my neck with a callused hand.

"I'm not talking to you! Don't make trouble, Cooper."

"Trouble don't scare me." Nicky pulls my hair. "Neither does a nigger."

I fling his arm off my neck. He laughs and shoves me.

"Knock it off, Nicky. Don't give this guy a reason to turn us away." Coop rubs his stomach. "I'm hungry." I can't believe he's gonna walk right up to Larkin.

"Oh, you want me to behave myself?" Pappo straightens out of his slouch, brushes the sleeves of his grubby cotton work shirt, struts up to Larkin and bows. "Sir, may we have the honor of dining at your illustrious establishment?"

I bend my knees, ready to run. Pappo stands straight, expecting an answer. Larkin leans against the doorjamb, thumbs hooked in his belt loops. His rifle, to my surprise, rests beside the door. A little wiggle plays around his lips. Does he think this fool is funny? Pappo might be dumb, but I'm not. I know Larkin's strength and fear it. He's a guard dog, fiercely protective of Wixumlee. He can— and will—squash Pappo like a stink bug.

"Would you like your regular table, sir?" Larkin smiles politely.

I gasp. Look to Coop with wonder.

"My regular table! Did you hear that?" Pappo grins at Cooper, who raises his eyebrows in surprise. "He's got my regular table waiting for me. I didn't even know I had a regular table."

Larkin bows his head slightly and opens the door. Coop pulls me forward and Nicky's jeering laugh chases us inside. Somehow that jeering laugh sounds familiar.

Within minutes, Savannah fills our water glasses. When I ask quietly how Talbot's feeling, his mama's real eye drips instant tears. She says her little boy fell down a hill through some wild blackberry bushes and got pretty cut up and isn't working right now 'cause he's healing. She turns her fake, happy eye on me. But he's gonna be okay, she says, 'cause Mariana's nursing him. Then her teary eye comes back into view.

"I sure feels bad about my little fella getting scratched up like that. I can't remember where I was when it happened and I feels like I ain't taking proper care of him."

"Savannah," a voice calls from the kitchen.

"But mama says, 'Don't worry, honey, we're all taking good care of Talbot now,' so I feels a little better. Just a little."

"Savannah, honey. Come on back."

I recognize Wixumlee's patient voice. So different from her vengeful one. Savannah trots back to the kitchen.

"That gal's crazy as a loon." Pappo drinks down his glass of cold water then he drinks down mine. "Did you get a load of that eyeball?"

"She made it herself." I know it's a mistake as soon as I say it. Pappo slaps the tabletop and rears back in his chair laughing.

"Did she? Well, she's a talent, that one. Hey, Coop, maybe we can get her to make us some fancy eyeballs, too, what ya think?"

Cooper frowns. "She ain't all there, Nicky, leave her alone."

"Well, if she ain't all there, I wonder where she is. Do you know, girly?" He nudges me. "Where's ol' Savannah? That's her name, ain't it?" His voice scrapes like a rusty razor. "Hey, if that was my woman I'd lock her up in a cave somewhere. She shouldn't be out in public, that one. Wouldn't you, Coop? Would you hide her away in a cave?"

Coop ignores him, but a chill creeps across my shoulders. I want to shut Pappo up, blast him nasty. He gets any louder, Wixumlee will swoop down like a hungry hawk and her claws will sink into me, too, just for being here. But Pappo won't shut pan. More words slop off his tongue.

"Where-oh-where is Savannah? Maybe that coffee-colored guy outside knows where she is. They're about the same color. Him and Savannah. Two cups of milky coffee."

I wish I had a club. Pappo laughs and rocks in his chair.

"Should I go ask that coffee guy?"

A deep growl rumbles in the pit of my stomach, and it's not from hunger. I really, really hate Nicky Pappo, and am mad that Coop doesn't pay him any mind. Maybe talk like this is common on the canal. He's heard it for years and it don't mean squat to him. Coop stretches, rubs his stomach and looks around. Maybe he just wants to ignore Nicky and hope trouble doesn't blow our way.

"Be nice to get some service here." As soon as Coop says it, Pappo lets out an ear-piercing whistle. And it accomplishes just what Nicky wants and I want least. Wixumlee springs to our table, waving her hands to calm her startled customers.

"Hey! You boy! What's wrong with you? This is a respectable establishment. Are you some crazy cowboy? Stop that noise."

"Good evening, madam," Pappo drawls. He leans back, hands behind his head, and puts his feet up on an empty chair. I sit rock still. "How good of you to wait on us yourself. You are the owner here, correct? I can tell by your lovely gown — is that a ruby at your throat? — that you are the proprietress. How surprising, but pleasant, that you agree to *serve* us yourself."

Sweat slides down my temples. Mouth ajar, Coop stares at Nicky. Neither of us looks at Wixumlee.

The large woman looms over Pappo and makes a big show of inspecting his shabby work shirt, broken fingernails, torn pants, grimy neck and scuffed brogans. She isn't the least intimidated by this sorry excuse for a southern gentleman disgracing her dining room.

"Look, you pitiful pool of pig pee."

Pappo's greasy grin disappears behind his thin lips.

"You pompous jackass."

Pappo's eyes bulge.

"You are a guest in my tavern. In my *home*. Keep your feet on the floor, your hands on the table, and your tongue in your mouth. Be rude or abusive to me or my guests and your skinny rump will bounce down the Slip and across the lake to Canada!"

Pappo jerks upright in his seat and glares. Wixumlee snaps her fingers and Quin strides from a dark corner of the tavern. No one in the room moves — not even the foofoos who can't understand a word she's saying but catch the tone — and the volume. I make myself as small as I can. Quin's twice Pappo's size. He and Wixumlee can easily grab Nicky's arms and haul him to the door where Larkin will finish him off.

"Feet on the floor," Quin growls.

Pappo hesitates then slowly pulls one foot off the chair, then the other.

"Hands on the table."

Pappo draws himself up into a proper sitting position.

"Now talk in a normal tone of voice and eat like a gentleman." Wixumlee dismisses him with a swift view of her long, straight back and sails into the kitchen. Quin remains an extra second to eyeball Pappo then struts back to his corner.

"Well, who ever thought coloreds would get uppity like that," Pappo whispers after Quin leaves.

"Shut up, Nicky! You almost got us thrown out." Coop's ready to slug him. "That's the last woman I want to tangle with."

I'm surprised, but not disappointed, that Wixumlee completely ignored me and Cooper, concentrating her fury on Pappo.

"Aw, that was a joke! I come in here all the time. She's just playing with me."

"Yeah, she is."

Mariana, her head wrapped in a blue and yellow kerchief, necklaces swinging like tow ropes, appears beside our table. "Tonight it's chicken, corn on the cob, mashed potatoes."

"What if I don't want chicken, corn and potatoes?" Pappo grins at the gypsy and reaches up to finger her shiny beads. Instead of slapping away his hand, Mariana pulls the leather bag tied around her waist to the front of her apron and stretches the hide to show the outline of her pistol. Pappo drops his hand.

"Tonight it's chicken. Corn on the cob. Mashed potatoes."

"Sounds great to me!" Coop smiles widely and rubs his stomach. I nod eagerly.

Nicky Pappo shrugs. "I guess it'll do."

"So, this—Wixumlee—stole your colored girl?"

"She's not our colored girl!" I hate this fool with my entire heart and soul. "Her name's Beany and she's our friend."

Pappo butters another piece of bread. "Don't take offense, girly, but you don't look to me like folks with servants." Said as if he hasn't just heard me say she isn't our colored girl, like we own her. Pappo takes a bite of bread and sneers.

"She's the cook's daughter," Coop says through a mouthful of chicken and gravy. "At the boarding house our folks run. We don't own the place."

I'm mad that Coop blabbed about Beany's kidnapping to Nicky during lunch one day at the granary. From what I can tell, Pappo doesn't know anything about the jailbreak in Seneca Falls, August's death and our escape on the canal. Cooper isn't stupid enough to let him in on that secret, I hope.

Nicky gnaws a chicken leg. "So, let me get this straight. You," he jerks his head at me, "came here with this Beany kid for lunch and wild Wixy Lee nabbed her. Is that right?"

I nod wearily.

"Then, you stole her grandkid, this Talbot — whose ma's that crazy, fake-eyeball gal Savannah — right?"

"Yeah." Cooper drains another glass of cider.

"Then you," he jerks his head at me, "let this Talbot get chewed by wild dogs, right? And now Wixy Lee won't give the girl back."

I hate Nicky Pappo. Hate everything about him.

"So, what you gonna do?" Despite his running mouth, Pappo looks to be shoveling as much food as Cooper. "I mean, you're gonna get the Bean back, right? The question is how. How you gonna do it?"

I don't know what I hate about Nicky Pappo most. His ugly, scarred, balded head. His sloppy southern drawl. His nosiness. His crudeness. His hatefulness. The list goes on.

"We don't really have a plan, Nicky. We're just mainly trying to survive here. But now I got this granary job, we'll be eating regular, and maybe we can hatch a plan to get Beany back." Coop burps, satisfied, but I'm mad. I'd never share a plan with Nicky Pappo.

Pappo's quiet for a minute, then raises his arms and scratches the back of his scabby head. "Well, you know — you snatch that kid, you say goodbye to your granary job." When Coop looks surprised, Pappo says, "You think you'll survive a day in Buffalo when Wixy finds her kid gone?"

"Beany's not her kid!" There's just so much lip I'll take from this bum.

"Ain't the point, girly girl. Point is, Wixy's taken a shine to that kid for whatever reason and wants to keep her."

"How do you know?"

"Plain as day! If she didn't want her, she'd have tossed her back. Tossed her back in a box when you showed up with chewed-up Talbot."

"Stop calling him chewed!" And is he saying Wixumlee would purposely hurt Beany? Badly? Permanently? Send her back in a box? A pine box? My supper sours in my stomach.

"What you need, Coop, is to get inside."

"Inside where?"

"Inside here." Pappo leans his head in close and drops his voice. "Inside this tavern. Get in good with Wixumlee."

Cooper snorts. "She don't want no part of me, bub."

"Hey, maybe you could be one of her bodyguards." Pappo's face lights up. "Like that chocolate mug in the corner or that milky one out front."

"His name's Larkin." Dang! Can't I keep my mouth shut?

Pappo pops up in his seat. "Larkin?" A slow, sickening smile smears his face. "Larkin, is it? You seem to know an awful lot about these colored folks, girly. You know their names. You know they make their own eyeballs. How you know so much? You in with them somehow?"

"How could I be *in* with them, fool? They hate me." I want to crack a plate over Nicky's crusty head. Maybe that's how he got those scars. People beaned his brain with sharp objects.

"Hey, maybe we both could get roughneck jobs here. You and me, Coop."

"Yeah, like she'd hire you!" I snicker. "She hates you more than she hates us!" I'm itching to leave, knowing we've outstayed our weak welcome.

"Shut up, girly, I'm talking to your brother here, the brains of the outfit." Pappo's sloppy smile twists into an ugly sneer.

"She called you pig pee!"

"Tess." Coop shakes his head, but I can't stop.

"She never called us that, not even when we brought Talbot back." I scoot back in my chair. I should shut my mouth. Quin's staring at us.

"She was prob'ly so mad she couldn't talk."

"Nicky, drop it. Come on, we're done here." Coop glances toward the kitchen. Mariana walks over with our bill and stands by our table while Cooper pulls out money for me and him.

"Pony up, Nicky. Two bits."

"Two bits! For that lousy meal? I'll prob'ly get food poisoning."
Mariana raises a hand to her leather bag.

"Two bits for a bony chicken leg, half a potato and two kernels
of corn? That's robbery!"

"Cripes, Nicky, you got money. Pay up!" Coop looks apologet-
ically at Mariana.

Pappo, his lashless eyes clamped on the gypsy, digs in his
pocket, draws out two coins and tosses them on the table. She picks
up the money, mumbles "son of a dog" and leaves. Pappo yawns,
stretches, makes a lot of noise scraping his chair away from the table
and saunters outside. Knowing Beany's in the tavern somewhere, I
cast one longing look behind me as Coop and I head for the door.

CHAPTER ELEVEN

The next morning, I sit in the dirt, chin planted on my knees, and stare across the street at the Black Pole. The tavern looks locked, deserted. Not a soul goes in or out. I'm hoping somebody will take Beany for a carriage ride. Maybe Mariana will head off to the market. I wouldn't even mind seeing Larkin strut down the street.

"Here you go, girly." Nicky Pappo flaps a piece of paper in my face.

I swat it away. "Get outa here!"

He picks it up and pushes it at me again. "Read it. Then get off your butt and start pulling your weight."

Damn! Why won't this goon leave me alone? I glance at the paper.

"Read it."

I take the sheet.

HELP WANTED
Printer for Buffalo newspaper
Must be smart and quick
Apply in person
Black Pole Tavern
Canal Street

I ball the paper up and toss it in the street. Wixumlee. She controls the police *and* the papers.

"Well?" Pappo squats down in front of me.

"It's Wixumlee!"

"Yeah. So?"

"She hates me."

"She needs a printer."

"Not my problem."

Pappo slaps the side of my head. "Not your problem, gutter-snipe, your opportunity."

I shrug. Push back against the building, farther away from him. "Where'd you get that anyway?"

"Handbills are floating all over town. How'd you miss them?"

I grip my knees and stare past him across the street.

He moves to block my view. "You're a printer, ain't you?

"How do you know?"

"Coop told me." He retrieves the paper from the street, smoothes it out and waves the wrinkled note in my face again. "You need a job, right? Or you gonna mooch off your brother the rest of your life?"

I bite my lip. I can ignore his mouth. It just takes patience.

Pappo flaps his arms like a giant bird. "So, go on! Git over there. Talk to her."

"I want nothin' to do with her!"

Pappo runs a dirty hand over his scabby head. "Girly, you are dumber than a sack of flour." He grabs my shoulders and stands me up.

"Here's the *in* I was talking about. You gotta get *inside* that Black Pole if you're ever gonna see your Beany again."

I shake off his hands. "Cripes, Nicky, what's it to you? Why do you care?"

He shrugs. "I don't." Shakes himself as if to calm down. "Don't mean nothin' to me. None of you do. Not you, not even Cooper. Certainly not that string Bean you're moaning about. I just know Coop's been nagging you to get a job. I'm sure not gonna pick up your share of the rent."

"I don't even want to live with you."

Pappo punches my shoulder. "Put two and two together, sweetie. You need a job. Here's a job."

Sweetie? Gag. I stare at him suspiciously — hate to look at him at all. He's sneaky as the devil in church. He was nasty to Wixumlee yesterday and here he is pushing me to ask the woman for a job. What's his angle? What's he getting out of it?

Pappo stands up straight. "Don't this beat all. Here I am trying to be the nice guy for once."

I snort and turn my head away.

"Look, give it a try or don't. I don't care. Either way it's no skin off my nose." He turns as if to go, then stops. "Hey, if you're scared, I'll walk you over there."

"Yeah, like I'd have a chance for the job with you tagging along! You said you're going, so go!"

He waves both hands at me, disgusted. "Forget it, then. What do I care? You want to pass up your best chance to see your Bean-girl, pass it up. Just remember, you ain't worth shucks to her sitting in the dirt." Pappo spins on his heel and struts off toward the Slip, not looking back.

I stand before the Black Pole's back door, take a deep breath, lift my arm slowly and knock. One knock, then another even more timid tap. Maybe no one will hear and I can leave.

I agonized all yesterday about asking Wixumlee for the printer's job. I can do the work, yeah, but there are problems. Aside from being scared to death of her, there's my looks. I've worn the same denim pants and cotton shirt for the last week. I'm sweaty and smelly.

The bigger problem though—the problem that makes me hollow and hurting inside—is walking into the Black Pole and facing Wixumlee's gang. First that gun-toting gypsy Mariana, then those brutes Larkin and Quin. I'll have to run their gauntlet of jeers and insults before I even get to Wixumlee—if I get that far.

Then that evil, people-selling woman will stare me down, laugh in my face—that deep, husky, bad girl laugh. The laugh I used to club my own victims back in Seneca Falls, what seems like years ago.

I'm the last person she expects to hire for her newspaper job. Or even see apply.

"What you want?"

My head jerks up. I didn't notice the door open.

"I—I—came about—the job."

"What job? We don't need no dishwashers."

"Uh, the other job."

"What other job?" Mariana's face screws up. "Phew! You just crawl out of a swamp?"

I swallow hard, eyes on the ground.

"Don't waste my time here, gal. What you talking about? What other job?"

I turn to leave.

"Hey! Stop! You knock on my door and I answer it, now what you want?"

"The job."

"What job you talking about? Cookin'? Cleanin'? Cleanin' the outhouse? Maybe you did that already. You smell like you fell in." Mariana's chuckle stings like a boxer's jabs. I want to slug her, or at least rip her end to end with a string of ripe curses, but the gypsy's leather bag is tied snug to her waist.

"The printing job," I whisper.

"Huh?"

"The printing job." I know the wicked woman heard me the first time. I hate people who force you to repeat, just for the power it gives them.

"I came for the printer's job." I raise my head and manage to look Mariana in the eye. "I used to be a printer. Where I used to live. I worked for a famous editor."

"Ooohhh, famous!"

"A woman."

"Ain't no women editors. 'Specially famous ones. What bull you trying to pull? You gonna waste Wixumlee's time with your lies?"

"I ain't lying!"

"You just want to get in this house and bother that poor little girl you starved."

"That's not true!"

"What's not true? Trying to get in the house or starving my little Beany."

"She ain't your Beany!"

"Mariana, honey, who you talking to?" Wixumlee pokes her head around the corner. "Who you fighting with? Oh!" She pulls back in surprise. "What trouble you come to make this time?"

"Says she come for the printing job."

I expect Wixumlee to laugh, but she doesn't. "You're a printer?" I nod.

"Says she worked for a *famous* woman editor." Mariana crosses her arms. Her whole body says she thinks I'm lying.

"Yeah? For a newspaper? You're a printer, or you write stories."

"No."

"No? No what? No you don't write stories, or no you're not a printer?"

"I am a printer! Somebody else—my friend Lucy—wrote stories. I set the type."

Mariana rolls her eyes.

"I did. I set type for *The Lily.*"

"No! You hear that, Mariana? You worked for Amelia Bloomer? I don't believe it."

"I did! If you have a newspaper I can set the type. I can set type for any paper in this town!"

"Ooohh. She's getting huffy now." The women smirk at me. "Should we let her in? Test her skills?"

Mariana waves a hand in disgust. "She's just looking for Beany."

"Are you? You just want to get inside to see Beany?" Wixumlee's taunting voice turns suspicious.

I fight back tears. "I'm a printer. I—but—yes, I do—want to see Beany, but I am a printer and I can set type and I want a job! I need a job!"

Mariana shakes her head and disappears into the bowels of the kitchen, but Wixumlee's yellow eyes burn through me like sunlight through a magnifying glass. I try to stand up straight, look Wixumlee in the eye, but the blond woman's stare forces my head down once again.

"I won't bother Beany. I promise," I mumble. The lump grows in my throat. "I—I'm dirty, I know. I need a job to fix myself up." I pause, hating to plead. "If you don't want me to see Beany, or if she doesn't want to see me, I won't fight it. But please, please let me have this job."

Cooper would beat me raw if he heard. The harder Wixumlee stares, the more I wish I wasn't begging like a baby. Whiner! That's what Coop would say. *Please. Please give me a job.* What a crybaby! How did I ever turn into such a whiney weasel? I turn to leave.

"Wait!"

I glance over my shoulder, but continue down the steps.

"I said wait! You work for me, girl, you take orders. Get in the kitchen." Wixumlee grabs my arm and pulls me inside.

"You know Quin?" She grips my arm with one hand and pokes my chest with a sharp fingernail. "You know Larkin? Those big, tough men? They follow my orders, no questions. If those bruisers can do it, so can a little worm like you. When I say *wait*, you wait.

When I say *go,* you go. It's that simple, girl. You do what I say. Is that clear?"

I'm nearly as tall as Wixumlee, but the tyrant makes me feel tiny.

"You ready to do my bidding, girl? Follow my orders?"

"Yes."

"What?"

"Yes."

"Say it like you mean it, gal! I don't surround myself with wishy-washy whiners. I need strong men and strong women in my business."

And you don't mean the tavern business, do you? A chill ripples the skin on the back of my neck. But I can't pass up this chance.

"I'm the boss! Of men and women both. Black and white both. Can you do it?"

"Yes!"

"Can you follow my orders? Can you print what I want when I want it?"

"Yes!"

Wixumlee drops her hands and laughs. "Heh, heh, heh." A lazy, doubtful laugh. "We'll see. Heh, heh. You're hired! You're hired, girl! We'll see how good you do. We'll see soon enough. Mariana! Give this brave gal some food."

CHAPTER TWELVE

The newspaper's name is *GosSlip*. When I look at her blankly, Wixumlee explains that it's a take-off on "gossip on the Slip." Stupid name.

After laboring as much for love as money on Amelia Bloomer's tidy, honest *Lily*, I'm stunned by Wixumlee's tattletale rag, a twice weekly mush of legal notices, church services, jokes, farm reports, shipping news, political feuds, police reports, casual rumors and downright lies. I scan a dozen issues and the only item I think has any accuracy is the Black Pole's weekly menu called Good Eats. Well, the shipping news and farm reports are prob'ly true.

But the paper's balderdash. A half page is dedicated to Pigs in the Pokey, a list of who got locked up for being drunk, who got locked up for fighting, and who got locked up for fighting drunk.

Slip of the Tongue is a column of the dumbest jokes I've ever heard. Only a fool like Nicky Pappo would split his gut laughing at 'em. The town board report is so boring I expect to get the nervous shakes setting the type. Wixumlee says the church services stay the same, week to week, but the shipping news and farm report— Goods on the Go and Barnyard Bonanza—change with every issue.

"I won't tolerate mistakes with Goods or Barnyard. People rely on those reports, you know—what gets shipped where." Wixumlee paces the tiny print shop, giving orders my first day on the job. "And make sure my menu's perfect. Folks like to know what I'm serving. The regulars, you know."

I twitch at the idea I'd be sloppy with my work. My face is scarred, my nose bent and my clothes shabby, but I'm neat as a pin setting type. I'll be careful with the shipping and farm news even though I'm stumped as to why they appear in Wixumlee's rag.

Voters and elected officials will go right for the town gossip. Sailors and canawlers will scan Pigs in the Pokey. But does the general public care what gets shipped across Lake Erie to Canada, what goes west by wagon or rail from Buffalo, or what's dropped off by Erie Canal cargos in Rochester, Syracuse and Albany?

When I ask why all the fuss about farm reports, Wixumlee shouts that she doesn't have to explain anything to her employees, they just do what she says. If I can't obey simple orders, I can quit right now. I shrug and tell myself that as long as Wixumlee pays me $5 a week — unbelievable, dang good money — I don't care what the crazy screamer prints in her slander sheet. I don't care, but I wonder.

Is it important that six bales of cotton leave Baltimore next Wednesday and ship through Philadelphia, Scranton, Albany, Utica and Auburn before being unloaded in Rochester?

And is it news that a special shipment is coming to a Mister Neils in Buffalo: two crates of molasses, one crate of dried corn, two boxes of flour and one pack of cotton gloves? Mister Neils most likely gets a telegram from whoever's shipping something to him long before the *GosSlip* broadcasts that blarney.

But I won't quiz Wixumlee about it. I don't care what that woman wants printed. The important thing is I get paid for printing it. I have a job and even though I haven't seen her yet, I'm close to Beany. Or closer than I've been in weeks.

I don't know who I hate hanging around more — Larkin or Nicky Pappo. Larkin's spying for Wixumlee, no doubt about that, but Pappo? What's he want? Doesn't he have a job at the granary? Cooper works hard from dawn 'til dusk, while Pappo clutters up the Slip — and the print shop — day and night.

"Get out of here, Nicky! You're in my way."

"Ain't botherin' you. Just come in to sneak a peek at the jokes. Only thing worth reading in this rag."

"Well, take the rag outside. This shop's too small for your carcass flopped over the counter."

Sometimes he leaves, but mostly he sits yammering at me until Larkin comes with new copy and throws him out. Then Larkin sits and stares at me — silently. I don't know which is worse — Pappo's mouth or Larkin's eyes — but I don't dare tell the big man to move.

My tormentors can't be more different. Larkin—tall, tan-skinned, muscular, brooding, soft black curls framing ebony eyes. Pappo—bald as a boulder, thin as a pin, white as a ghost, beady-eyed, running his mouth like he's running for election. Still, once Nicky called my name from the doorway when I was in the back room setting type and when I came out front I was shocked to see it was really Larkin standing at the counter.

"Don't you work anymore?" I squeeze past Nicky, careful not to touch.

"Sure I do," Pappo mumbles into the *GosSlip*.

"Then why are you hanging around here?" I grab a handful of type and begin spelling out words in the tray. "Larkin comes in, he'll boot your butt right out. Better leave now."

Pappo grins over the edge of the paper. "You want to be alone here with Larkin?" His teeth are small and tobacco-stained.

"Shut pan, Pappo! Beat it! Or I'll get Larkin myself."

"Oh, sure you will. That's just what you want. A little private time with the coffee-skin man behind the type case." He folds the newspaper slowly.

It won't do any good to say, "Shut pan, Pappo," again. I turn back to my type.

"I saw Beany today."

I stiffen and hold my breath.

"I said I saw that Bean girl you're moaning about losing."

I refuse to face him. "How'd you see her? She never leaves the house."

"Sure she does."

"Only with Wixumlee."

"Or Larkin."

My hand closes around the type tray. Where would Beany go with Larkin?

"That boy, now he's a looker ain't he? All the girls are crazy for Larkin."

I poke around for another handful of slugs.

"That Beany, she's a looker, too, now that Wixumlee put some meat on her bird bones. Yeah, she's been getting out more and more. You never see 'cause you're locked in this cave day after day jugglin' slugs. You gotta get out more, girly girl."

"You gotta get outa *here*, Nicky." My heart pounds and I don't really know why. "Get back to work. Rent money's due. Got your share?"

"Don't worry 'bout me. Money's never a problem for your Nicky."

I pause over the type. The next time I need to puke, I'll swallow the idea of him being *my* Nicky.

The door slams and Larkin's bulk looms over Pappo's hunched frame.

"Get your butt out, Pappo."

I'm surprised when Nicky hops out the door like a spooked toad without one smart remark. Larkin pulls a piece of paper out of his shirt pocket and hands it to me.

"Wixumlee says put this in."

I glance at the paper. "The farm reports done. Type's set. There's no room for this."

"Make room. Take something out."

"But—."

"You gonna argue with me?" Larkin sits on the stool Pappo just left and folds thick arms across his chest. "Are you saying no to Wixumlee?" A wiggly smile plays at his lips. He's laughing at me again.

I swallow, shake my head and read the latest addition to Barnyard Bonanza: "Leaving Philadelphia Monday morning for points west. Four crates of cider, two crates of dried plums, three boxes of soy beans. Deliver to Mister Bolan, Rochester, New York, after stops in Scranton, Elmira, Utica, Seneca Falls and Pittsford."

Seneca Falls. Familiar faces flash through my head—Lucy, Amelia, Ma—and I can't stop a sob from squeezing past my lips.

"What's the matter with you?"

"Nothin'."

"You bawlin'?"

"No!"

"You crying 'cause your boss gave you an order?"

"No!"

Larkin leans against the wall and closes his eyes. "Good. Print it. I'll wait."

I set the type swiftly and ink the press. Larkin shifts his feet and sighs. I look up nervously, hoping he doesn't think I'm stalling.

"Beany says hi."

I stop, ink brush in hand. "What?"

Larkin opens his eyes and sits up straight. "Beany says hi."

"To me? She asked you to tell me hi?"

He shrugs and looks away.

I feel a smile stretch my scarred face. "She knows I'm working here?"

"'Course she knows. She has ears, don't she?"

Butterflies tickle my stomach.

"Did she say anything else?" I hold the ink pot in one hand, brush in the other. I'm not sure, but Larkin looks kind of — guilty.

I take a chance. "Can I see her?"

He shifts on his stool, annoyed.

"I mean, do you think Wixumlee will let me?"

"Don't be stupid. She doesn't trust you."

"What does she think I'll do? Steal her back?" Instantly I regret the word *steal*. Larkin's eyes narrow. He slips off the stool and I take a step back.

"You think Wixumlee kidnapped Beany, huh? That's the way you have it in your ugly, selfish head. Well, Beany would be dead if Wixumlee didn't take her. You weren't helping her. She was dying!" He's not just angry. I hear something else in Larkin's voice.

He slaps his hand on the counter. "Run those copies."

Obediently, I set the press and pound out a half-dozen sheets. He grabs them before they're dry and pushes out the door, leaving me shaken but with a tiny bit of hope.

I'm washing the press when Mariana, carrying a large grocery basket, crowds into the print shop, turning up her nose at the heavy ink smell. The gypsy scans my blackened hands, smudged face and stained shirtfront. "Clean yourself up and get over to the tavern right after work. For supper."

I stare at her, stunned.

"You got anything to wear besides those filthy pants and shirt?"

I shake my head.

"Nothing clean?"

I shake it again.

She scowls. "Well, come anyway. Maybe we got something decent for you."

Right now, I don't care if that *something* is one of Mariana's flowered skirts.

Not a skirt, but a brand new shirt and blue denims await me when I walk into the Black Pole's kitchen. Mariana pours a tub of hot water and sets a towel and bar of soap in the wash room for me. I'm not insulted. I'm glad to wash up and would shower under an icy waterfall to see Beany. The cook doesn't say Beany will be there, of course, but I can't figure another reason Wixumlee would invite me for supper. Give me new clothes. I expect to still look like a tramp next to the primped up Beaner, but I don't care.

At seven o'clock Mariana points me to a large oak table by the front window just like the one I sat at in Black Rock the night Wixumlee stole — the night me and Beany met Wixumlee. I have to put that word — stole — out of my head. Not say it ever again. Things are going good. I can't mess up. I sit down at the table set for three, ignoring the room full of jabbering foofoos.

"Hi, Tess." Talbot smiles and pours me a glass of water.

"Hey, Talbot. How you doin'? Feeling better?"

"Yeah. Pretty much healed. Lots of scars though."

I stare at my empty plate. "I'm sorry about that. You know I am."

"Not your fault."

"We left you tied up. You couldn't defend yourself."

"Yeah, that was your fault, tying me up, but not the other part."

"What other part?"

Talbot wipes the water pitcher with a napkin. "Nothing. Never mind."

But I know. He's talking about me not coming to his rescue. Me backing down to a growling dog. Letting Talbot get chewed alive 'til Cooper crawled in with a pocketknife. Just a pocketknife. That's all Coop needed to save Talbot's young life. I hang my head.

"I said never mind, Tess." His voice is soft, tender. Then his face brightens. "Hey!" He laughs. "You're lucky. It's *not* Polish night." He has a nice smile. "Mexican meal tonight."

A tear slips down my cheek.

"Enchiladas. You ever eat 'em?"

I shake my head.

"And black beans and rice. You're in for a treat. Don't cry, Tessie."

There's movement and Quin pulls out a chair for Wixumlee. Then Quin, inky snakes hidden by sleeves buttoned at his wrists, takes the third chair. That uses up all three seats. There isn't one for Beany.

Wixumlee shakes her head. "Dang that girl! Talbot, I told your mama to set this table for four."

I draw a small, happy breath.

"Get another plate, honey, and some silverware. Quin, pull

another chair over, please."

But it's Larkin who struts across the dining room and sits down on the other side of Wixumlee, not Beany.

"I thought—."

"What'd you think, huh?" Wixumlee smiles, but I catch an unpleasant undertone.

"I thought B-Beany would be here."

"B-Beany? Now you stutter? Lord, girl, add up all your problems and you ain't worth shucks."

I swallow hard. Larkin and Quin stare at me like I ain't worth shucks. Hot, mean thoughts crash through my head, but not one escapes my lips. I wish I had the nerve to slap the grin off Larkin's face.

Quin runs a hand over his short, black hair and smiles across the room at Mariana carrying a large tray. Genuine pleasure blesses his nut brown face as he helps her set the platter of fragrant food on the table.

I look at the tray with dismay. I don't need food. I need Beany. I need to sit close beside her. See her sweet face. Talk to her. Ask if she's feeling better. If she's well enough to come home to me and Cooper.

Instead I'm sharing a mysterious meal with three people who never have a good word for me. Who take every chance to tell me how dumb and ugly I am. Everyone fills their plates, and I wonder how far I'd get if I got up and ran.

"What's wrong, girl?" Wixumlee picks up my plate and fills it with beans, rice and some long, doughy things. "Pick up your fork and get to it. You want Larkin to cut up your food?"

The men snicker.

I slice clumsily through one of the rolls. Ground-up meat and melted cheese spill out. I fumble with a steaming forkful and wonder why I'm sitting here with Wixumlee and her plug-uglies. Can only be trouble. Maybe I printed something wrong in that fussy farm report. But then why treat me to a meal? The last time Wixumlee did that, things turned out pretty bad. I'm probably in for a—.

"Put that bite in your mouth, girl. How can we get to the important part of this meeting if you haven't even started eating? Look at my boys here."

Quin and Larkin refill their plates. They remind me of mill girls in pants. Forks poised like lances, they eye the last *in-cher-lader* or whatever Talbot called it. Larkin and Quin both stab into the last doughy roll.

"Boys, boys. None of that. No fighting over food. You know there's more in the kitchen." Wixumlee beams like a proud grandma, although she isn't anywhere near old enough to be even Talbot's granny. I'm sure she isn't any older than my own ma. Maybe younger. 'Course that crazy Savannah doesn't look much older than a kid and here she birthed Talbot thirteen years ago.

I force down a forkful of spicy rice. "So, what's to talk about?"

"You'll find out. After you eat. And you clean up everything on your plate, you hear?"

I sigh. If Wixumlee's gonna slam me for messing something up, I might as well go down on a full stomach. I drop my head and don't stop shoveling until the Mexican goo is gone. I wipe the last smear of tomatoey sauce off my plate with a thin piece of warm bread, swallow a glass of cider and wait. The dining room's quiet and I realize the foreigners are gone. Piled on top of a wagon—a few sad colored folk packed underneath—and carted back to Sandy Town.

Quin rolls up his sleeves to let the snakes out then picks up a toothpick. Larkin pushes his chair back and crosses a booted ankle over one knee. Wixumlee sets down her coffee cup, brushes crumbs off her shiny red dress and looks me straight in the eye.

"Tell me about Beany."

My mouth drops open. "What?"

"Don't play dumb, girl. Tell me about Beany!"

Tell her? By now she should know all about Beany. It's been weeks.

"Talk!"

"What do you—? Hasn't she—?"

"No, she hasn't! I don't know anything about her! Do you think if I did I'd be wasting my time pulling words out of your tight little mouth?" Quin and Larkin lean forward like they might pull out my tongue. Wag it. Make it talk.

"She—she—."

"Start at the beginning. Who is she?"

"She's—." Beany must still be as miserable as when I lost her. Fancy clothes and a full stomach don't mean squat. Beany's still heartbroken. I expected her spirit to be soothed, pampered by food and shelter, but it isn't.

"Good Lord! Larkin! Make her talk!"

The big man grabs my hand, presses my thumb and a thin, hot pain shoots right to my brain.

"Ah!" I try to yank my hand away.

"Who is she? What happened to her?" Larkin presses again.

"Ow! Stop! You said Beany said hi." Larkin drops my hand and stares at the tabletop.

"What?" Wixumlee whips around to face him. "Said hi? She talked?"

Larkin sits stone-faced.

"Answer me. Did Beany speak?"

His hands ball into fists. "Yes. But she only said one word. *Her* name." He jerks his head at me.

"Tess? She said 'Tess'? Lordy." Wixumlee grips the table's edge. "When? Why didn't you tell me?"

Larkin hangs his head.

"You know better than to keep secrets from me." Wixumlee tone seethes with authority. A tone very different from the sarcastic one she uses with me.

"It was just one word, and —." Larkin spreads his strong hands flat on the table.

"And what?"

"I was afraid. I didn't want — you — pushing her."

The room becomes church quiet. Larkin draws tiny circles on the table with one finger. Quin rubs an eyebrow. Neither of them grins. Neither one smirks or looks down his nose at me. Not now.

Wixumlee glares at Larkin. But when his shoulders sag and he looks, reluctantly, into her face, her eyes soften and she touches his arm. "She asked for Tess?"

Larkin nods. "She said her name. Just that. I thought it meant she was asking for her."

Larkin had told me "Beany says hi." I don't know now if she really said that, or if she'd just said "Tess" like he told Wixumlee. Whether she said one word or ten wasn't important. She'd said *something*. Finally. And she'd asked for *me*. And Larkin had told me.

Wixumlee drums her fingers on the table. "So that's why you put this idea in my head about inviting this girl to supper."

"Yes. Beany's in so much pain."

I wince at the ache in his voice.

"Tess knows what happened to her. She can tell you everything."

Wixumlee nods slowly.

"The information you had from…" Larkin stops, connects with Wixumlee's warning eyes.

"…wasn't enough," she finishes smoothly. Larkin nods.

I rub my sore thumb. "Someone told you about Beany?" Who knows Beany besides me and Cooper?

"Quiet!" Wixumlee switches her attention back to me. "I get information from many places. From many people. And now I'm going to get it from you. Spill it, girl. Tell me everything you know about that child. Right now!"

Everything? I've known Beany her entire life. But what does *everything* mean? Should I tell the good parts or just the important parts? Or the recent, horrible parts? Should I start at the beginning and tell her that Beany was taught not to speak in public. To keep her eyes down when walking the street. Or that she can make a foolish clown dance with a swipe of charcoal? That she loved her mama more than herself? What's important? What is *everything*? And was any of it Wixumlee's business?

Larkin and Quin stare at me, willing me to talk, and suddenly everything *important* pours from my mouth like a flash flood.

"Beany's mama was a runaway slave. The cook at our boarding house. Slave catchers captured her and Beany in our backyard. We broke them out of jail. Slavers found us by the towpath. We fought. Beany's mama killed herself so they couldn't take her back. We escaped on the canal."

I sit back, glad to have shocked them. Larkin slumps in his chair, slack-jawed. The snakes on Quin's arms writhe on flexing muscles. Wixumlee leans across the table ready to swallow me whole.

"She saw her mama kill herself?" Her yellow eyes blink like lanterns in a fog.

I tremble. Bloody images splash inside my head.

"No. She saw — ."

My voice cracks.

"August ran — 'round the curve in the towpath."

Chills claw the back of my neck.

"Beany ran after her, but it was all over when she caught up."

I see us piled, the three of us and Cooper, bloody meat.

"August stabbed herself in the chest. With her own knife."

Wixumlee sucks in air like a dying woman and collapses on the tabletop. Her shoulders jerk and she coughs up retching sobs. Quin lays a snake-laced arm across her back — the first time I've seen any-one touch Wixumlee. Larkin, dark eyes flashing, pounds his thick, balled fists together. No wiggly smile plays at his lips.

Suddenly Wixumlee's head jerks up. "Who fought? Who defended Beany and her mama on the towpath?"

"M-me and C-Cooper." I shiver uncontrollably. "The canawlers helped. Coop and his crew…"

My stomach heaves. I'm going to lose my meal.

"…killed the slave catchers."

I take a deep, steadying breath. "Dumped them in the swamp."

"Canawlers killed them? Whose boat?"

"Captain Beale."

Wixumlee nods slowly. "Captain Beale. I know Captain Beale."

She waves Larkin and Quin in close. Huddled together, they mumble, looking up at me now and then. I watch them guardedly, taking shallow breaths to control my need to spit out poisonous memories. Suddenly, all three stand and I cower in my chair.

"You, Tess. You'll sleep here tonight. Get up, girl! Stand!"

Quin jerks me to my feet.

Wixumlee jabs a pointed fingernail at me. "Go! See Mariana in the kitchen. She'll find you a bed for the night. Tomorrow morning you'll tell me everything — *everything* — you know about that child. Now get to bed."

CHAPTER THIRTEEN

Mariana has me dressed, fed and sitting in Wixumlee's bedroom by eight o'clock the next morning, spewing out everything I know about Beany — thirteen years worth, which isn't much, really.

I've been told that Beany's room is connected to Wixumlee's, but I don't hear movement in there 'til around ten when Savannah bustles in singing. At the sound of her daughter's voice, Wixumlee stops grilling me. Stops ringing from me every tiny truth about Beany and August. From my first memory of a little brown baby stumbling around the boarding house kitchen to Pa's pestering August. From the Woman's Rights Convention to our work at *The Lily*. From Pa's thievery to my revenge to the brutal fight for freedom on the towpath.

I'm exhausted when Wixumlee finally says, "Enough! Go to work." I leave the woman sunk in her chair, one arm thrown across her forehead, tears streaming down her cheeks, a fist pounding the seat cushion.

No one — not Larkin, not Nicky Pappo — pesters me at the print shop, but around noon Talbot walks in and tells me to come to the Black Pole for supper. I close up at six o'clock, wander over to Mariana's kitchen, and plunk down on the bench near the wall. It's been a long, long day.

"Somebody going on a picnic?" I ask.

The gypsy, packing food into a large basket, jumps like she's been snipped by a snake.

"Sweet Jesus! What you doing here?" She looks uneasily from me to the basket and back.

"Talbot said come eat."

"Well, that don't mean you bust into my kitchen anytime you want. Go, girl! Get outside!"

"But—."

"Git! Sit on that stoop 'til I call you."

I slink outside. Cripes, I'd be happy with a sandwich and glass of milk. These people are more than strange. Every one of them. They pull me in, they push me out. Pull me in, push me out.

I hear bustling in the kitchen, scrapes across the floor. Think I hear Larkin. I'm tempted to peek through the window, but if Larkin really is in there, he'll smash me for snooping.

Finally, Mariana sticks her head outside. "Get clean, girl, supper's ready."

I rinse my face in the wash room, pour a few cups of cold water over my chopped hair and shuffle back to the kitchen. I expect a plate in the corner, but the cook waves me into the dining room, where foofoos laugh and guzzle beer, and Beany sits with Larkin at the round, oak table near the window.

My heart races but my feet are glued to the floor. There she is. Don't spoil it, Tess.

"Go on, you been asking for her." Mariana gives me a push. "And next time knock before stomping into my kitchen."

I walk slowly to the table and stare at the back of Beany's dark head. Larkin grunts and points to a chair. I sit down.

"Hey, Beany. How you doing, girl?" I pull close and smile. "It's me. Tessie."

Beany wears a yellow dress with small, green leaves scattered across the skirt. I guess it's silk, only because silk is supposed to be the best. Beany's hair glistens and the side curls are pulled back and fastened with clips made of deep green feathers with yellow streaks. Hanging around her neck on a silver chain is August's blue stone knife.

"You look pretty, Beany."

Her hands move from her lap to the knife around her neck and her head turns slowly toward me. She fingers the knife, strokes it, searching my face with hard-candy eyes, not the soft pudding eyes I knew back home.

My stomach stiffens. Maybe this is a bad idea. Maybe my scarred face brings back memories best forgotten. For a split second Beany looks like she might scream or jump. I glance at Larkin, who studies the girl with both expectation and dread.

"Thanks, Tessie."

I spill a sigh of relief, but my eyes fill with tears. Beany did not say one word the entire length of the Erie Canal from the Montezuma swamp to Black Rock. Not a word during the days I carted her back and forth scalpin' tickets, and from what Wixumlee said, not a word in the weeks she's been under the blond woman's care. Finally, after all that time, only my name—Tess—escaped Beany's lips, spoken first to Larkin and now again at this table.

Larkin leans on his elbows. His eyes are kind.

"Yeah, Beany. I been saying you look pretty, and now here's your friend Tess backing me up." He smiles at me, a beautiful smile filled with short, straight teeth. One dimple pokes a hole in his left cheek. I tear my eyes away.

"You put some meat on your bones, Beany." It's true. She's gained a little weight. Just enough to wipe away the hollow look and pad her sunken cheeks. It hurts me to say it, but I add, "Wixumlee's taking good care of you, girl."

Beany wraps her slim fingers around the knife.

"I like her."

I swallow the lump in my throat.

"That's good, Beany." But a chilling fear spreads down my arms and legs. Through my own dumb fault, I let Beany slip into Wixumlee clutches. Now Beany has gone over to the woman, but it isn't the clothes, food and fancy carriages that snagged her. It's Wixumlee herself—a bossy, threatening, queenly, light-skinned colored woman. So different from August.

The platter of food Mariana sets on the table smells so good it makes me giddy. Sheets of wide noodles layered with thick, white cheese and red gravy. Brown bread. Some chopped, raw vegetables in vinegar.

Mariana scoops noodles onto Beany's plate. Butters her a piece of bread. Lifts a few cucumbers out of the vinegar into a small bowl near her plate.

"There, dolly girl. You eat now. Larkin, you see that she eats." The big man nods solemnly. Mariana strokes Beany's head and leaves.

"Get your food," Larkin orders.

I shovel noodles and gravy onto my plate. Scoop some vegetables into my small bowl.

"Get enough?"

I nod and Larkin switches his empty plate for the oval platter. Replaces his small bowl for the larger one holding the remaining cucumbers.

"Get some bread."

I snatch two pieces and drop a slab of butter on my plate, afraid he might grab that, too.

"Wixumlee hates it when I do this," he grins, "but I love this Italian stuff." He crams a forkful of noodles and cheese into his mouth, then opens it wide, huffing to let the hot steam out.

"Isn't there always more in the kitchen?" It's out of my mouth before I can stop it.

But Larkin chuckles. "Yeah, I'll get to that, too." And chuckles again. Pleasantly. "Come on, Beany. Take a bite. It's good."

I spread the noodles around on Beany's plate. "There you go. Cool it down a bit." I cut off a bite with my fork and raise it to Beany's lips. "Try some."

After a few seconds I stuff the food into my own mouth. "Mmmm, good." And it was. Delicious. I offer another bite to Beany.

"Eat up, Bean, or Larkin here will swallow yours, too." I glance at him quickly, hoping he catches the joke. Larkin grins through a mouthful of bread.

Beany's eyes float over to the young man, who winks at her. Her mouth opens and I pop in a noodle.

"Mmmm. Ain't that good? Come on. Chew it up. That's a girl. And here's another one." I manage to get a few more bites into Beany's mouth and several forkfuls into my own before I see Wixumlee hovering in the kitchen doorway.

Dang! Don't butt in, woman! As if getting the message, Wixumlee withdraws.

"I'll get more." Larkin disappears and I worry Wixumlee will tag back out after him, but she doesn't.

Larkin shares more noodles and gravy with me and butters another piece of bread for Beany, which she allows him to place in small pieces in her mouth. She eats about half the slice and Larkin's pleased.

But I don't like this feeding business. After all these weeks, is this the only way anyone can get her to eat? Beany acts like her fork doesn't exist. Her hands lay flat in her lap like two dead birds. She's eating, but her empty stare and the heavy way she sinks in her chair scares me. Her body is mending. Her soul is weak.

Talbot brings apple pie for dessert, but Beany doesn't touch hers. I think of August's fresh fruit pies and wonder if Beany remembers, too. Maybe food reminds her too much of her mama.

Beany grew up in the kitchen. It was her entire world. Cooking and scrubbing dishes. Maybe she's given up on food like she's given up on life.

Larkin scrapes the last smudge of apple pie off his plate, drinks down his third glass of milk, and gazes fondly at Beany. This is the cheeriest I've ever seen Larkin. Despite his bearish size gentleness drifts around him like soft light.

The eating and drinking complete, the three of us sit quietly. When Beany turns sad, watery eyes on me, my heart jumps to my throat.

"Stay with me, Tessie."

Before I can answer, Larkin bolts to the kitchen and comes back with Wixumlee.

"We'll put another bed in Beany's room. Larkin will take you up. You're the only one who can unlock her soul. So you make yourself at home, Tess Riley." Wixumlee gives Beany a hug and glides back into the kitchen.

I stare at her retreating back. I've been kidnapped, too.

CHAPTER FOURTEEN

"Here's your lunch." Mariana pushes a small black pail across the kitchen table where I hang over a plate of eggs, bacon and toast. I can get used to three meals a day real quick. "And tonight you tell your brother come get supper."

When I woke this morning, I found a dresser full of brand new denims and colorful shirts stocked quietly by someone during the night. A clean bed. New clothes. A warm breakfast. Will Wixumlee shower this much attention on Cooper, too?

Last night, before she let me climb the stairs to Beany's room, Wixumlee made clear what my purpose is. I'm a mule. My job is to draw Beany out. Pull her out of her shell. I'm the only one who knows everything there is to know about Beany. I'm the connection to her dead mama. I'm the link between the dull, silent, grieving girl upstairs and the gentle, artistic, loving girl murdered on the towpath.

"You bring back that sweet child her mama loved," Wixumlee told me sternly. "She's locked inside a broken heart. You find her and lead her out."

I wipe up the last of my eggs. Mariana's scrambling up more for "the boys."

"How was it last night?" Wixumlee, clutching a large cup of black coffee, slides into a chair beside me.

"Fine."

"Fine? Spell it out, girl. What'd you two talk about?"

I crumble a piece of bacon with my fork. "Nothin'. We went to sleep."

"At nine o'clock? Two young gals? Young gals stay up all night gabbing!"

I poke my lower lip with my fork. "Well, I was tired, and Beany, she—."

Should I tell Wixumlee how Beany sat motionless on the edge of her bed while giggling Savannah undressed her? How Beany let Savannah take the feather clips out of her hair, brush it, slip a night-gown over her head, push her gently onto her back, bring up her knees, and cover her up in bed? How Beany didn't cringe when Savannah brought that bold eyepatch down near her face to kiss her goodnight?

Beany showed no emotion at all. After asking me to stay with her, she didn't act like I was even up there in the bedroom watching her. Didn't even say goodnight to me.

"She just laid down and went to sleep."

But that wasn't true either. When I realized Beany didn't go right to sleep — that she was, in fact, staring wide-eyed and unblink-ing at the ceiling — I sat down in the chair next to her bed with a book and read.

Sneaking looks at her now and then, I wondered what was going on behind those blank, dark eyes. Was she thinking about August? Did she ever stop thinking about August? Could she stop?

Savannah had hung that blue stone knife back around her neck and rested it on her nightgown amid a cluster of embroidered roses. Beany had pulled that knife out of August's chest on the towpath, and, truly, it was the only remembrance of her mama Beany had.

But cripes, to hang it around her neck?

So now, this morning, when Wixumlee presses me for a report — against my own best judgment — I lash out.

"It's true! We didn't talk about anything. Beany just laid there staring at the ceiling, fingering that stupid knife. Why'd you have to do that? Put it on a fancy chain and hang it around her neck? That's the knife that killed her mama!"

It was a sick thing to do and I have to tell her, even if Wixumlee throws me out. The woman sets her jaw and leans across the table.

"That's right, girly. That knife killed her mama. I knew it killed something, crusty with dried blood like it was. And the way she clutched it, I knew it had stabbed someone dear to her. And if she was locked off from the world because of that killing, I knew that knife was the only thing gonna unlock her soul."

"You said I was the only thing gonna unlock her soul." I stand up. "Take it off her. *Please*. Let her forget what happened."

"Oh, no, no, no." Wixumlee leans back in her chair and shakes her head slowly. "I don't want Beany forgetting her mama! Her slaughter was Beany's life lesson. What's gonna change Beany's life forever. Beany must remember her mama—absolutely—and the bloody way she died."

Wixumlee grins wickedly. "That's the important thing—that she killed herself to escape slavery."

When I shudder, she asks, "You think that's unnatural? It's not. Lots of colored folk kill themselves to escape the plantation or being dragged back to it. You just happen to know one of them."

I watch Wixumlee with a new fear.

"Sit down."

I sit.

"Now here's what I want from you, Tess Riley. You can work in my print shop. You can eat at my table. You can sleep in Beany's room. But you must pour all your energy into drawing that child out."

"Of course I will! I said I would. I want to bring Beany back!"

"And you'll give me detailed reports on your efforts. Any help you need just ask."

"What kind of help?"

"Anything! Anything that'll make her come alive. You said she likes to draw. Made pictures of a circus, the canal. Where are they?"

I hesitate. Beany also drew pictures of August's slave stories.

"Where are they? Back at that boarding house?"

I nod.

"Then write your mother. Tell her to send them. Send everything. Maybe those pictures will jiggle that little girl's mind."

I shake my head. "It could be bad! They might just make her think of August."

"I want her to think of August! Didn't I just say that, stupid girl? Forgetting her mama is not gonna bring Beany back. Remembering gives life. Forgetting brings death."

I truly hate this woman.

"So, that's where we'll start." Wixumlee spits out orders. "We'll send a telegram. Your mother will send everything from Beany's room. Everything that child and her mama owned!"

It won't take Ma long to pack *that* box.

My feelings about writing Ma are mixed. I miss her so bad my heart melts and I want to let her know me and Coop are safe. But the telegram Wixumlee wants to send would be an easy trace if the law is still looking for the constable's killer.

Wixumlee slaps a piece of paper and a pencil in front of me. "Write."

I pick up the pencil slowly.

"Dear Ma! Come on, girl. Write!"

I write "Dear Ma" at the top of the paper. My arm is heavy, my hand leaden.

"Send everything that belongs to—Good Lord, girl, what's wrong with you?" Wixumlee snatches the pencil from my hand, pulls the paper across the table and writes in bold strokes.

Send everything right now from Beany's room in care of Wixumlee, Black Pole Tavern, Buffalo, New York. She especially wants all of Beany's drawings. Hurry!

"Now run this down to the telegraph office before you go to work. Remember to sign it with your own name. Oh, and put a little note to your ma on there. Tell her you're all right. She must be worried sick."

There's no way out. The evil woman is testing me. She can easily have Larkin or Quin send this message. Or take it herself if she's in such a dang rush. Instead she's forcing me to obey. To become one of her stooges.

Blind obedience. That's what she demands.

And that's what she gets.

The day Beany's box arrives Talbot comes to the print shop and tells me to come home. *Home.* Yeah.

I see Wixumlee sitting in the kitchen, eyes red and swollen, long fingers twisting a wet handkerchief. August's two raggy dresses, a couple wrinkled sacks Beany'd worn, an old brush wound with dark hair, two sketchpads, a small box of colored chalk and a prayer book are scattered across the tabletop. The book lays open to a picture of a saint tied to a post, her heart pierced with arrows. Ma gave August that prayer book one year for Christmas, and the cook stared at the pictures every morning before starting her chores.

Wixumlee picks up one sketchbook and thumbs the pages, shaking her head as slave scenes slip by. Scenes of weary looking black people bent over in long, endless fields of tobacco. Pictures of old women cooking in pots hanging over holes dug in the ground and filled with fire. Sickening scenes of men, women and even children tied to trees and posts being whipped, and the agonized faces of people forced to watch. I see that every other page has words written on it. August's slave stories. Beany had written them down just like she said she would. But she'd never shown me the book.

Wixumlee slaps the sketchbook shut. "This is it! The history of Beany's thirteen years on this earth." She looks at me as if it's my fault. "Did your mother send it all? This can't possibly be everything."

"It is."

"They must have had more than this." But I can see on Wixumlee's face she isn't really surprised this is all Beany and August have to show for their short, tortured lives.

I shake my head. "August didn't want nothin'. Claimed she didn't need nothin' more than a roof over Beany's head. Food in her stomach."

"Well, if that's all she wanted than that's all she got!"

I don't like Wixumlee's blaming tone. "August loved Beany. They didn't need nothin' but each other."

"Ha! A lot good that's doing Beany now. She needs someone else now."

"And you think it's you?" Clean clothes, good food and my position as Beany's savior give me a small amount of courage.

Wixumlee glares. "Right now, it's *you*! Tonight after supper you show her these pictures. You talk about that circus. Tell her about that other girl. That rich kid."

"Lucy. Her name's Lucy."

"You tell her about those hungry mill girls she used to sweat in that hot kitchen to feed. You bring up everything you can think of. You keep telling her those stories until she wakes up. Talks! Comes alive!"

"And if it doesn't work?"

"You make it work, Tess Riley. Even if you have to bring your mama and that Lucy girl here to Buffalo. You make it work. And don't let it take forever. I don't have forever!"

At night scraping sounds—like furniture being moved—keeps me awake. I glance at Beany's bed. She's asleep, worn unconscious by my storytelling, my attempts to make her remember. I strain to hear voices murmuring downstairs then cover my head with a pillow, trying to block them out.

I know what's going on. Today, on my way in from work, I surprised Mariana filling another basket with bread, cheese and chicken. Mariana rules her kitchen like a kingdom, but she was shocked when I came up behind her instead of angry at my intrusion. And at supper I was ordered to pass out extra bottles of wine to the foofoos. Wixumlee sent the families home in a wagon but waylaid the single men, showing them card tricks and filling them with more and more whiskey.

After supper, Larkin steered Beany and me upstairs, past the merrymakers. Shouts and songs kept me up long after Beany fell asleep. All this means one thing: Wixumlee's preparing to cart off more people in the bottom of a farm wagon.

The mumbling and scraping continues. I sit up in bed. Should I go downstairs? If Larkin and Quin are marching people at riflepoint out the back door, there's no way I can stop them. I'll only make Wixumlee mad and then they'll get rid of me. Wixumlee will find other means to bring Beany back to life.

I lay back down and pull the covers over my head. It's a cool, late summer night. Winter, which comes early to western New York, is around the corner. I don't want to get tossed out and have to live with Cooper and that fool Nicky Pappo.

Pappo. I shudder beneath the covers. Tonight, he tried to sit down to supper with us. Just walked into the Black Pole with Cooper and pulled a chair over to the oak table. Larkin looked to kill him.

"Get your scrawny carcass out of here." Larkin's voice was quiet, but with a knife-like edge.

"I can pay for my meal." Nicky tossed a wrinkled Buffalo newspaper — not the *GosSlip* — onto the table. "I don't have to mooch like my buddy Cooper here."

Coop laughed, but I wanted to club the bum. Beany, me and Coop are family and Larkin eats with us on Wixumlee's orders. Pappo isn't family and he isn't one of Wixumlee's henchmen either.

"We don't want your money, Pappo." Larkin scraped his chair back. I knew if the big man stood, Nicky would be rolling outside in the dirt. I hoped it wouldn't come to that. I wanted Pappo out, but I didn't want a ruckus to upset Beany. But then the poor kid hadn't even noticed Pappo — as usual.

Nicky raised his hands and grinned. "Okay, don't go wrathy on me. I'll risk ptomaine over at that other slop bucket across the street.

Never mind, Coop, you just sit here and wolf down free food. Good thing I'm working. Can pay for mine."

"Coop's working, too, mule ball." I resisted the urge to stab him with my fork.

"I can handle him, Tess." Larkin picked up Nicky's newspaper and slapped it threateningly on his open palm, until Pappo got the message and slithered out the door.

I pull the covers off my ears. The mumbling and scraping downstairs stop. Outside, drunken men sing and wagon wheels crunch. Wixumlee and Talbot come tiptoeing up the stairs saying their goodnights. A minute later Mariana follows and the house falls silent.

CHAPTER FIFTEEN

I'm furious when a letter arrives from Ma and another from Lucy Manning, both sent directly to me in care of the Black Pole. Cripes! Does the whole world know I'm here?

Ma's letter mixes anger and love, hope and despair. Thank God, you're safe, she writes. Is Cooper with you? And Beany? What a tragic scheme to break August out of jail, she scolds.

Lordy, does the whole town suspect me and Coop, or has Ma just figured it out herself?

She doesn't blame us for August's death. The poor woman thought she had no choice, Ma writes, and she really is in a better place now. Ma's your typical churchy type. Always talking about a better place *up there* after the miserable one down here crawls or crashes to a close.

The good news—in a twisted sort of way—is that Constable Parker is still alive after Cooper cracked his head with a frypan busting me, August and Beany out of jail. Parker's stuck in bed for the rest of his life—his head fuddled and his body lopsided—but he's definitely not dead. Coop's face isn't stuck on the post office wall. No price hangs over his head. In fact, from what Ma writes, no one suspects Coop and Lucy busted us out. I bet her big bug father Abner Manning had something to do with that.

Come home, Tess, please, Ma begs, no one's after you. I should visit. I owe Ma that. But go back for good? Uh, uh. For a while I thought that's what I wanted, but not anymore. I got out of Seneca Falls the hard way. As much as I miss Ma, I'm not going back.

I wonder how Lucy knew where to send my letter then read that Ma ran into her mailing Beany's box at the post office and the news was out.

I rip open Lucy's envelope. After cautious questions about our health and safety, Lucy turns lively. She's going to college! Old man

Manning is lending her the money. *Lending*? I read that word five times before I believe it. Yeah, Lucy has to pay back the money to her pa after graduation. When she has a job. He's giving her a loan and Lucy is happy about it!

Well, she's finally going to Oberlin, that college in Ohio she never stopped yammering about. I sag at the thought of the heavy, velvet money bag Lucy pushed into Beany's hands on the towpath. Money earned painfully, given with hardship and lost by neglect — no, cowardice. I put a couple dollars away each week from my printing job to pay Lucy back.

"You write your ma again, Tess." Mariana's husky voice invades my thoughts.

I nod.

"I mean it. Stop her worry. You tell her you're okay. Got food, a bed. Tell her you're working."

"Cripes! Okay, I'll write."

Me and Mariana have worked out a truce. She orders and I obey. Still, there's a shade of humor to it. Sometimes I balk, offer just enough resistance to make her steam, then I look sheepish and mumble, "Okay, all right." Like I'm giving in. Which I am, but the game makes it easier on me. I even catch the gypsy smiling now and then.

Still, I know I'm an outsider. Know that if Mariana has to choose, I'll be last on the list to be tolerated, helped or saved. Maybe one notch above Nicky Pappo.

Pappo! I saw him yesterday, slinking onto Canal Street from behind the tavern. What the heck was he doing back there? He's gonna get himself beat or worse. Only a fool would keep invading Wixumlee's territory. She can't stand the worm and makes no bones about it. But Pappo keeps taunting her — and Larkin — building up bad feelings, poking in their business.

Nicky Pappo takes joy in being wicked.

I push Pappo away to concentrate on Beany. I can't wait to tell her about Lucy's college plans. Lucy stories are safe. Good memories. The fun days at *The Lily*. The circus giraffe Beany gaped at parading down Fall Street and that turned up graceful and sweet in her sketchbook. The time Lucy helped Beany buy August a pretty purple-flowered dress. No. Not that one. That story has a murderous ending.

Beany's charcoal drawings are still in the box in our bedroom. I didn't show them to her, although I wanted to, badly. At least some of them. Drawing is Beany's gift. Each page mirrors her feelings. Maybe I can show just the happy ones. Hide the slave pictures.

Would Wixumlee let me hide the bad ones? No, Wixumlee will not hide anything. To Wixumlee, the worst pictures are the best pictures.

I bring the letters from Ma and Lucy to supper. Cooper reads aloud the one from Ma and listens keenly when I read Lucy's news to Beany.

"So, what do you think, Bean? Lucy's going to college, just like she wanted." I fill Beany's plate. We're eating German food tonight. Sausage and sauerkraut. The tavern stinks, but it's a good stink. August cooked a lot of sausages, and Ma always laid in a big supply of kraut in tall, clay crocks. I wonder if the strong odors bring back memories to anyone but me.

Beany watches silently as Larkin butters a thick slice of black bread and I cut her meat. The foofoos are lively, toasting one another in what sounds like curses and war whoops. Wixumlee opens another keg of German beer right in the dining room, and the young men guzzle and cheer. Larkin stares uneasily at the rowdy bunch. One man has already bumped Larkin's chair on the way back from the keg, sloshing beer out of a pitcher overflowing with foam.

"I'm surprised Wixumlee lets these guys get corned this bad." Coop leans forward, allowing a mug-toting diner to sway past. "These guys are skunked."

"You questioning Wixumlee's judgement?" Larkin's eyes narrow. He's grudgingly accepted Cooper into the fold but challenges him constantly.

Coop grins. "What I'm questioning is whether you and I can take one, two, three. Four, five. Maybe six of these bruisers."

"They're sloppy drunk."

"And big."

My hands sweat as the big blond boys splash beer on Wixumlee's rosy carpet and knock over chairs. They're laughing, but it only takes one bump, one bad joke—in any language—to set someone off.

Beany faces the room but doesn't seem to see or hear the ruckus. If all hell breaks loose, what will I do? I won't fight. I'll protect Beany, that's all. Pick her up and carry her into the kitchen. And stay there. Coop and Larkin—and Quin, wherever he is—can handle it themselves.

I turn my attention to Beany. "Hey, girl, how about picking up your fork?"

Despite the racket, Beany turns her head. I grin, trying to shake off the chaos building around us.

"See that shiny, pokey thing down there?"

Beany looks at the tabletop.

"Yeah, that's a fork. For eating."

Beany runs her finger down the long handle.

"Pick it up. Stab one of those sausages. You like sausage. Mmmm." I pop a large piece into my mouth, make a funny face and chew.

A large lug at the next table slaps the head of a little guy next to him. The little guy slaps him back.

"I don't like this." Coop scrapes his chair back a couple inches. "I've enjoyed some ball-bustin' brawls, but I don't want to see one in Wixumlee's dining room."

Larkin nods, his eyes glued on the two slappers. "Tess, take Beany to the kitchen."

I freeze. Can I get through the crowd? The slappers have turned into shovers. Guys at other tables jump up, expecting trouble. Hoping for it.

"It's too wild. I can't—Ugh!" A heavy weight lands on my back, knocking my head into my food. Coop grabs the fallen drunk and pushes him back. I wipe mashed potatoes off my eyes. The drunk twirls clumsily and lands on me again, pinning me beneath him.

Then he screams.

Twisting my head, I see a large, silver fork sticking out of the drunk's neck. Beany stands beside me, staring at him with a blank face.

"Jesus! Beany!" Cooper yanks out the bloody fork. The drunk slides screaming to the floor. "Get her out of here!"

I throw my arm around Beany and haul her toward the kitchen. Larkin punches drunken men out of our way and shouts for Quin as the dining room explodes in a free-for-all. Someone swings an empty beer pitcher, catching Cooper on the ear. He roars with pain and launches into a slugging, kicking frenzy. He and Larkin send drunken foofoos crashing into piles of smashed dishes and broken glass.

Suddenly a loud *crack!* cuts through the tumult.

Crack! It sounds like a rifle shot but is really Wixumlee swinging a bullwhip.

Crack!

"Stop!" she shouts.

Crack!

"Stop!"

Fighting men separate as Quin moves into the crowd leveling his rifle first at one drunken foreigner then another. Mariana points her pistol at one particularly burly man.

"Sit." Wixumlee raises the whip. "Down." They sit. Larkin sidles next to Quin. Wixumlee nods to Cooper, and he joins her side of the room. From my post near the kitchen, I see him whisper to her and point at the floor near our table. She jerks back, startled, and looks around the room.

"Who speaks English? Anybody? English?"

One man raises his hand.

"Get a friend and bring that injured man to me."

The two foreigners lay him at her feet while the others grumble and stretch their necks to see how serious a fate befell their writhing, moaning comrade.

"Cooper, carry him to the kitchen. Send Talbot for the doctor."

Coop raises the man to his shoulder and disappears through the doorway. A few foofoos move to follow, but Quin jerks his rifle and they back off.

Wixumlee smiles at the English-speaking foreigner. "Tell them I've sent for a doctor and their friend will be well cared for."

He tells them in their language, but the men are angry. A few shake their fists.

"Tell them to sit down, and I'll bring a wagon around to take them back to Sandy Town."

The men sit down, griping in their own twisted tongues. One or two point to the keg, but Wixumlee shakes her head and raises the whip.

"Tell them they can have more food, but no more drink."

Most of them can barely straddle their chairs. Wixumlee looks back at me and Beany standing in the kitchen doorway.

"Tess, take Beany upstairs."

Gratefully, I pull her up the steps away from the turmoil.

I cuddle Beany on her bed, stunned by what she's done.

Stabbed a man with a fork. A white man! Beany, unaffected by her violence, sits peacefully, waiting for Savannah to undress her.

Downstairs, the dining room is quiet. Horses hooves clump up the side alley and onto Canal Street. From the upstairs window, I watch Wixumlee march drunken foofoos into the wagon. There's laughter. Good spirits have returned. The wagon carts the revelers off to Sandy Town and, once again, I wonder who's hidden beneath.

The next day Wixumlee sits me and Beany down and demands an explanation for the fork-sticking scene. I give her the blow by blow but don't offer more than a shrug as to why Beany suddenly turned vicious. Secretly, I think Beany was defending me against the clumsy drunk but don't tell Wixumlee 'cause that would make it my fault. Yeah, I wanted my face pushed into mashed potatoes — twice — by a lumbering drunk. But that's what she'd say.

Wixumlee demands to know why Beany — taught by her mama to hide — would suddenly take to stabbing white men with forks? What pushed her fear aside? Not getting any answers from me, she turns to Beany.

"What were you thinking, child?" Wixumlee rubs her forehead. "You almost killed that man! Lucky you didn't hit something vital."

Beany stares blankly over Wixumlee's shoulder until the woman throws up her hands and walks away.

One good thing comes out of the uproar. Wixumlee — impressed with Coop's loyalty and fighting ability — moves him into the house, making Nicky Pappo mad as a sweat bee. He comes to the restaurant after supper, demanding to see Cooper.

"Yeah, go on, mooch off that weird woman," Pappo complains to Coop and me outside the tavern. "First free food. Now a free room. What else did she give you, huh, Coop?"

"A job."

"Doing what?"

"Whatever she wants. Look, Nicky, I can't pass this up. Why should I pay two bucks a week for a dirty cot in a drafty room over a gin hole, when I can get a warm, clean bed for free?"

"'Cause we're friends, that's why."

"Yeah, and we'll stay friends. We'll just live in two different places."

"Get me in there, Coop."

"Wixumlee doesn't like you."

Pappo feigns surprise. "Why not?"

"You rub her the wrong way."

"Naw."

"You go out of your way to make her mad."

"Not me."

"What you got against her anyway?"

"Nothin'. I hardly know the gal."

I hold my tongue, determined to steer clear of Nicky Pappo. I don't trust him. Can't understand Coop's friendship with him. And now that Wixumlee has taken me and Coop in, I don't want Pappo spoiling it. I'm back with Beany. Wixumlee expects me to nurse her soul. It's a job I want and need. The last thing I need is Nicky Pappo.

A couple days after the fork-sticking scene, I bring out Beany's old sketchpads and prop the one she called her circus book in front of the silent girl. A bit nervous, I turn to the first page — a picture of a graceful clown in striped pants skipping down Fall Street back home.

"Well, looky here, Beaner, remember when we went to the circus? You, me and Lucy?" Beany's eyes flick to my face, pause, then float down to the picture. Not much more reaction. No smile. No recognition.

I turn the page. "Well then, look at this one." Beany stares at the drawing. "Here's that tall animal you liked so much. What'd Lucy call it? I can't remember."

Mariana looks over Beany's shoulder. "Lordy, look at that thing. Why would God make a creature like that?"

I stiffen, hoping the gypsy won't say something dim-witted — like the animal's ugly or something. The giraffe was Beany's favorite circus animal.

"Look at that tiny head way up there on that long, skinny neck." Mariana skims her finger up the page, laughs, and returns to the sink.

I sigh. This isn't working. Beany could care less about these pictures — her own sketches, drawn with her own hand. The circus was a good time. If pudgy clowns and spotted giraffes can't cheer up Beany, how can I show her the second book? The slave book. I try a different tack.

"Hey, Beaner. Lucy's going to college — end of this month. Remember Coop read you her letter?"

Oops. That was the night Beany stabbed the burly German. I

hurry on. "Her pa's lending her the money. She has to *pay it back*. Ain't that something?"

Mariana dries her hands on a towel. "That girl Lucy. She lives in your hometown, right?"

I nod.

"When's she going to school?"

"Don't know exactly. Her letter just said the end of September."

"And you said her pa's an abolitionist?"

I already told Wixumlee everything I know about everybody who'd had anything to do with Beany. Abner Manning had contact with her on only two occasions, but they were both violent events in Beany's life—Pa's attack on August that left her with an injured shoulder and August's capture by slave catchers.

"Yeah, he's an abolitionist," I reply.

Mariana bobs her head thoughtfully and turns back to the sink.

"Well, I gotta get back to work." I plop my brand new newsboy's cap on my head "Beany, you want me to leave this sketchpad for you? Look, my ma sent your pencils. Maybe you'll feel like drawing."

Mariana looks over her shoulder and chuckles. "Maybe she'll draw a picture of me standing here at the sink. A picture of my big, broad back."

Well, it would be something anyway. I leave Beany staring at the tabletop.

But it isn't a picture of Mariana's big, broad back I find in the sketchbook that evening. It's the face of the stabbed foofoo, mouth twisted, shrieking, eyes wild with surprise, a silver fork plunged into his crooked neck. An ugly portrait carved in bold strokes. A few dark lines to illustrate Beany's anger, her hate.

Did Wixumlee see it? Mariana said nothing, but I know it's just a matter of time before one of them pages through the pad. Wixumlee set a deadline. If I don't find the soft, sweet girl straining within that sorrowful shell soon, Wixumlee will toss me out. Fire me from the print shop and this new life. Wixumlee will find her own way to save Beany's soul and it won't include me.

I rip the shrieking face from the pad, crumple the page and stuff it into my back pocket.

CHAPTER SIXTEEN

"Pack your bag. You're coming to Black Rock."

This order from Wixumlee is easy to take. I've been worried about being separated from Beany, when Wixumlee takes her to the other tavern. Still, I have a job in Buffalo.

"Hear me? Pack up."

"But, don't—don't I have to work?"

"Don't you want to come?" Wixumlee jams her fists into her hips and scowls.

"I do! But the print shop—."

"The print shop? Listen to me, girl. If I hand you copy, you print it. If I say pack up, we're going to Black Rock, you jump in the wagon."

"Okay."

"Okay." Wixumlee shakes her head and raises her hands in the air like I'm the dumbest gal on the Slip and a complete waste of her time.

"You hear that, Mariana? She asks me if she has to work."

The gypsy waves a bangled arm. Too busy packing to be bothered with my stupidity.

Wixumlee turns on me.

"Everything you do for me is work, girl. If I'm feeding you and putting pants on your butt and giving you a real bed to sleep in, it's because you're working for me. No other reason I'd pay you the slightest never-mind. Doesn't matter if you're setting type or setting the table. Or spending time with my Beany."

Her Beany! But I shut pan. Don't want the bossy blabber to leave me in Buffalo to bunk with putrid Nicky Pappo.

Pappo! I saw him again—when he should have been down at the granary—slinking behind the tavern. How he gets away with not working is a mystery. Coop always hit the granery at dawn and slaved 'til dusk when he had that job. But Nicky, he turns up any time he wants—or doesn't turn up at all—and still gets paid. At least he's always rhino fat, flashing pockets full of cash.

Now that Coop works for Wixumlee, Pappo shows up even more often, getting into squabbles with Larkin and Quin. Why can't he leave Coop alone? He's gonna spoil it for us and if he does, I'm gonna kill him!

For the first time in my life, I'm riding in a carriage. A fancy, dark green brougham. As coachman, Larkin drives the matched pair of jet black geldings, while me, Wixumlee and Beany lounge inside on soft, goat-leather seats.

Behind us, Quin drives a Dearborn carrying Mariana, Talbot and Savannah. Trunks packed with clothes and supplies are strapped on the backs of both carriages, but my corduroy bag is stuffed under the seat. It's a sturdy satchel with enough room for a spare pair of pants, a clean shirt and Beany's pads and pencils. I bought it in a second-hand shop after my first week of work.

I'm still surprised Wixumlee pays me a salary besides giving me room and board. And covering my butt with pants. I'm breaking in a new pair of brogans and getting used to the feel of cotton stockings. I know I have a good thing going. I'm with Beany and nothing is going to spoil it.

"I hope Savannah settles down." Wixumlee twists her ruby ring.

Savannah raised a stink over not riding in the brougham. Wixumlee ordered the seating, so I don't feel too guilty, but the gal's tears upset Beany, who rarely raises an eyebrow over anything. She started to fidget and whimper, so Wixumlee pulled her onto her lap, and that upset Savannah even more.

"Mariana said she'd help Savannah make a new eye patch, if she behaves."

Wixumlee winces. "That's why I put her in the Dearborn. I hate having that blazing eyeball glaring at me all the way to Black Rock."

Such cruel talk makes me mad. Savannah's her daughter, for cripes' sake. Wixumlee could have a little sympathy. Even Larkin has more patience with Savannah than her ma does. The woman goes hot or cold on the poor girl without warning. And every time she squawks at Savannah, she brings up how much she hates that blazing eye patch.

I consider pulling out the sketchpads, hoping to cheer Beany, but remember the frantic foofoo she drew and get afraid it might backfire. I'm painfully aware I'm not making progress with Beany. She's as heavy as a basket of wet laundry, except when someone else in pain—like Savannah—gets her feelings flowing. Getting on better terms with Wixumlee—who Beany likes—might help me, but the woman's too scratchy. All she does is give orders and damn those who don't obey.

"Who hurt Savannah?"

We both jump when Beany speaks.

Wixumlee stares at me over the top of Beany's head. I stare back, shocked and expectant.

"How'd she get hurt?" Beany's voice is surprisingly strong.

"Lord, child, who says she's hurt?" Wixumlee's yellow eyes flicker. I wonder what startles her more—Beany speaking or the questions themselves.

"How'd she lose her eye?"

Wixumlee eases Beany onto the seat. "Well, darlin', it's nice to hear your voice." Wixumlee takes a deep breath, exhales and fusses with her skirt.

"Who hurt her?"

"Hurt her?" Wixumlee fumbles with her shawl. "Hurt Savannah?"

Beany's dark gaze pins the tall woman to the back of her seat.

"Well, somebody hit her." It's barely a murmur, but then she repeats it, a bit stronger. "Somebody hit my baby. Knocked her little eye right out. And she was just a bitty thing."

Wixumlee spins toward me on the seat, suddenly on fire. "That hit—that meanness—changed my whole life."

She falls back against the seat, brings long fingers to trembling lips and stares out the window. I watch her pained reflection and know the powerful woman has shared more about herself than she intended.

I lay on a bed in Beany's Black Rock bedroom. It's a gussied-up space just like the one in Buffalo. Beany's wide bed has a frilly curtain over the top and a white blanket covered with daisies. My bed, pulled into the room by Larkin and Quin, is narrow, plain and covered with a faded brown quilt. No curtain—or canopy as Wixumlee calls it—threatens to float down and smother me.

Mariana brings a glass of warm milk and tells me the switching between houses stirs Beany up, makes her restless at bedtime. I don't think Beany sleeps much, riled or not. Black Rock or Buffalo. Tonight she drinks her milk, lies back against her pillow, folds her hands on her chest and stares stony-eyed and silent at the canopy, making me wonder if it really was her voice that shocked us with questions in the carriage.

I give up trying to talk to her. Just say, "Goodnight, Beany," and close my eyes. Just like every other night.

Around midnight, I awake to shuffling, rustling. Is the noise downstairs? In our room? I'm not sure if I'm awake or dreaming.

No, that's definitely movement. And a loud *thud*! I prop up on one elbow. See the bedroom door partially open. I glance at Beany's bed and turn cold. The daisy blanket is pushed back, the bed empty.

I jump up, dash through the doorway, but come up short in the hall. Where am I? This isn't the house on Canal Street. I shake my head, get my bearings—I'm in Black Rock—and stagger down the stairs, colliding at the bottom with a black woman whose forehead and mouth are creased with angry frowns. Quick as a lick she points a long-barreled pistol at my head.

"Git over there." She grabs my nightshirt collar, twists it around her hand and yanks me into the dining room. I cough and gasp for breath. She pushes me into a chair and without letting go, and without pointing the pistol anywhere but at my forehead, demands answers.

"Who you, gal?"

"T—Te—" I reach toward my neck to let her know I'm choking and feel the sharp crack of the pistol barrel on my knuckles.

"Ooow!" I grab one hand with the other. Tears swamp my eyes. "Te—ss," I gasp. There's shuffling nearby, but the woman keeps my head turned away from the movement.

"Why you here?" She twists the collar tighter, "Huh?"

"Live—here."

The woman pushes her horrible face closer to mine. "With Wixumlee?"

I nod.

"You white?"

I nod again.

"White gal living here with Wixumlee?"

"Harriet, she's okay."

Larkin!

"Let her go, please."

The woman releases my collar slowly, reluctantly. The pistol disappears from sight and Larkin's black eyes glare down at me.

I take a ragged breath. "Beany's gone."

"I found her," Larkin growls. He and the woman flank me threateningly.

"Where? I heard a thud. What's going on?"

"What we gonna do with her?" The woman's tone is menacing. Like she has to decide what to do with people often and the outcome rarely turns out good for them.

"Wait for Wixumlee." Larkin places a hand on the woman's shoulder, draws her to a chair. She sits, the long-barreled pistol cradled in the crook of her arm.

Larkin spins back toward me and punches one fist into the other. "Damn you, Tess! Why are you downstairs?"

"I heard noise. Beany's gone."

"I told you, I found Beany."

"I didn't know! I didn't know the house was full of people."

"What people?" When the woman jumps toward me, I yelp. "Who you see?"

I hesitate. "Just you and Larkin."

"But you hear something, right?" The woman waves the gun in my face. "Noise? Moving around?"

"Up—upstairs," I lie. "I thought it was Beany."

"No, you hear it down here. Something falling. A thud. That's what you said."

I don't know if the woman is asking me or telling me. I look helplessly at Larkin, who looks worried. That scares me. Larkin never looks worried. Never looks scared.

"She seen something, we get rid of her," the woman mutters firmly.

I try to rise, but Larkin's big hand on my shoulder and the woman's pistol in my chest push me down. I start to sweat. Coop's in Buffalo and I'm alone in Black Rock. This fierce woman is talking about getting rid of me—killing me?—because I heard shuffling downstairs.

"I didn't see anybody. I didn't."

Mariana would laugh at my whine, call me a sissy, but this black woman with the angry face only glares, her slightly misshapen forehead looming large before my frightened eyes.

"Take her outside."

I scream "No!" as Wixumlee walks into the room.

"Shut your mouth, fool!" The slap across my jaw stings like a whip. "Can't you do anything right?" With the same hand that stung my cheek, Wixumlee lowers the terrible woman's gun. "It's okay, Harriet. She's stupid, but harmless."

"Stupid people is dangerous people."

"No, honey, there's not a lick of fight in this one. I brought her along to watch Beany, but she can't even do that."

"How is Beany?" Larkin dark eyes blink rapidly.

"Mariana put her back to bed. She'll sleep with her tonight. This fool," pointing to me, "can sleep in the shed."

"Did Beany—did she see anything?" Larkin doesn't hide his worry.

Wixumlee hesitates. "Yes. And I gave her a simple explanation."

"What do we do with this one?" A vein in the corner of the black woman's head pulses like a ticking clock.

I grip my hands together. "I didn't see anything!"

"Shut up! We'll talk later, Harriet. Don't worry. I won't let anything get in the way. Put her in the shed, Larkin."

"No!"

"To sleep! Mariana took your bed—were you listening to me? Get yourself out there and don't come back 'til breakfast."

Larkin marches me outside, but the shed turns out to be just another room with a bed in it. He doesn't lock me in. Maybe they want me to run, so they can chase me down and kill me to keep me quiet. I might be lucky and escape, but I'd never see Beany again. Should I stay? Run?

Wixumlee told homely Harriet I'm harmless. Don't have a lick of fight in me. I fall asleep wondering if I'll ever have a lick of fight in me again.

When I creep into the kitchen the next morning, Beany is sitting up straight at the table dressed plain as a pumpkin.

"I found this dress in the back of my closet." Her stream of words startles me, but Mariana, slicing ham at the counter, doesn't turn around. "I'm gonna ask Wixumlee for more like it."

She's clean and tidy, but the frills are gone. No ribbons. No feathers. No silk. Her dress is light brown cotton. The blue stone knife still hangs from her neck.

"But you know, I'm thinking maybe I'll take up pants, like you." Beany smiles.

Mariana cracks eggs into a frypan, but doesn't hum like she usually does cooking breakfast. I sit down slowly. What the heck is wrong with Beany? She sounds—normal. I should be happy. Instead I get the feeling Beany is completely crazy. 'Cause what could change her overnight?

"Uh, I don't know about pants, Beaner. Wixumlee likes those fancy frocks."

"I dressed myself this morning. I'll be dressing myself from now on."

"That's good." I look over my shoulder at Mariana, busy cooking.

"I have work to do, Tessie, and I can't be dragged down by swirly skirts and stiff shoes. You knew that years ago. Everybody laughed at you—at the clothes you wore—but you didn't care. You were smart."

"Beany."

"I'm gonna get me some brogans just like yours."

"Beany."

"You can come along if you want."

"Where?"

"Wherever we need to go."

"What are you talking about?"

"Clear the way!" Mariana sets down platters of fried potatoes, pancakes, eggs and ham. Beany picks up her fork, scoops some egg onto a plate, sticks a forkful into her mouth, and snaps off a bite of bread. She could have just bitten off the head of a chicken for the way I gawk. Then she stabs a piece of ham, pushes on more egg with her bread and crams it all into her mouth.

"This is good." She swallows then gulps down black coffee. And smiles. "Eat, Tessie. We're gonna need all the strength we can get."

I'm more scared now than when Harriet pointed her long-barreled pistol at me. Who is this new Beany? The change is too quick.

Wixumlee and Harriet float ghostlike into the kitchen and pull chairs up to the breakfast table.

"Good morning, Beany." Wixumlee's eyes drift over the girl's drab dress.

"Good morning, Wixumlee. Good morning, Harriet."

Harriet grunts a dull "hullo" and slides three fried eggs over a plateful of potatoes. Her eyes drift once, twice, over to me, giving me goose flesh. Wixumlee acts like Beany's cheerful greeting, bright eyes and clean plate aren't worth mentioning. She shakes out her napkin and covers her silk skirt.

"Well, darlin', aren't you chatty this morning." She jiggles a fried egg onto her plate. "It's good to hear your voice." She flips a piece of ham next to the egg. "You've come back to us!"

Wixumlee's tone is sweet, but she jabs her egg yolk and the goo slides over her ham like yellow paint.

"Now that you've rejoined the living, it's time we had a serious conversation." Wixumlee glances at Harriet. Beany smiles and reaches for a muffin.

I haven't taken a bite of breakfast, yet something nasty lurches in my throat. Beany and I are in big trouble. She saw and heard the same stuff I did in the kitchen last night. The same shuffling and thudding I'd heard in Buffalo's Black Pole kitchen. Wixumlee is running the same scam in both towns.

It's scaring me stiff but has the opposite effect on Beany. What she saw and heard brought her back. Caused her to rejoin the living, as Wixumlee put it.

But to me — and maybe even to Wixumlee — Beany's recovery is bittersweet. Beany's smiling and talking, eating and dressing herself, but now Wixumlee's faced with the dilemma of letting us in on her treachery — or silencing us.

I have no doubt she'll choose the latter — at least where I'm concerned — to protect herself and her gang. If she spills all in this serious conversation she wants to have, I have a feeling I'm gonna wind up stuffed in the bottom of a farm wagon.

Dead.

CHAPTER SEVENTEEN

The serious conversation takes place right after breakfast in Wixumlee's bedroom. Just the five of us — me, Beany, Mariana, Harriet and Wixumlee. Larkin and Quin stay downstairs, helping Talbot mind Savannah, who's complaining about being left out of the woman talk. The bedroom is quiet as a wake, a vase of yellow lilies scenting the air and the mood. Wixumlee leans against the window frame, grim. Her usual spark flickered out.

Mariana bends to set a tray of lemonade on the low table in front of Wixumlee's pink and green striped sofa. My fear swells when the glasses rattle and lemonade splashes out of the clear pitcher. Mariana nervous is like Larkin worried: It never happens. The gypsy wipes the yellow drops off the tabletop with her skirt hem and sits down heavily.

Wixumlee spins the big red ring on her finger and chews fake color off her lips. She doesn't look at anyone. Harriet, coaxed into leaving her pistol in the kitchen, watches me as if I'm a thief waiting to swipe something. I bet the woman can count the number of people she trusts on one hand and Wixumlee is one of them. I sit nervously on a chair covered in gingham check, feeling as welcome as a toad in a punch bowl.

Beany plops into a wing-backed chair and tucks her feet under her plain brown dress. She stretches toward a plate of cookies, swipes two and tosses one to me, smiling.

"Tess and me gonna help. Don't worry." Beany's clear voice snaps Wixumlee to attention.

"Good Lord, child!" The big blonde pulls a handkerchief from her sleeve, rolls it into a ball and bites down hard.

"We ain't afraid. We're good fighters."

My neck sinks into my shoulders. Don't volunteer me, girly! I don't know what you're talking about, but if *fight* is in it, it can't be good.

Mariana settles into the sofa and motions for Wixumlee to join her. "Come on, honey, sit with me. Don't fret now. Just start telling from the beginning. Come on, girl."

Wixumlee lays one hand on the window frame and bows her head. Then she raises it quickly and clears her throat.

I fight the urge to jump up and run. "Look, you don't have to tell me nothin'. Really."

Wixumlee sets a hard look on me and clenches her fists.

"Start with your baby, honey," Mariana croons. "Start with Savannah."

Instead, Wixumlee strides toward me and jabs a long, painted fingernail at my face. "You weren't supposed to have a part in it! And I curse myself for bringing you to Black Rock."

I press back into the checked chair as far as I can go.

"Honey, honey, that's no place to start," Mariana whispers. "That's the end of the story."

"That's the middle!" Harriet folds her arms across her stomach and hunches in her chair. "This story's far from over!"

"Sit down, Wixumlee. Calm yourself." Mariana pours lemonade and passes the glasses around. "Want me to start the story? Here, let me start." Mariana reaches for Wixumlee's ruby-ringed hand and pulls her onto the sofa. She pats the long, thin fingers gently, lovingly.

"Once there was a little yellow girl lived on a rich plantation in Mississippi."

Mariana looks at me like I asked for the tale.

"She was the plantation owner's granddaughter, but instead of living in the big, white house with the tall, white pillars, she lived in a scrubby shack some hundred yards away along the tree line. And instead of calling the owner granddaddy, she called him massa, 'cause that's what he was. He owned her. Like he owned her mama and her grandma, and every other person of color who picked his cotton. Yeah, her mama and grandma were light-skinned, but they were still slaves."

With an angry twist of her head, Wixumlee snaps out of her trance and takes up the tale.

"Her mama and grandma told the little yellow girl who she was. Who her daddy was. Who all her relatives were. All her aunts and uncles, all her cousins. In both houses. The mansion and the shack. She couldn't understand that story. She couldn't understand, either, how the massa—her granddaddy—could beat his kids and grandkids and wrap them up in chains when they ran away. And she decided it must be that white blood made him do it, so she decided she would someday have babies only with the blackest boy on the plantation. To try to boost up that good black blood. And she did."

Wixumlee looks straight at me. "And when she was thirteen, she had herself a little girl baby, who wasn't yellow like her mama or black like her daddy. She was darker than her mama—and didn't have her yellow eyes—but was still lighter than her daddy's polished black."

I stare back, numb.

"And that girl baby was a delight. The sweetest child—she still is."

Savannah. Wixumlee is only thirteen years older than Savannah. She had a baby when she was three years younger than me.

"And that girl baby played in the dirt with the other babies and, since she was too young yet to beat, had a pretty good life, giggling and eating bugs."

Wixumlee smiles crookedly.

"And her mama—being not much more than a baby herself—sat in the dirt with her—after working in the fields or slopping hogs or pulling weeds, of course. And they played and had a good time and the yellow girl was pleased her baby was darker than she was."

Sweat beads up on Wixumlee's forehead.

"Just before her baby turned four years old, the yellow girl's grandma died from a fever and her mama was sold to another plantation in another state. So the yellow girl was all alone, 'cept for her baby girl."

I glance at Beany. Her eyes, pinned on Wixumlee's face, reflect an understanding I can never share.

"Then one day when baby girl was five years old, someone in the big house—a great aunt or great uncle maybe—decided she was old enough to serve at the dinner table. She was a pretty child and happy as a kitten. She sang songs and even her cousins in the big house liked her. But it was her mama who loved her."

Wixumlee's eyes lock on Beany's.

"And her mama was happy her baby girl was picked to set the table and carry in the bread and jam, instead of being in line for the field crew."

Wixumlee stops talking and draws a couple long breaths. Mariana strokes her hand. "Take your time, honey. Tell it when you're ready."

Wixumlee sits up straight and sets both hands on her knees.

"But one day, one of baby girl's uncles in the big house tells a joke just as she's setting a pan of blackberry cobbler on the table for dessert. When everyone at the table laughs, baby girl jumps and that pan of blackberries tips right over into uncle's lap, right on the pants of his brand new white linen suit.

"And that uncle flies into a rage. He grabs that baby girl by her soft, curly hair and punches her tiny face. Once. Right on her little brown eye. Smashes it. Smashes it so bad the white doctor digs it out and throws it away. Says it's a useless eye. Will never work again."

My pounding heart ricochets through my chest. Mariana bows her head. Harriet rocks, stony faced.

Wixumlee's painted eyes drip color onto her cheeks. She sniffs, blows her nose, sniffs again.

But I see that Beany sits at attention. Alert and alive. She doesn't cry. Hasn't cried once, not even at the mention of anybody's mama.

Wixumlee takes a deep breath and spills out more.

"It healed, yes, it did, that eye healed over. It never worked again—shoot, there was nothin' in that blank hole to make it work—but it healed.

"And when the bandages came off, the yellow girl bundled her baby girl into a sack she tied to her back and hustled out of there. She left that miserable plantation and all those uncles and aunts with the mean white blood and went north. She carried her baby girl with the blank eye through the swamps and weeds and woods. Through fields at night.

"They didn't get caught, no sir. That yellow girl wouldn't allow it. She looked up into the night sky, picked out the biggest, boldest star and followed it straight north."

Wixumlee's tale tumbles across her tongue like trout slipping downstream.

"But by the time they got to Louisville, the yellow girl knew that mean punch had let something loose in her baby's head besides her eyeball. She was not right after that. She'd been a happy child before, but now she was just silly. Giggly goofy for no reason. So the yellow girl was especially glad she ran away, 'cause no massa would keep a giggly goofy girl. No profit in it, he'd say.

"The yellow girl, she found ways to keep alive in Louisville—

some better than others. Her baby girl was never hungry, no sir, she ate good. The yellow girl didn't care what she had to do to get food for her child. Baby didn't walk barefoot either. And she wore a warm coat in winter."

I watch Beany inhale Wixumlee's words like they're jasmine-scented.

"I still think that way." Wixumlee sits up straighter. "I got irons in the fire, and I make things work."

She looks at me as if I might challenge her.

"Nothing — and nobody — will stand in the way of me reaching my goal. Whether it's feeding my baby girl or —" Wixumlee leaps from the sofa —"helping runaway slaves escape to Canada!"

I gasp. Fall back in my chair. Escaped slaves! Shuffling through the Black Rock kitchen last night! That thud I heard. Somebody dropping a sack. Or a basket of food.

I remember weeks ago busting in on Mariana in the Buffalo kitchen, while she packed fruit and bread. How shocked — and nervous — the gypsy was. How she pushed me outside onto the stoop.

Beany'd been in both Buffalo and Black Rock houses for weeks. Everyone thought she was as blind as she was silent, but who's to say she never heard — or saw — runaways slipping in and out of hiding places at night. All that time Beany'd been silent, she'd been watching. And the encounter downstairs last night between her and escaping slaves — well, it's obvious Beany won't be silent any longer.

"In wagons." I look straight at Wixumlee. "You put them under the wagons and pile drunks on top to disguise their escape." I should shut pan right now, but I can't help asking, "Where do you take them?"

Harriet shifts in her seat. Pats her pockets. Searching for her pistol?

"It's okay, Harriet." Wixumlee suddenly seems at ease, relieved. "We take to the harbor. We load them on ships to Canada."

Wixumlee smiles. "Don't worry, Harriet. Tess lives in my house. She works for me. She belongs to me. It's time she heard the whole story."

Wixumlee extends her arms. One toward me, one toward the scowling black woman. "Tess Riley, meet Harriet Tubman. Harriet is like Moses to her people. A heroic conductor on the Underground Railroad."

CHAPTER EIGHTEEN

So the tragedy of Savannah's lost eye changed Wixumlee into a savior and a lawbreaker—a station master on the Underground Railroad.

In all my sixteen years, I'd never heard of the Underground Railroad, even with pistol-wheeling Harriet "Moses" Tubman sheparding runaway slaves through western New York and across the water to St. Catherines.

Me, who thought I knew everything going on, didn't know that farmers and bankers, merchants and tavern keepers, teachers and housewives fed, sheltered and guided runaway slaves through one tiny town after another until they reached the southern shore of Lake Erie where sympathetic ship captains sailed them to Canada.

All abolitionists were not do-nothings like Abner Manning.

It dawns on me that I've been a blind participant in this outlaw gang. I'm amazed by the simplicity—and slyness—of the Underground's tactics.

"Four crates of molasses, two crates of dried corn and three boxes of soybeans" means four adults, two old folks and three children—a large family of runaway slaves hidden in numerous northern towns before being "delivered" to an Underground Railroad conductor who ships them to Canada or sends them on to other conductors farther west. I've been printing "farm reports" like that—and similar railroad schedules in Goods on the Go—for weeks and wondering why someone would care about tracking a few boxes of soybeans so carefully.

And as I fear, hearing the whole story brings me inescapable trouble. Since I *belong* to Wixumlee, I also belong to the Underground. I'm Wixumlee's tool and so now are my friends. She knows Lucy Manning will soon be traveling across New York en route to college in Ohio and she wants Lucy to bring along a special run-away slave disguised as her maid.

The day after spilling her story, Wixumlee orders me to send Lucy a telegram about linking with a Railroad contact in Seneca Falls. The Underground Railroad operates in Seneca Falls!

"I—I don't know," I stammer.

Bring Lucy into a mess like this? Turn her into a criminal? Lucy is finally going to Oberlin! Her future is hopeful! I'm scared sick to be trapped in dangerous, illegal activity and just as fearful of dragging Lucy into it.

"What do you mean you don't know? Lucy helped break Beany and her mama out of jail!"

"Yeah—."

"And gave her own college money to Beany on the boat! You told me that."

"Yeah, but—."

"Money you lost!"

I hang my head. Wixumlee grabs a handful of my hair, poking her sharp fingernails into my scalp until I raise it again. "So what makes you think she won't help us now?"

"She won't trust you. She doesn't know you."

"She knows you! And her father's an abolitionist."

"That doesn't mean—." I look at Wixumlee helplessly.

"That's who runs the railroad, Tess! Abolitionists!"

"But—." I shake my head.

"But what?" Wixumlee looms closer. "What!"

"Her pa's just a talker! He was useless when they locked Beany and August in jail. He just spouted the law. He didn't do nothin'!"

Tears spill from my eyes as I remember the frustration and anger I felt sitting on the steps of Lucy's Washington Street house after Abner Manning washed his hands of August's plight.

I jump at the sting of Wixumlee's slap on my ear.

"Stop that blubbering!"

She smacks me again.

"Listen here. Her pa might be useless, but that white gal's different, I know it! Any working girl who hands over her hard-earned money to help the child of a runaway slave is someone special!"

Wixumlee jabs my head again with her pointy fingernail.

"She's got guts! That's what I like. A gal with guts!"

Salty tears sting my eyes. A gal with guts. That ain't me.

I suck up snot through my broken nose and look at Wixumlee through a window of water. Instead of a wicked woman I see a shimmering Satan, a demanding demon. She may be doing something good, but she's evil. This telegram she wants me to send to Lucy is just the beginning. Wixumlee will demand more and more and more from me. And me—I don't want anything more to do with runaway slaves and their branded thighs, whipped backs and slave catchers chasing all over them.

Wixumlee slaps her hands together angrily. "Dang it, girl, stop that whimpering! Don't make me sorry I brought you into my house."

I look away, hiccupping on my tears.

"You send that telegram to Lucy! I'll write the whole dang thing out for you. All you'll have to do is send it."

I lean over the kitchen table and drop my head onto my arms, but Wixumlee yanks it back up.

"And forget Lucy's pa—useless as a box of bones. That girl will do it on her own. Your gal Lucy will take charge."

When I read Wixumlee's telegram, I wish I'd been quicker—and smarter—and sent off one of my own to warn Lucy away from this Underground conspiracy. I would have written something like:

Dear Lucy, please meet a runaway slave behind the grey barn on Whipple Road. Dress her as your maid and bring her to the Black Pole Tavern in Buffalo one week from Saturday.
Tess

That way, Lucy would never get the telegram. It would be hand-delivered to her father—or maybe even the sheriff. Lucy would be questioned, but she wouldn't get in trouble. Abner Manning would pretend it was a bad joke, a hoax. And Lucy would be saved.

But, of course, I'm not quick or smart. I'm slow and stupid and standing at the telegraph office with Wixumlee's message in my hand. A message that carries no warning, but is, in fact, tempting to a young girl with spirit:

Lucy, see Mister Pavin at his shoe store in Seneca Falls Wednesday afternoon. He'll have a surprise package for you from me.
Tess

The telegraph man back home will not hand that message to the sheriff. And if Lucy's parents read it, they might question their daughter's continuing friendship with a jail-breaking hooligan like me, but they won't stop Lucy from getting a surprise package from her friend. At least Wixumlee doesn't think so.

When Lucy arrives at the store Mister Pavin will hand her a wrapped shoebox and ask her to open it right there, quietly. Inside she'll read a short letter from an unknown woman commanding her to break the law. Mister Pavin will explain the details.

Since Lucy helped a runaway slave once before, Wixumlee is convinced she'll do it again. But Lucy's headed for college—her life's dream—and I'm hoping she'll be afraid to do anything this brainless—anything to knock her off the track.

And who knows if or how Lucy's been changed by what she saw on the towpath. Sending me a newsy letter is one thing. She might not want anything to do with me or Beany, chased as we are by the shadow of death. She may have turned against us and our schemes. I almost hope she has.

"What if she tells?"

"What if who tells what?" Wixumlee sits with me and Beany at supper the night before we return to Buffalo.

"Lucy. What if she tells her pa."

"Why would she? From what you told me, that man hasn't given her any reason to trust him. He refuses to educate her. Bullies her. Fails to help her friend. He finally *loans* her money for school after squandering it on his precious son who couldn't give a hoot about a college education, from what you told me. Your Lucy can't wait to be rid of her father, believe me!"

"She might tell her ma. Miz Manning's a nice lady. She tried to help August."

"Only if she believes her mother *can* help. Lucy's not going to tattle."

"You don't even know her. She might have changed."

"People don't do something that daring—break a runaway slave out of jail—just once in their lives. It's not her one-and-only final good act. Lucy has courage. It's part of her character. It's who she is."

Courage. Courage! I'm sick of talk about courage. It burns me from the inside out. Mostly because I don't have any. Not anymore. I know a person can change, oh yeah, definitely. Change from a dirt-loving gal itching for a fight to a cowardly scamp scurrying to the shadows. All I have to show for my courage is a crooked nose and a face scored with scars. A human being—given into my care—is dead. My courage—and I had buckets full—didn't save August.

A couple days later, when Wixumlee shows me Mister Pavin's telegram, a shiver races from my tailbone to the roots of my hair. But all I can do is take the message down to the print shop and set it into Barnyard Bonanza.

Sorrel mare arrives in ten days.
Special delivery to Mister Simms in Buffalo.

Couragous Lucy has accepted the assignment.

"So, who *is* this sorrel mare?" I poke at the dumpling stuffed with cheese Mariana plops onto my lunch plate. Beany, finishing her third dumpling, eyes the heaping platter in the center of the kitchen table. She's gaining weight fast. Filling out. Looking healthier than I can remember.

"Eat, Tessie. We gotta build up our strength if we're gonna help Wixumlee."

I ignore her and take a bite. The cheese is sweet, the dough eggy. "Who's the sorrel mare?"

"None of your business." Mariana drops into a chair and reaches for a pierogi. "Whew! Summer turned around and came right back." She hikes her flowered skirt above her knees so the air can dry off her thick thighs. "That's better."

"It's my business if Wixumlee wants me to help." I stuff my mouth with dough and cheese.

"Who says she wants your help?"

I tilt my head toward Beany. The crazy kid has been twisting Wixumlee's ear about her and me teaming up to rescue runaway slaves—starting with the sorrel mare. I wish Wixumlee would shut pan about Underground Railroad business when Beany's around.

"Mmmm. Try this one." Beany holds out a forkful of dough and sauerkraut. She even likes the ones stuffed with prunes.

"Don't pay attention to that." Mariana grabs a towel and wipes her forehead and neck. "That ain't gonna happen." It's early October and still summer hot. The big bugs in Albany are taking advantage of the weather and keeping the canal open a little longer, but nobody's fooled. October snowfalls are common in western New York.

I study the new Beany, who's blooming with ideas and the energy to carry them out. All she talks about now is the Underground Railroad and how we're going to guide runaway slaves to freedom. The thought of it makes my stomach roll. I want no part of it—but I get it anyway.

My assignment comes that night at supper. Beany will stay home, but to my absolute agony, I am meeting Lucy and the sorrel mare in Rochester and bringing them back to Buffalo by wagon. Alone.

"Me?" I droop onto the kitchen table and bury my head in my arms. "Why me?"

"Stop shrinking like a wilted weed!" Wixumlee whisks at my hair with her flat hand. "Pick your head up! Sit up straight! Why you? Because you're Lucy's friend. You've worked together before."

I groan. Wixumlee doesn't know it, but she's making a big mistake. Why does she believe everything Beany tells her? Like the falsehood that I'm a fighter. I'm not. Not anymore.

"I need a wagon driver," Wixumlee says.

"There's Quin. Or Larkin." Big, strong men with muscles. And guns.

"They have other jobs. Don't argue with me, girl. I don't believe I'm listening to this! You butted your nose into my business—."

"It was an accident!"

"Well, now you're involved. Up to your eyebrows. And this is a special delivery. Very special. Can't be no mess-up." Wixumlee hates mess-ups. Hates weakness. She applauds only strength. It takes all my strength to hold up my head.

Wixumlee shakes out her napkin and spreads it on her lap. "Your job is simple. Take a packet to Rochester, put them in the wagon, drive them to Buffalo."

"But what if there's trouble? Slave catchers!" I feel the sting of One-Eye's fist cracking my nose and rub the ugly bump.

"Not likely."

Yeah, not likely in sleepy Seneca Falls, either. But it happened.

"All people will see is a young woman traveling with her maid."

I feel like I swallowed a bellyfull of live snakes.

"Listen! Lucy will be a stranger to you. Don't act like you know her. You're just the wagon driver. Be polite, but ignore them both. Don't draw attention to yourself in any way. Mister Pavin will tell Lucy the same thing. They'll be waiting in Rochester on Monday. Pick up your head and listen to me! You take a packet to Rochester, hire a wagon, drive them to Buffalo. It's that simple."

Take a packet to Rochester. Hire a wagon. Drive them to Buffalo. Yeah, simple.

I hunch in the packet's stern, knees and corduroy bag clutched to my chest. It's my first time on the Erie Canal since my escape from Seneca Falls nearly two months ago. Most other passengers seem to enjoy the trip, but cold sweat soaks my back. I shut my eyes and see the dead slavers laying like bloody sacks beside me. Feel Beany's light, limp weight in my arms. Hear the shattered girl humming August's kitchen song.

Just take a packet. Hire a wagon. Drive them to Buffalo. That's all. That's easy. I repeat the words, blocking out the chattering passengers. Blocking out Lockport, Middleport, Brockport, Spencerport. Blocking out every blasted port. All the way to Rochester.

CHAPTER NINETEEN

She's still short and pointy-faced. Still has that mixed up yellow-red hair. Still fidgets like a busy body. When I pull the wagon up at the depot at the smack of dawn, I almost expect Lucy Manning to declare, "You're late!"

"Are you my ride to Buffalo?" An actress playing the part.

"No. You'll ride the wagon. I'm the driver." Ninny.

Lucy scowls. "Will you please help us with our baggage." The words should have been a question, but Lucy doesn't ask it. No, she orders it. Part of her role, I guess, as a young miss with a maid.

I jump off the wagon and lift suitcases and trunks into the back. Now I know why Wixumlee didn't send a carriage. Lucy is going to college and, as a rich girl, taking everything she owns.

What the heck! I stop loading and look hard at the back of a wiry guy scurrying around the corner of the mercantile a few doors down from the canal's ticket office. Dang! If that don't look like Nicky Pappo. What's he doing in Rochester? I shake the thought from my head. Can't be him.

Miss Priss, of course, doesn't heft one single satchel. The older woman standing quietly beside Lucy tries to help with the larger trunks, but Lucy stops her.

I toss the last bag into the wagon and wipe sweat off my forehead. "That's it. Ready to go?"

"Yes." Lucy holds out her gloved hand. I stare at it until it dawns on me I'm supposed to help the little fox into the wagon. Cripes! Put this gal on stage! I take Lucy's hand, and while I really want to boost her in the butt, allow her to use me as a handrail to mount the wagon. Her maid climbs up behind, not needing any help at all, even though she's three times Lucy's age.

I climb aboard, slap the reins across the horse's back and we're off. So far so good. The towpath is bustling with passengers fighting for packets, canawlers tossing cargo and babbling foofoos wandering around lost. No one pays the least attention to Lucy, me or the sorrel mare. Relief washes over me. With luck we'll be in Buffalo in three days and the sorrel mare will be off my hands.

The trip is uneventful — thank you, Jesus, as Ma would say — and by the end of the second day we meet up in Batavia with the main road heading west for Buffalo. But after ignoring me for two days, Lucy now complains we're traveling too fast and points out that the sorrel mare looks weary. Weary from sitting on her butt all day long? How about me being weary driving this horse and wagon from sunup to sundown?

"We can make it to Buffalo by tomorrow night if we push it," I tell Lucy at supper.

"Why push it?" She looks at the sorrel mare, who doesn't look the least bit interested in time or distance, and back at me, as if giving some kind of signal. Then she lowers her ruddy eyebrows, telling me, I guess, that I'm just the driver and to shut pan.

So, we don't push it and it's not until late afternoon on the third day that we stop at a tavern in a little mill town called Williamsville to sleep and sup.

We're on the road early the next morning, and now the silence is killing me. We're supposed to be strangers, but three days of dead quiet, of dull driving on rutted roads — of constant rock and bump — is making me cranky.

Who'll hear if we exchange a few pleasantries? If I ask a few questions about home? I grudgingly admit I'm eager for news of Seneca Falls, but Lucy turns a thin shoulder to me. Doesn't even talk to her maid. Playing the role of what's proper.

I'm getting pretty steamed, dreaming up nasty insults to sling after we reach the safety of the Black Pole, and don't notice the tree limbs piled in the road until the horse shies.

"Lordy! Do you intend to drive us right through that?" Lucy shrieks.

The words barely leave her mouth before two young toughs with drooping soaplocks jump out of the bushes. One twirls a heavy leather sling shot. The other points a rusty rifle. My stomach drops. No! No! No! My clammy hands slip on the reins.

Lucy explodes out of her seat like a firecracker. "What do you think you're doing!" Again, it isn't a question. "Get those limbs off the road. How do you expect us to pass?"

Rifle Boy chuckles. "Well, that's the point, darlin'. We *don't* expect you to pass."

"Oh, wait! Yes we do," Sling Shot laughs. "We expect you to pass your money. To us." Cocky — and mean — they amble closer.

Lucy passed a heavy bag of money to Beany two months ago, and I know the girl ain't gonna part with one more shiny coin.

"Don't point those guns at us." Hands on her hips, elbows sticking out like bent corn stalks, she stamps her foot.

"Shut up!" I mumble, pulling her back onto the seat. Why can't these baby outlaws practice on somebody else?

Rifle Boy grins wide. Jerks the gun barrel at Lucy — then me — then at the sorrel mare. Taps the trigger threateningly. I flush hot and cold.

Sling Shot tosses a heavy stone up and down in his left hand. With an exaggerated motion, he drops it into the pouch and twirls the weapon menacingly. If he's any good at all, he can kill one of us. I don't know what to do — other than fight — and I definitely want no part of flying fists and bashing boots.

"Get 'em, Tess!"

Cripes! Lucy's siccin' me on them like I'm a dog!

"Jump 'em!"

The boys yuck. The colored maid does not move.

"You're a funny little gal." Rifle Boy approaches my side of the wagon, but his eyes are on Lucy. "Kinda cute, too."

He glances at me. "This your boyfriend?"

With one quick move, he yanks me off the wagon seat and knees me in the stomach on the way down. Lucy gasps.

I land on my belly in the dirt, the wind knocked out of me, the sole of Sling Shot's boot pressing on the back of my neck. Sickening pictures of Big Slaver kicking August flash through my head. Beany's tragic screams echo in my ears.

Rifle Boy pulls Lucy off the wagon and snatches at her small black purse. "Gimme that!"

"No!" Lucy slaps his hand.

Chuckling, he flashes green teeth.

"She's a feisty one, ain't she?"

But his face turns cruel. He knocks Lucy down with a whack to the side of her head and yanks the purse away. Up on the wagon seat, the maid sits still as a stone. Obviously, she knows better than to get tangled up in white folks' squabbles.

I struggle to regain my breath. If I lay here long enough, these thugs might just take the loot and run. Rifle Boy stuffs paper money into his pants pocket and throws Lucy's bag in the dirt.

It's almost over.

He bends over Lucy laying on the ground, stunned.

"Thanks, honey. Ain't you a sweetheart to come driving down the road just when I need some cash."

Any minute now, they'll leave.

"But, you know what? You're so cute, I'm gonna bring you along for company." Rifle Boy jerks Lucy to her feet.

She struggles and kicks at him. "Let go of me!"

Rifle Boy laughs.

Sling Shot takes his foot off my neck and kicks playfully at my side. I steel my gut for a real shot from his pointy toed boot.

"Look at that! Your boyfriend here ain't worth squat!" Sling Shot draws back his foot. "You need a real man!"

The gunshot scares me so bad I wet my pants. Lordy, did that devil shoot Lucy? The maid?

"Move your asses!"

I roll over. Two men in baggy pants, flannel shirts and wide-brimmed hats pulled low over their faces point guns at the young hoodlums.

"I said *move*! Away from those girls!"

Harriet!

"Drop your weapons."

I stare at the long-barreled pistol pointed at Rifle Boy's pants. He drops his grip on Lucy's wrist, lets his rifle slip to the ground, and looks down fearfully.

"Yeah, that's right, weasel. You don't have to worry 'bout me shooting your simple brain out of your simple head. I don't want to kill you—just make you lonely for the rest of your life." Harriet jerks the pistol quickly, telling me to get up.

"Move those branches so that wagon can pass." Harriet aims her pistol at one failed thief then the other. Rifle Boy and Sling Shot rush to move the debris blocking the road.

"You girls jump up and drive off."

We scramble into the wagon, and I urge the horse into a fast trot. Beside me, Lucy trembles and the maid puts her arm around the girl's waist and holds her hand.

"Who saved us?" Lucy's voice quivers.

"One's Harriet Tubman." I slap the reins. The Moses of her people. "I don't know the other."

"The other's my daughter," the maid replies. "Wixumlee."

CHAPTER TWENTY

"No, honey, it's not that I thought you'd fail. Don't think that, Lucy. That's not why we were there."

A royal blue dressing gown drapes Wixumlee's tall frame, her scruffy pants and shirt barely a memory. She pours tea into a tiny cup and hands it to the maid with a smile.

"I just needed to be there, behind the scenes. To take extra care with my mama."

Lucy accepts the next cup of tea. "I'm so sorry it didn't go off smoothly, like you planned."

Wixumlee waves her hand as if the botched rescue means nothing, but Harriet snorts.

"Damn good thing we showed up." She frowns at me, hunched in a corner. "That one might as well have two broke arms. Peed her own pants, she did. And all that scrawny kid did was pull her off the wagon."

No use telling them it was the gunshot that scared the pee out of me. Makes no difference to Harriet and Wixumlee. All they saw when I got up off the ground was the wet spot between my legs and drew their own conclusions.

"You did fine, Lucy. You did just what we asked you. You can be proud." Wixumlee smiles.

"Thank you. I'm glad to help."

"You did just what we expected." Wixumlee looks over at my corner, letting everyone in the room—Mariana, Beany, Quin, Larkin, Wixumlee's mama Cleo—know that Tess Riley did not do what was expected. When she and Harriet caught up with us at the Buffalo Black Pole, Wixumlee didn't ream me out, cuss me out or bawl me out. She shunned me.

Well, dang, I didn't want to be part of their big rescue. I told them point blank I didn't want to do it. Wixumlee forced me when she could have easily sent Quin or Larkin. But I was sent and in everybody's eyes—including my own—I failed. I couldn't take a skinny boy with a rusty rifle that maybe couldn't even fire. Or a dumpy kid with a flabby sling shot. All I could do was lay on the ground sniffing dust.

And Beany, pouting because she was left behind, made it worse. The girl threw herself into Lucy's arms like they were long-lost sisters. And when Wixumlee and Harriet returned—who knows what they did with those greasy highwaymen—Beany demanded to hear the whole story of Cleo's escape from a Georgia plantation, her long trek north following that damn star they all worship, and, of course, Harriet's version of what took place on the road, when Lucy stood up to two boarder ruffians and I ate dirt.

When she heard the story, Mariana waved both gold-bangled arms at me like I was worthless, worse yet, dangerous to have around.

"Mama, I been looking for you for eight long years." Wixumlee sits on the parlor sofa next to Cleo, tears trimming her eyes.

"How you ever find me, honey?" Cleo sets her tea cup on the table and reaches for her daughter's hands. "I been missing you for so long. Over twenty years I been without you. All that time, I never stop thinking 'bout you. Worrying 'bout you. You just a young girl when they sell me away from you. How you ever find me?"

Beany watches them with the same hungry look Lucy wore chasing down stories for *The Lily*.

Wixumlee raises Cleo's hands to her lips and kisses them. "I did whatever I needed to do, Mama. That's all you need to know. Your hard days are over. You're with me now, and I'm never gonna let you out of my sight!" She smiles lovingly. An expression foreign to Wixumlee's face, at least when I'm around.

Beany's hand creeps slowly up her chest to the blue stone knife hanging around her neck.

"Now tell me about this beautiful child you have." Cleo touches Beany's knee gently.

"Well, this is my Beany." Wixumlee beams like she birthed the girl herself.

My stomach tightens. She's not your Beany! She's *my* Beany! Wixumlee has her claws in the girl now, but someday I'll get her back.

Larkin pulls a cot into Beany's room after she insists Lucy sleep with us. I half expect to be booted out to the shed, but instead end up on the cot with Lucy curled in the bed that has been mine for the last two weeks. Never mind. Lucy will be off to Ohio tomorrow. Out of my hair—maybe. Tonight Wixumlee talked about how active Oberlin is in the Underground Railroad. She's pushing Lucy to get involved. Now, as we wash for bed, Beany fills Lucy's head with plans for the three of us to work together helping slaves escape to freedom.

"I have to do it, Lucy." Beany sits up in bed, wide awake. It hits me that Beany never talked to Lucy before. Always used me as a go-between. Back in Seneca Falls, Lucy could barely squeak a "hey" out of the little mouse.

"I have to do it for my mama." Beany doesn't cry when she says "my mama" like I expect her to. Beany is strong now, in body and spirit. She's Wixumlee's eager student, mimicking her worst traits. Pretty soon she'll be marching off with these war parties—with or without Wixumlee's encouragement. Or permission.

"Next time there's a slave rescue, I'm going. I can do it." She gabs like a crazy girl.

I lay on the cot, tortured by confused emotions. I want Beany—but I also want out. I took the printing job to get close to Beany—to help her back from her misery—but Beany's gone from lackluster to loony. Overnight.

Beany has spirit and energy and she has Wixumlee. She doesn't need me. I'm not sure she wants me either. Maybe I should hit the road. Ride with Lucy to Ohio and just keep going. Or maybe I'll ride the Erie to Albany. Naw, the action's to the west, not east.

Action. I roll over. The word that used to excite me now scares me raw.

Lucy takes a stagecoach west the next morning. I see her off at the Buffalo depot.

"Is that all you're carrying?" I survey the small trunk and satchel the driver hoists onto the roof. "What happened to all those crates and trunks I loaded into the wagon in Rochester?"

"Oh. That was part show and part charity," Lucy whispers. "Those crates were full of children's clothes from me and my brothers. Also my mother's old things and dresses that don't fit me anymore. I gave them to Wixumlee for—you-know-who."

I give her a funny look. "Don't fit you? You don't look any fatter." Maybe a little rounder.

Lucy blushes. "I'm not. But I've stopped wearing a corset, so last year's dresses don't fit."

I stare at her natural tiny waistline.

"Someday I might be bold like you, Tess, and give up dresses completely, but not yet." We sit quietly on a bench. I throw an ankle over a knee and play with the shoestrings on my brogans.

"You gonna do it?"

"Do what?" She looks at me innocently.

I pause. "Smuggle slaves."

"Shhhhh." Lucy glances at other passengers waiting on benches.

I wait for an answer.

She sighs. "I don't know. Maybe. I mean, I want to. After what happened to August, I should. We all should."

I wonder if Lucy knows I lost her money. I could fess up, but what good would that do? I'll just pay it back one day in a heavy, velvet sack.

"Beany's enthusiastic about working for the U-R-R."

"The what?"

"You know," she whispers, "the Underground—."

I grimace. It's all Harriet's fault. Beany is Harriet Tubman's favorite audience. The bold woman rambles for hours about daring escapes, near captures and jubilant reunions of long separated families in Canada or the northern and western territories. According to Harriet, she's rescued hundreds of runaways, guiding them by the North Star from the sorrow of the south to the joy of the north.

"Beany gets too wrapped up in Harriet's tales," I say. "Just like she did in Coop's canal stories. She believes every word."

"But she's drawing pictures again," Lucy counters. "That's a good thing. Expressing her feelings."

I screw up my face. "Did you see the last one she drew? The one with Harriet pointing that dang gun at a slave who tries to change his mind in the middle of an escape?"

"Harriet told Beany she wouldn't risk him turning back and being forced to tell on the others," Lucy explains. "He had to make the choice. Move forward with his mouth shut—."

"Or die? She was willing to plug a hole through him? Is that what she's teaching Beany?" Lucy wasn't here when Beany stuck the fork in the foofoo's neck. It won't take much encouragement for her to put a bullet in someone.

Harriet is Beany's hero—right after Wixumlee. Beany thinks Lucy is brave, too, for bringing Cleo from Rochester to safety. I wonder where I rank on Beany's bravery list.

The stagecoach pulls up, and Lucy sticks out her small hand. "Goodbye, Tess. Thanks for all your help."

I study her face for a smirk. "What help?"

"Picking us up in Rochester. And on the road."

Is that supposed to be funny? I shoot her a sharp look, but Lucy's face is smooth, her eyes sincere.

"Yeah. Okay."

"I'll write to you. Will you write back?"

I shrug. "I dunno."

She reaches up and hugs my shoulders. "Don't give up, Tess." Gives me a little peck on the cheek. "I'll write as soon as I get there."

Surprised by her intimacy, I watch the little fox hop into the coach and ride away.

The second surprise comes seeing Beany walking along Commercial Slip with Talbot. Sweet Jesus! Scared little Beaner roaming among white folks in broad daylight. They smile and wave as I draw near, and I have a flash memory of prying Beany off the front porch and dragging her across Fall Street to Lizzie Stanton's convention. *Mama's gonna be mad! Mama's gonna kill me!*

"What you doing, Beany?" I put my arm around the girl and draw her out of the foot traffic.

"Walking."

"Why?"

Beany laughs. "'Cause it's a beautiful day!"

She swishes her skirt and moves back onto the Slip. The once shy girl is changing and changing fast. Talbot follows like a perky puppy.

"Wixumlee know you're out here?"

"'Course she does. She sent me to the store. Hey, Tessie, did Lucy get off all right?"

"Yeah."

"She said she'd write to me."

"Yeah, me too."

Passengers ooze left and right around us, just like they do when Wixumlee strolls the Slip. Beany holds her head high, and I swear the girl is strutting—like Wixumlee. I remember August's warnings, preached to Beany from the time she could walk. *Keep your eyes on the ground. Don't look nobody in the eye.*

Beany's eyes are everywhere but on the ground. She stares even the most grizzled canawler down and doesn't back off. I don't like the way the sailors and teamsters grin at her. I trail Beany and Talbot into the general store where she places her order with authority.

Wixumlee grins when Beany walks through the tavern door, bright-faced, with the smell of sunshine on her hair.

It's hours later, as we prepare for bed, that I get a chance to talk to her again.

"Lucy noticed — just like me — that you're all excited about this Underground Railroad business." I splash water on my face and neck. "Why you want to get tangled up in that? It's dangerous."

Beany stops brushing her hair. "It's important."

I dry myself with a towel. I don't really want to bring up August.

"Your mama wouldn't want you messing with these people, Beany."

"My mama's dead! And it's her own fault!"

Beany's temper is an unexpected flash of lightning. She sits ramrod straight on the edge of her bed, fury swelling her slim body.

"You don't mean that."

"Yes, I do! My mama was scared of everything. And stupid. If she'd been smart she would have hauled herself and her big belly as far north as she could go, where she'd be really free. Not drop herself in Seneca Falls, where she was too scared to pee."

My hand trembles with the urge to slap her. These aren't Beany's words. They can't be. Beany never talks like that. Never uses that language. Never says a word against her mama.

"Wixumlee's my mama now. And she ain't scared, and she ain't stupid! And I ain't either."

I lay down shaking in my bed. What's happened to Beany? To her love for August? To talk that way about her mama! The new Beany is strong, but in a bad way. A dangerous way. Her loyalty to Wixumlee — this blind devotion — will hurt her. I'm sure of it.

Beany drops her hair brush noisily on the nightstand and walks to my bed. I look up uneasily.

"You know what I like about Wixumlee?"

I shake my head.

"She ain't *nothin'* like my mama."

CHAPTER TWENTY-ONE

Harriet Tubman disappears the next morning—thank you, Jesus!—and the rest of us get back to normal living, which at this moment does not include worrying about runaway slaves.

I'm not sure why I'm still a member of the gang. I don't feel part of it—this tough, violent branch of the Underground Railroad. Wixumlee brought me into the fold to bring Beany out of her shell. Well, dang, the girl's out, though I had little to do with it and hate the result. Maybe Beany insisted Wixumlee keep me. The woman wants Beany happy and that gives the girl power. I don't want anything to do with these cutthroats, but my gut tells me to stick with Beany.

"Hey, girly girl, where you hiding? I been looking for you."

My stomach rolls at the sight of Nicky Pappo. Wixumlee has me clearing tables in the Buffalo dining room and Pappo—knowing darn well he ain't welcome—plunks his sorry butt into a chair and demands service.

"Not talking?"

I want to ask if it was him I saw scooting off the Rochester towpath when I picked up Lucy and the sorrel mare. But I don't.

"Where's Cooper?" I wipe the table with a damp rag.

"Don't know. Ain't my day to watch him."

I stop wiping and stare.

"That's a joke! Get it? I don't know where he is 'cause it ain't my day to watch him. Watch over him. Get it?"

Donkey brain! I heft a pan of dirty dishes and make for the kitchen.

"Hey! Bring me a plate of whatever slop that mean ol' gypsy tossed together today!"

I turn and mouth, "Shut pan." Wixumlee hates shouting in her dining room. Mariana hates hearing her cooking called slop. I dump the dishes in the large kitchen sink and sit down in a corner.

"Pappo wants a plate."

Mariana wipes her forehead with her sleeve and looks me up and down. "What's wrong with you?"

I shrug.

"Well, get lively. Savannah's not feeling well. You'll have to help Talbot serve these meals."

I groan. Work for Wixumlee can take any form at any time, that's what the bossy crone says. One day I can be printing newspapers, the next day smuggling slaves, the next day waiting tables. Variety, that's what I have. I miss boredom.

"Take this to him." Mariana hands me a plate with enough gumbo on it to feed a freighter full of foofoos. "And put a smile on your face, pickle nose."

I'm a bit flummoxed why Mariana doesn't spit over feeding Nicky Pappo. He's as rude to her as he is to Wixumlee and she's shown him the outline of her gun many times. Sometimes he gets away with strutting into the Black Pole and other times Larkin or Quin toss him out like he's gutterscum. Which he is.

I set down Nicky's slop, and he dives into the food. I hope he pays the bill. If I can't get the money, I'll have to call over Mariana and her pistol to make the coins jump out of his pocket. Then the crabby gypsy will toss me the look that says "Can't you do nothin'?" and I'll have failed again.

"You been to Rochester lately?" The words spill from my lips before I know it.

"When?"

"I dunno. Last weekend." I turn to go, but Pappo grabs my elbow.

"What you doing in Rochester?" He squeezes hard enough to make me wince.

"Nothin'."

"You're there doing nothin'?"

"Never mind. It's none of your business anyway." Cripes, me and my mouth. I'm supposed to say I was helping a runaway slave? I try to pull away, but Pappo's pinching grip slides to my wrist.

"Forget it, Nicky!"

"You think you saw me in Rochester?"

"Geez, what's the big deal? Must have been somebody else." But I know it wasn't. It was Nicky Pappo, I'm sure of it. Now he's all fired up, mad 'cause I caught him. I have the slave secret. But what's his?

Pappo drops my arm. He spoons gumbo and stares at me as he swallows. Mariana yells for me to serve some foofoos. Ten minutes later, when I clear his table he has his money ready.

"So, what you doing in Rochester, girly girl?"

I snatch the coins and rush from the dining room.

My own supper's spoiled. Mariana hands me a plate and says Wixumlee's called a meeting to plan the next rescue — and I have to be there. The last thing I want is to be dragged through another failure. After supper, I sit alone in a corner while the others — Beany included — crowd both sides of the long kitchen table.

"This trip just came up." The General parades before her troops. "Pretty quick after the last one, but it's an emergency. We have to get these people out." Mariana, Quin and Larkin lean forward. Cleo's gone to bed, but Beany sits at attention.

"It's a young mother and two very young children. One a little older than the other, but both still babies. That's what makes this mission so hard. What makes it necessary."

Wixumlee pauses, looks over to my corner. I remove my hands covering my ears, and she continues.

"The mother tried to get out last spring with her husband and parents — when the kids were even younger. They didn't get far. The babies started crying. Couldn't keep them quiet. One would cry and get the other going. The Underground has methods for dealing with that. Stuff these folks didn't know about."

I glance up suspiciously. If Harriet Tubman's in charge, that'll prob'ly mean smothering them.

"The babies had colds and were miserable and cranky. But their daddy — he'd escaped twice as a boy and was recaptured — their daddy was determined to get out for good the next time, and he was afraid those crying babies would give him away. After several close calls, he told his wife to take the children back to the plantation. He'd take her parents north then send for her. She didn't want to do it, but it was plain nobody would get free if they were caught. At least some of them had a chance if she took the babies back."

Mariana takes a pot of coffee off the stove and pours cups for Quin and Larkin.

"When she showed back at the plantation, the master didn't believe her story that she'd just taken the kids to visit an aunt at another house. He beat her. Tried to make her tell where her man and folks were, but all she would say—could say—was that they went north. That's all she knew."

Wixumlee pauses and takes a cup of coffee from Mariana.

"Here, boys, have some pumpkin bread." The gypsy sets a plate between them. "I put raisins in it for you, Larkin, and almonds on top." Thick slices of bread disappear in a few bites, washed down with full cups of hot coffee. Larkin and Quin settle back in their chairs, muscled arms across their thick chests, stomachs full, faces serious.

"The woman suffered, but her husband and parents had good luck and made it to Rochester."

I shudder at the mention of that city.

"The husband had skills—carpentry and such—and got work pretty quick. Started attending meetings with our good friend Mister Douglass."

I come to attention and Wixumlee notices.

"You know Frederick Douglass?"

I shrug. "I heard him talk once back home, that's all."

Beany's face lights up. "Me, too. At Miz Stanton's woman's rights convention. Me and Tess went both days."

And I had to drag you, you little ninny. Now you're all perky about it.

"Yes, I heard about that." Wixumlee smiles. "Well, Frederick heard the husband's story and said he could reunite him with his wife and children. That he had a system. It would take planning, patience and courage, but he could almost guarantee he'd get that mother and her babies to Rochester."

I can hear it now. Take a packet to Rochester. Put them in a wagon. Drive them to Buffalo. Me, a black woman and two squawking colored kids.

"The family wants to move to Ohio. We already have a contact out there. Our friend Lucy Manning, who helped get my mama home. I'll send her a telegram tomorrow with the details."

I groan inside.

"We have conductors going down to South Carolina to guide that family through the most treacherous part. Harriet's taking care of that. We have conductors through Pennsylvania to the New York border, and we have shelter and food planned for them up through New York state. Our conductors in the Binghamton and Ithaca areas have been especially generous." Wixumlee stops for a sip of coffee.

"What's our job?" I don't like the way Beany asks that. *Our* job. Putting herself — and me — in the thick of it. Wixumlee smiles, pleased with Beany's enthusiasm.

"Well, we're going to pick them up in a little village called Avon and take them up the Genesee River to Rochester. Then we'll put the whole family on canal boats going west and bring them to Black Rock. Then we're going to pass them along like we usually do to conductors who'll take them to Ohio and pass them on to Lucy Manning."

"So — let me get this straight," Larkin says. "They're coming up through Pennsylvania into New York, we're taking them up to Rochester, but then the Railroad's taking them back through the western corner of Pennsylvania into Ohio?"

Wixumlee nods.

"Awful roundabout route, don't you think? Why don't they just cut straight west across Pennsylvania to begin with?"

"The woman wants to meet up with her husband and parents in Rochester. Doesn't want to travel without them."

"Why don't the daddy and grandfolk go west on their own and meet up with them in Erie, close to the Ohio border?" Larkin butters another piece of pumpkin bread.

"He wants to keep working until his wife and babies arrive. Build up his savings. And they just plain want to travel together. They feel safe now that the Railroad's in charge." Wixumlee sips her coffee.

I shoot her a dark look. Yeah, the Railroad's invincible. The Railroad's so well organized it can parade people up and down one state and across another. I sink my head deeper between my shoulders. Go ahead. Parade 'em. Just leave me out of it.

"Well, that's true. They'll be safe with us. But it's a whole lot easier to hide people in twos and threes than in sixes." Quin speaks firmly and reaches for another piece of bread.

Well, Wixumlee's just fine with everybody contradicting her and asking questions isn't she. Everybody except me.

"I agree," Wixumlee answers peaceably. "But we've moved large groups of people before. It's more difficult, but not impossible."

Larkin and Quin accept that and content themselves with more bread and coffee. Two loaves are already gone.

"I'll work out the details and make the assignments. Our phase of the operation will begin in one week. Meeting's over. Goodnight."

I go to bed dreading my assignment. Wixumlee will surely give me a dangerous one, just for spite.

And I'm right. Her plan has me and Larkin posing as Allegheny fur trappers moving north up the Genesee River. A Railroad conductor in Avon will bring the mother and babies to a trapper's shack near the old Indian settlement on the west bank of the Genesee before midnight. Paddling all night, we'll take the family up the river and connect with the Erie Canal in Rochester before dawn.

Wixumlee nails down more details but I stop listening. This is crazy. How will we keep two notorious squawkers quiet during a long river trip?

"I expect you to hold your own this time, Tess." Wixumlee eyes me firmly. "You're big and you're strong. Lord knows I've been feeding you enough. I was ready to boot you out when you turned to mush on the Rochester road but decided to give you another chance. Don't disappoint me."

CHAPTER TWENTY-TWO

We hop out of Quin's wagon in a field near a little town south of Rochester called Geneseo, hike to the river and follow it north back to Avon. The backtracking is supposed to hide our real identities. I hope it has some good purpose, 'cause my feet are wet and cold before we tramp two miles. It's mid-October, has been raining all week, the nights are frosty enough for two blankets, and I expect the rain to turn icy any minute.

I've never been alone with Larkin before and so far it isn't pleasant. For starters, he barely talks. Not one word during the long wagon ride from Buffalo to Geneseo and so far hardly anything on the river walk, except to say, "Hurry up" or "Stop draggin' your tail." He's big, strong and walks quickly, several paces ahead, and loses me a few times in the tangle of wild grape vines and staghorn sumac. When I catch up, the disgust on his face is enough to wilt a warrior.

We're dressed alike in oily buckskin and dirty coonskin caps. Larkin carries a bulky backpack, and I have a necklace of smelly animal pelts draped across my shoulders. Rain has smeared the mud on our faces, drawing dark and light stripes from forehead to chin. We look like we've been on the trail for months. Last summer I would have jumped at the chance to stomp around the woods in deerhide pants, but right now I wish I was clean and didn't smell like wet dog.

I stare at Larkin's broad back moving steadily ahead.

"What if someone's in that shack when we get there?"

"Won't be."

"You sure?"

"Somebody squatting there will get booted out."

"By who?"

"Our people."

Our people. Those aren't comforting words. I'm not one of *our people*. Don't want to be. I don't belong in the Underground. Don't have the stomach for it. But I've been forced to join the band of big bad brothers. No one asked me, but I'm in now, like it or not. And if I mess up again—who knows what Wixumlee will do to me.

My buckskin suit is covered with a thin film of ice when we trudge up to the empty trapper's shack just after sundown. A tilting box of weathered boards, it crouches a few feet from the water, close enough to be snatched away if the river swells.

I scrounge for driftwood and start stacking a meager pile of half-damp twigs.

Larkin kicks them apart. "No fire!"

"I'm froze to the bone!"

"No fire, no light. Grab some sleep. You'll be paddling all night."

No fire. No hot food. I pull a blanket from my pack, wrap myself tight as a sausage, kick some rusty cans into a corner of the shack, and curl up shivering on the dirt floor. Larkin sinks to the ground beside me and holds out some jerky. I stare at the stiff strip.

"What'd you expect?" He shoves it under my nose.

I take the dried meat and touch it to my tongue. Might as well be holding one of those damp twigs between my teeth. I try to muster enough spit to soften it and picture a plate of Mariana's tender chicken. Her buttery mashed potatoes. A slice of black bread soaked with strawberry jam. Larkin pokes a canteen into my shoulder.

I take a swig of lukewarm water. "Why didn't Quin come with you?"

Larkin fusses with his blanket. "Who says he didn't."

"Where is he?"

"Not far. Lucky dog's prob'ly sacked out in a bed at the inn right now, while we roll around on possum bones and tin cans. Come midnight he'll be working again, though. Just like us."

Larkin flops around in his blanket, trying to get comfortable and his loose black curls bounce around his forehead. Like Beany, he has large, dark, almond-shaped eyes. Big buckets of chocolate pudding.

"Stop gawkin'!"

My face burns hot. At least he can't see me flame in the dark.

"Is Beany coming on this rescue?" I mumble.

Larkin stops his flopping. "Are you crazy?" Then his eyes melt in an unfocused stare somewhere behind my head. "No. She's not coming, but she'll help Mariana pack food and clothes. Dress the kids when they get to Black Rock. She'll have to be satisfied with that for now."

I pull my blanket higher up on my chin and whisper, "I'm worried about her."

"Why?" The whites of Larkin's eyes blink in the dark. "Why you worried about Beany?"

"She's so keen on this rescue stuff." My voice trembles. "I'm afraid she'll get hurt—somehow—I don't know."

"That's why she's not here. She's not ready."

I'm not ready either. Why am I here? It's a big mistake.

"She's changing so fast," I say. "Ever since Harriet showed up. I've known her all her life. She used to be a scared little girl. Now she wants to lead an army!"

Larkin laughs softly. "And that's bad? We need women fighters."

"She's a kid! And she's never been a fighter!"

It's pitch dark inside the shack, but I feel Larkin's eyes on my scarred face. I hide my humped nose in the blanket and fight back tears.

"Those slave catchers beat you good."

Yeah, they did. My nose runs and I have to either suck the gunk in or wipe it off on the blanket. Larkin pokes the top of my head with his finger.

"Listen up, Tess. You fought for Beany and her mama on the towpath. That means a lot to Wixumlee. To everybody. Once she started talking, Beany told us the story, blow by blow. You got beat bad, but you gave as good as you got. The way Beany told it, you can be proud of those scars."

I pull the blanket down below my eyes. He isn't smiling, but he isn't scowling. I sneak a swipe at my dripping nose and feel a warm glow tweak the edges of my heart.

"And you're gonna do good tonight."

The glow vanishes quickly, replaced by stone cold dread. "I'm scared, Larkin."

He tosses his head. "Me, too. Only stupid people ain't scared. It'll all come back to you—how to fight. And anyway, we got this rescue planned so good, nothin' can go wrong."

I feel a nudge on my hip and open my eyes.

"Get up." When I don't move, Larkin leans over, grips my shoulders, stands me straight up and strips off the blanket. "Quick! Roll it up. Dump your pack in the canoe. Move!"

I stumble out into an inky night. I can barely see the canoe pulled up on shore. Larkin gives me a push, and I wobble over the rocks toward it. I feel for the edges and toss in my pack. Its weight and motion make the boat quiver and slide into the water.

Larkin spits an angry oath and drags the canoe back up onto the gravelly bank. He grabs my hand and slaps it onto the edge of the boat.

"Hold tight. Don't let go."

He presses the long stem of a paddle into my other hand, then climbs into the canoe, working his way carefully to the back. Dry-mouthed and trembling, I hang on.

Shadows near the treeline change shape and two large figures pass something from one to the other, while a smaller shape hovers close by. Then one big shape and the smaller shape glide toward the shoreline.

Quin and the runaway mama each carry a bundle. He helps her into the canoe, and she lays her package on a nest made by our packs and animal skins. Quin hands the woman the second bundle, then motions me to climb in.

For one, quick instant I consider dashing off into the woods, but a nudge from Quin sends me tumbling into the canoe.

No one says a word. No baby cries.

To my surprise, Quin taps me on the head in friendly farewell then pushes the canoe into the river.

CHAPTER TWENTY-THREE

Flowing north to Lake Ontario, the Genesee River is a windy stream, cluttered with large rocks, and the canoe bangs into them in the blackness. Each time it smacks a boulder lurking beneath the surface, I cuss softly, fearful the jolt will jar the babies from sleep. The mama has pulled the blankets back from their heads, and the brisk night air scrapes their faces, but the babes sleep on. She holds one kid, while the smaller one burrows in the packs and skins. Larkin doesn't speak, just drives the canoe with powerful strokes, and my arms ache from keeping up with him. After several hours sliding past sleeping farmland, I take to paddling once to his twice, and he doesn't complain.

Woods and farmland give way to a city taking shape along the river's edge. I can almost make out factories dribbling yesterday's smoke. Tall church spires poke at the still dark sky. We are approaching Rochester, a boomtown famous for a man-made arch that carries the Erie Canal up and over the Genesee River. During my painful journey with Beany from Seneca Falls to Black Rock, I heard Captain Beale call it an aqueduct—and a remarkable achievement. I didn't marvel at the time. I barely noticed.

And now, here it is, less than a mile ahead. I can just count the aqueduct's seven arches and realize Larkin and I must guide our canoe in the darkness through one of those curves.

I glance back at the sleeping babies. See black curly hair and soft, round cheeks. Mouths puckered like rose buds. They were sleeping when Quin put them in the canoe, and they haven't stirred since. The mama doesn't need to croon lullabies or pat their tummies. They sleep like they're dead.

Something long scrapes the bottom of the boat. Boulders, deadly enough in daylight, are impossible to see in the blackness, but this doesn't feel like a boulder. Despite the peril of traveling the Genesee, Wixumlee says runaway slaves sometimes go up the river in boats and somehow make their way across Lake Ontario to Canada. Of course, I can't be that lucky. My runaways have to zigzag their way west to Ohio.

Boom! Something heavy bangs the side of the canoe and the mama yelps.

"Shhhhh," Larkin hisses, holding his paddle out of the water and letting the canoe glide. I do the same, both of us searching the dark river.

Boom! The second jolt wakes the baby laying in the skins. It mews softly, and the mama pulls the blanket farther away from its face to give it more air.

Boom! *Knock! Knock! Knock!* I flinch as a large log bounces along the side of the canoe — and look across the water to see a swarm of downed trees sliding toward us.

"Dang! Where are these logs coming from?" I push at them with my paddle, but they're clumsy and heavy, pulled along with the canoe by the current.

"Push them behind us! *Push*!" Larkin stands in the canoe and shoves his paddle against a huge log — only one of a half dozen circling us like warriors, attacking the canoe, colliding with each other.

I stare at the logs, then at the curving arches ahead of us.

Shaken by the vibrations, the baby in the skins cries louder — loud enough, I'm sure, to be heard on shore in the silent night. Besides factories and churches, I now glimpse houses and stores. Panicked, I turn to Larkin.

"Get that one." He jerks his head at a large log sliding straight for the canoe's right side. I stand up in the wobbling boat, brace my paddle's long handle against my shoulder and aim the rounded end at the approaching log. The impact jams the thick, round handle into my shoulder, making me yowl with pain. The paddle end slips off the log, and the canoe turns sideways, buffeted now from all directions by mean, dead trees. Silent for so long, the baby on its mama's lap shrieks as if it's being skinned.

"Get the bottle of sleep!" Larkin strains against another log and manages to steer it past us.

"The what?"

"Bottle of sleep!"

I look from Larkin to a gigantic log, covered on top with globs of mud and raccoon dung. It slams into the side of the boat and knocks me to the floor. I scramble up quickly. The bigger baby screams again. I feel water on my feet.

Larkin cusses angrily. "Small bottle. In the satchel."

"Where?"

"Bottom—of—boat." He groans with the strain of keeping another log away from the canoe. "Next to—my pack."

I lay my paddle down and yank at a small bag I didn't even known was in the canoe. I also don't known the satchel supports the skins on which the smaller, fussing baby lays. With a screech, the kid rolls face down into the boat bottom, sloshy with water.

"Sweet Jesus!" I make a one-handed grab for the baby's blanket. The mama reaches, too, squashing the kid on her lap. The baby blasts a murderous cry.

"Bottle of sleep!" Larkin hisses angrily.

I dig around in the bottom of the bag. "I can't find any bottle!"

The mama strains to pick up her gurgling baby and hold on to its sibling.

"Toss it to me."

"What?"

"The bag!"

I toss it right over the back of the fumbling mama and its contents spray in all directions.

"Idiot!" Larkin adds a few choice curses. "Help her with those kids!" He scrambles in the soggy boat bottom, while babies wail, logs ram and the curving arches loom.

The mama holds the bigger kid on her shoulder, whispering and patting its back. I pluck the smaller squawker out of the watery bottom, and stare at its wet, stretching mouth. I put my hand over the wide-wiggling hole and press down, but the mama slaps my hand away.

Larkin cusses and fumbles and finally comes up with a small brown bottle. He taps the mama's shoulder. "Turn around," he tells her. "Keep us in the middle of the river, Tess."

"I'm holding this dumb kid!"

"Don't drift to shore!" He unscrews the rubber stopper and drops some liquid into the older baby's mouth. "Okay, switch."

I pass the squalling squirmer to its ma and am rewarded with the bigger brat. I stuff it under one arm, brace my legs, grip the long paddle one-handed, and struggle to keep the canoe aimed at one of the rapidly approaching arches. I'm sweating like a farmhand and cussing like a canawler. "Somebody take this brat!"

"Okay, ma'am. They'll sleep now. Get your other baby back." He stuffs the bottle of sleep into his shirt pocket and picks up his paddle.

"Aim for that middle arch, Tess. The river angles down on the other side of the aqueduct. Prepare for the drop."

The *drop*?

We shoot through a curved arch and slide down a rock-strewn slope, paddling frantically around boulders as big as cows. But we past them quickly, and I take a moment to gulp huge lungs-full of cold night air. Maybe now the trek will ease up.

"We gotta move." Larkin sounds more worried than angry. "With all this racket, somebody's gonna spot us. It's getting near dawn."

I slice my paddle into the black water. All this racket! Next time one of those brats opens its mouth, I'll throw it overboard.

CHAPTER TWENTY-FOUR

"Go right! To shore! Now! Right! Right!" Larkin is on his knees in the bottom of the canoe, straining every muscle in his back, arms and thighs, digging his paddle into the black water.

A thundering noise shouts at us and a powerful current drags us toward a curtain of mist shimmering above a roaring waterfall. And our canoe is flooding. A log has punched a wide crack in the side below the surface. We've been so busy quieting screaming brats we didn't notice water seeping in.

"Paddle! Hard! Dig!"

Searing pain shoots through my arms and chest, and I can't take a big enough breath to clear my head.

"That's it. Good! We're close. Keep us turned to shore." The canoe strains toward the riverbank. "Grab something! Anything!"

The mama sets her babies on the pile of skins and reaches over the side to grasp tree roots sticking out of the bank. Her hands slip but she reaches again, shoving her fists through the buckled roots and getting a strong, determined grip. Groaning with the strain, Larkin fights the current with his long paddle.

"Tess! Grab those vines." I drop my paddle and snag handfulls of wild grape vines hanging from maple trees guarding the shoreline, and wince when the ragged bark cuts my hands as the current tries to yank the canoe away. "Nobody let go! Hear me? *Don't let go!*"

Larkin drops his paddle and snatches a handful of hanging leaves, gingerly inching hand over hand to pull down a stronger tree limb. "You can't let go, Tess. *Hang on!*"

With thunder in my ears and my heart pounding, my head has room for one thought only—*hang on.*

"Toss those kids up there. Toss 'em!" The mama hefts one baby than the other onto the steep, slippery bank. They land with soft thuds, slide, and she whines with fear, but their blankets catch.

"Climb out. Go!" Without testing the tree roots, the mama pulls herself out of the canoe. Her feet catch on the side, tipping the boat, but she kicks them free. Digging her fingers into the soft, slippery mud, she claws her way to her children.

"How in hell we gonna get out of here?" Half of me dangles in the boat, the other half is suspended above the water, attached to the grape vines by throbbing hands. The waterfall screams for the canoe, and the potent current works to please it.

Larkin's tree limb bobs, threatening to rip him from the boat. He's stretched like a bow string and struggles to grip the edge of the canoe with his boots to keep it near the river bank. If the tree yanks him out, I'm lost. Over the falls. And if I jump onto the bank—and if the taunt tree limb doesn't catapult Larkin out—he'll be drawn with the canoe to his death.

"Climb out. Go!" Larken shouts.

"No!"

"Jump!"

"You'll go over the falls!"

"Then we jump together. You got a good grip on those vines?"

"Yes!"

"When I say jump—*jump*."

"No, Larkin!"

"Jump, Tess! Jump or die!"

Damn that Wixumlee! To stick me in a mess like this!

The runaway mama, clutching both babies, rocks on the muddy river bank as if in mourning. I hate the sight of her and her screaming brats. There they are, safe on shore, while Larkin and I wriggle like worms on hooks.

"Tess! Listen! On the count of three."

I wrap the vines once more around my fists. Pull to test them, tighten them. I can barely hear Larkin above the thundering waterfall.

"Ready. One—two—*three*!"

Larkin releases his feet and shoots through the air like a cannon ball, landing with a crash somewhere behind the mama. I kick the canoe free, but hang waist-deep in whirling water, the current tugging possessively at my thick buckskin breeches. The tightly wrapped vines bite into my hands, cutting off circulation. If they break, I'll slide screaming over the falls.

"Here, girl!" The mama stretches on her belly down the muddy river bank and holds out her small, brown hand. I try to shake one hand free, but my weight holds me down, and I can't unwind my fingers from the vines. The mama lets herself slide a bit farther down the bank, grabs my shirt behind my head, and takes some weight off my hands.

"Get your feet up."

I pull myself a little higher out of the water and try to swing a leg up over the bank. Try to jam the heel of my brogan into the greasy mud, but my foot keeps slipping. I yell as I fall back into the water, dragging the mama with me.

My hands sizzle like they've been plunged into hot oil. I'm so tangled in the vines, I can't let go if I want to. I'm on the brink of passing out from fear and pain, when Larkin grabs my buckskin shirt and hauls me up even with the top of the bank. He pulls my legs up and turns me around. I'm out of the water, but hanging upside down, handcuffed to the grape vines. Then his sharp knife cuts through my bonds, and blood boils through my hands and fingers. Out of the water, the three of us lay gasping in the near light, shivering under a layer of mud and cold sweat.

The babes sleep on.

CHAPTER TWENTY-FIVE

We stand on shore near the top of the waterfall. The drop into the swirling pool below looks about a hundred feet. And it isn't the only waterfall tumbling through this stupid town. Larkin says the Genesee drops twice more—right through the middle of Rochester—before dumping into a bay and spilling out into Lake Ontario. Dumb place to put a city.

"Now what?" I look wearily at Larkin, staring over the cliff at the remains of our smashed canoe. Wixumlee told us to meet up with abolitionists in Rochester's Third Ward on the river's west bank. Larkin calls the area Corn Hill but won't tell me why. We're now on the east bank with the river and a waterfall between us and safety. Or as much safety as I've come to expect with the Underground Railroad.

"Somebody's gonna find that canoe." I wipe bloody hands on my buckskin pants.

Larkin shrugs. "Doesn't point to us. Could be anybody's canoe."

He says he knew about the waterfall but got rattled by the log attack and overshot our landing spot on the west bank, where a Railroad conductor was waiting to take us to a safe house.

"There's always another plan," he says.

"Does another plan include crossing this river?" I wipe mud from my eyes and strain to see across the wide waterway.

Larkin stands grinning, hands on hips. Is he enjoying this? The mama holds her smaller baby and I'm stuck with the bigger one. I'm pretty sure the kid's pooped his pants. I'm guessing he's about two years old, dead weight, and the thought crosses my mind—briefly—to ease everyone's burden and toss the stinking bundle over the falls.

"Maybe we should just find some place to hole up," I suggest when Larkin doesn't answer me. "The people we're supposed to meet—they'll look for us, right? Let's walk south, hide in the woods and wait. They'll find us. Maybe they'll bring a boat and ferry us across the river."

Larkin stares silently at the speeding water, and I wonder uneasily if there really is a second plan or if he'll just make one up on the spot.

"We'll wade across."

Dang! I knew it!

"Across the river! It's freezing cold water!" I'm shivering and so's the mama.

"Have to cross it. Can't wait."

"You're crazy!" Made bold by my recent triumph over death—and the fact I'm holding a baby—I stare Larkin down.

"There's no way around the falls except across the water." Larkin looks from me to the mama. "And it's almost daylight. Rochester is crawling with bounty hunters." He takes the bottle of sleep from his pocket. Fills the dropper.

"There has to be someplace to hide. You've brought runaways this way before, haven't you? Where'd you hide them?"

Larkin ignores me. Leans over the small baby and squirts brown liquid into its mouth. "I'm just giving them a little bit more, ma'am. Just a little. I know they just had some." The mama nods.

"I'm not walking through that water. I just got out of that water." I turn the bigger baby so Larkin can give it a dose. "It's too damn deep!"

Larkin jams the stopper back into the bottle. "We'll walk back south a little where it's shallower. Slower." I know his concern is for the runaways. Not a lick of it for me.

"It's still dangerous! We'll get killed!

Larkin's eyes flash. "This whole trip's dangerous. This is just one more piece of danger and there'll be one or two more after that. What'd you expect?"

"I didn't expect to get tangled up in your damn Underground Railroad," I mumble, shifting Stink Butt from one shoulder to the other.

"You were sent by Wixumlee to do a job. And you'll do it." He takes the mama's arm and leads her into the trees, not looking to see if I follow.

The mama looks back at her bigger baby. For a moment, I don't move. I want to drop the kid and run. Instead, I follow Larkin, cursing the fact that I'm gonna die holding a kid who smells worse than dog shit.

We backtrack nearly a mile before Larkin finds a suitable place to cross. "Our people expect us to make our way somehow to the west side of the river. Somebody's prob'ly there right now watching for us."

I don't believe a word of it.

"Wait here." Larkin steps out of the trees and scans the riverbank, up and down, both sides, then waves us out. "I'll carry this little one and hang on to you, ma'am."

And I'm supposed to get across this river myself holding this kid?

"Water's moving fast. You said it'd be slower." I hate the quiver in my voice.

"Not too bad," he lies.

"Looks deep. You said it'd be shallower." A shiver streaking across my shoulders wobbles the baby's head.

"I've done this before. Crossed right here."

Liar!

"We'll go first."

The bank slopes easily, and Larkin walks into the water, the mama following. He holds the baby high on his shoulder and wraps strong fingers around the mama's wrist. The water rises quickly to his waist and up to her chest. Yeah, this is the shallow spot.

"Come on, Tess! Hang on to that baby."

I'm shaking so hard, the baby's head bounces on my shoulder. Larkin looks back and with a commanding jerk of his head, orders me into the water. I swallow hard, shift the kid up a notch and step into the rushing Genesee. The cold water clutches my buckskin pants and creeps icily up my legs.

I wade farther into the water, telling myself Larkin wouldn't make us undertake an impossible crossing. If the mama starts to float, Larkin will tow her. He must know the water is shallow enough for me to walk through to the other side. He doesn't want me to lose the kid.

The river is at my waist now, chilling my bones. I hoist the kid's butt up near my face and try not to gag. I don't want water splashing his head and waking up the little monster. I'm almost at midriver. Not too bad. Should be getting shallower soon. I see the mama, safe in Larkin's grasp, look back at her bigger babe.

Then something hits them from behind. Thick and long, the log rolls over the mama and Larkin and they disappear under the water.

I strain to keep my balance against the current. Are they coming up? I don't see them but watch the hateful log twist away toward the waterfall.

Bam! Something slams into my lower back. My back snaps like a whip and the baby pops out of my arms.

I'm underwater. The hard, rough log rolls across my back. Bangs the back of my head. I'm on my hands and knees on the bottom of the river and can't stand up. What's wrong with me? I struggle to stand, but have no strength in my arms and legs.

Stop fighting and float, I tell myself. I break the surface and suck in great gulps of cold air. Fight for footing against the current. It feels like someone's holding a hot knife against the back of my neck. Pain ricochets up and down my spine and my back feels raw where the log pounded and scraped.

The baby! I paw the water. Scan the river's surface. Sweet Jesus! I've lost him!

I stumble with the current, dimly wondering if the baby is underwater or floating toward the drop. I take a breath. Squat beneath the surface and feel around the mucky river bottom. Coming up for air, I remember the baby exploding from my arms like the first burst of water from a pump. And know that baby isn't anywhere near me.

The water churns. I thrash frantically, expecting another log attack. Instead, Larkin thrusts a muddy bundle into my arms and without a word strikes out with strong strokes toward the falls.

With a crazed mix of awe and fright, I look at the soggy mass. It's the smaller baby. Not my baby. I scan the river desperately, fight the current's tug, and stare in numb terror as Larkin swims toward the drop.

Someone grabs my waist. I twist and stare into a stranger's face. Slave catcher! I strike out with my fist.

"I'll help you!"

I punch again, straining to keep my grip on the baby as the man tries to rip it away. Another larger man appears at my side. He has the mama's arm in one hand and grabs my flailing fist with the other.

"Stop! We're your people. Let us help you." The men wrap strong arms around us and guide us toward the river's west bank. I crane my neck toward the falls.

"Larkin!"

"Somebody went after him."

"The baby!"

Neither men speak.

"The bigger baby!"

They pull me and the weeping mama up onto the riverbank, where women in heavy coats and wide-brimmed bonnets wrap us in wool blankets and pour hot coffee down our throats. Then they load us in wagons and cart us to safety in the place called Corn Hill.

Me. The mama. And the smaller baby.

CHAPTER TWENTY-SIX

Ignoring the piercing pain in my back and neck, I lurch out of my corner and rush past the weeping mama bent over the kitchen table. Past the young husband hunched across her back, both of them shaking with grief and disbelief. Past the wailing and the misery, out into the cold Rochester night.

I stumble through a maze of twisting alleys onto Main Street. Braced against a lamppost, panting, bawling, I wonder I can run at all. My head feels like it's been whacked with a club. Pain stabs mercilessly from my tailbone to the roots of my hair, but the pang in my heart is worse.

I've spent daybreak to twilight in the Corn Hill kitchen, hating the whispers and the looks. Waiting for Larkin. Praying Larkin will return. Knowing he will not.

Larkin is gone. Gone with the bigger baby over the falls.

That's what *our people* said. Our people own this Third Ward safe house. Our people found the baby, smashed on the rocks at the foot of the falls and brought its tiny broken body back to its mama. But our people didn't find Larkin. Our people figure he'll pop up somewhere sometime. Or maybe not. Sometimes the Genesee never spits up the bodies it swallows.

I press my face against the lamppost. How could so much go wrong? Logs attacked us like a charging army — twice. One ruthless warrior knocked that little babe right out of my arms. I had a good grip on him, I know I did. But I heard the murmuring. Even though our people said it wasn't my fault, I heard their true, mumbled feelings, marked by guarded looks into my corner of the Corn Hill kitchen.

"We've never lost a child," one woman whispered to another as they sipped tea at the table. They blame me for losing that baby, I know they do.

After pulling us from the river, rescuers hoisted me, the mama and one baby into a wagon and covered us with hay. Two men held the mama down and covered her mouth with their hands for the short ride to their safe house. One of the bonneted women took the living baby from my arms and squirted it once more with sleep from a new brown bottle.

The husband, the papa, was at the safe house when our sorrowful group came up from the river. He'd heard the original plan had failed, but he was in the kitchen smiling—never expecting the worst. His grin faded when he saw his shaking wife. It was all misery after that.

They held the mama down again to strip off her wet dress and wrap her in warm quilts to fight the cruel chill that gripped her body and her soul. Someone rocked the living baby, and I shrank into the corner to suffer through the rescuers' story. They'd seen the first log hit Larkin and the mama and saw them go underwater with the smaller baby. They saw the bigger babe pop out of my arms when a log hit me in the back.

"Wasn't her fault," one rescuer told the papa. "That log hit her—*wham!*—and your baby shot out like a bullet. Log rolled right over that gal and by the time she came up choking, your baby was floating way out of reach. She couldn't even see him."

That's what they told the papa, but I know they blame me.

"We've never lost a child," they repeat. "Never."

I wander the night city, wounded. Pain locks my neck and shoulders, and I can't turn my head an inch to either side. It feels like I've been blindsided by a buffalo. And I gag on the thought that Larkin's dead. Somebody went after him—that's what the rescuer said. But no one came back with him, or even his body. I can't accept it, but I know Larkin is gone.

I have no reason to return to the safe house. New conductors will take the papa, mama, grandfolk and one living baby to Black Rock. They don't need me. Don't want me. I'm bad luck. A coward. I failed on the Rochester road with Wixumlee's mama, and this time I lost a baby. Couldn't hang on to a tiny, sleeping, peaceful child.

My feet follow an insistent, crashing sound to the foot of a waterfall somewhere in the city. Is this the greedy beast that swallowed Larkin? Which of the three wet witches is this?

Large rocks scatter around the waterfall's base. Spray mists my face. Something dark and sad swells inside me. Larkin might be laying here, drowned and splintered.

My eyes search among the rocks. Please, Larkin, where are you? When our people tell Wixumlee the story, Larkin's loss will be my fault, too. His loss will shatter Wixumlee.

I turn from the falls and stop dead. There, sitting on a rock looking right at me is Nicky Pappo. He doesn't wear his usual snotty grin and for a moment I wonder if he really sees me. Then he slides off the rock and walks straight at me. Panic grips me. What will I tell him? Why am I in Rochester? Think!

"Tess." That's all he says, standing before me.

"What you doing here, Nicky?" My voice is too husky, too shaky.

"Nothin'. What you doing here?" His pale eyes blink slowly.

"Nothin'." I didn't tell Wixumlee I'd seen Pappo in Rochester when she sent me for the sorrel mare. Or that he knew I'd seen him. Now he'll want to know what I'm doing in this city—again. But I can't draw attention to Wixumlee and her schemes. Especially this one, branded by death.

"Hungry?"

'Huh?" I gaze at him through blurry eyes. He's acting strange. Too quiet for Nicky Pappo.

"Come on, I'll buy you supper."

We walk slowly away from the falls, me wincing with every step. I notice Nicky has a knit hat pulled down over his eyebrows, and now and then he glances over his shoulder.

"Somebody following you, Nicky?" Stiff with pain, I turn my whole body to look behind us, then yelp when Pappo jerks me back around and pulls me inside a tiny saloon to a table in the back.

"Somebody's following me, yeah. The sheriff."

The word terrifies me. If the mama's owner comes looking for his property or sends slave catchers, it's the sheriff's duty to help. Maybe slave catchers floated those logs out to stop us.

"Stop it, Tess."

"Huh?" I focus on Pappo's face. "Stop what?"

"You're shaking out of your skin. They're following me, not you. Settle down. I gotta sit here staring at your sweaty, green face, you're gonna spoil my supper." The snotty tone is back. Then he sighs. "Hey, you feel okay?"

"Yeah."

He reaches across the table to touch one fingertip to my hand. "You move like you're real sore."

I pull my hand back. "Headache, that's all." Why would he care how I feel? Should I believe him? Is the law really after him? Or after me?

Nicky orders potatoes and sausages for us, and I study him as he eats. Why did Nicky Pappo suddenly turn up on the rocks by the waterfall? I poke at my food, queasy with a sickening thought. Maybe Pappo is a slave catcher. A man hunter. Maybe that's why he disappears from Buffalo so often. Why he's so hateful to Wixumlee.

"Eat, kid! You look weak."

I lift a forkful of potatoes. The movement sends pain slicing through my upper body, but the sting doesn't dull my suspicion. What the heck is Pappo doing in Rochester? Maybe he followed me and Larkin to Avon. Sent those logs down the river to stop us. Pappo wouldn't care that we had two little babies with us. And he hates Larkin. It was an easy way to get rid of him.

"Drink your cider. Warm you up. When you going back to Buffalo?"

I take a sip. "I don't know. Soon, I guess."

Is he holding me for the sheriff? Maybe the constables found Larkin's body and think he's a runaway slave. Maybe Pappo told them we were smuggling slaves. New York is a free state, but when it comes to capturing runaways, bounty hunters have the law on their side.

"Don't you like your supper? An Irish gal like you turning up your nose at bangers and mashers?"

I study Nicky Pappo over the edge of my mug, convinced he's the enemy.

He makes me sleep on the floor in his dirty hotel room, where I can't escape him or my dreams. During the night, I'm underwater — searching — searching — searching. I grip a soggy, shapeless mass and bring it to the surface, but it's only a coonskin cap that bites my hand and I fling it across the river, all the way to the other side.

"Wake up, Tess!"

There's a pounding in my ears — water crashing on rock. I see a blanket-wrapped bundle float toward a glistening mist that meets the sky. I try swimming toward it, but my boots are nailed to a log on the river bottom and I sway like a reed, helpless against the current.

"Wake up!" Somebody shakes me and starts the pain raging. "You're okay, Tess."

Shivering and sobbing, I look up into Nicky Pappo's questioning, lashless eyes.

The next morning a constable stops Nicky on Fitzhugh Street and I escape. Running with my pain, I hobble down side streets and alleys in a desperate attempt to flee Pappo the slave catcher. When a freezing rain starts to fall, I realize my forehead is hot with fever. But I can't go back to Corn Hill. I can't return to Black Rock either. Soon the grieving mama will be telling Wixumlee her story, and Wixumlee will be cursing my name.

"We've never lost a child," she'll say, weeping in the kitchen with Mariana and Beany. "We've never lost Larkin."

CHAPTER TWENTY-SEVEN

I'm on my back. Icy chills slide up and down my shuddering body, but my head and neck burn as if from branding. I open my eyes to pitch darkness. Not a sound teases my ears. There's dirt beneath my fingertips, sweat on my face. The air is cold, damp and smells like puke.

Scenes from a long journey flit through my aching head.

Riding in a farm wagon.

Walking the towpath.

Sneaking onto a canal boat.

Sleeping with mules.

Are they new pictures or memories of my escape with Beany from Seneca Falls? My head is too foggy to sort them out. Only two things are certain. I'm deathly ill and I've had the river dream night and day.

I'm underwater, searching. I comb the river, digging my fingers into the mucky bottom. Then a small, soggy bundle floats toward the mist. And I lose the baby.

I close my eyes. Last night the dream was different. Ma and Pa were in the water with me. Pa thrashed the black water, called Ma's name, and swiped at me every time I came up for air. Ma dipped her face into the river, holding it just below the surface. Every time she raised it up, a pitiful cry escaped her lips. "My baby, my baby." When a small form floated out of reach, I saw it wasn't the little slave baby floating over the waterfall. It was my baby brother, born too violently, too soon.

I swipe dully at tears trickling into my ears. Why dream about my baby brother?

My knuckles bump a rocky wall and the damp odor becomes familiar. My eyes adjust to the narrowness of the space. I'm in the cave behind the vine-covered apple tree guarding the entrance to the cove. Somehow I traveled through bustling canal towns, snuck by Black Rock, stumbled past the sand-washed foofoo cottages—avoided Wixumlee's thugs—and made it to the outskirts of Buffalo. Despite fever, hunger and sickness, I found the cave.

"Tess."

I jolt upright, banging my head on the rocky ceiling, and scream, so cruelly does the pain shoot down my neck and shoulders.

"Cripes, lay down. You almost knocked your head off."

"Who? Who?" My voice quivers, my body tenses.

"It's me, Talbot." A gentle hand rests on my shoulder. "Don't be scared."

Talbot. His granny Wixumlee sent him to find me.

"Coop went back for a wagon."

"Cooper?" The screaming pain in my head sends vomit rising in my throat.

"How long you been here?" Talbot strikes a match and lights a small lantern. The sharp light jabs my eyes.

"Off!" I cover my face with one hand, my churning stomach with the other.

"I gotta take a look at you. Cripes, you stink." Talbot scans the lantern up and down my body. "Why'd you run off?"

"Huh?"

"Why'd you run from Corn Hill?"

Yes, the story got back to Wixumlee.

"Why didn't you come back with the rest?"

Because I lost Larkin. I close my eyes.

"Grandma has everybody out looking for you."

My throat fills with tears.

"She waited three days and you never showed. They've been looking for three more. Beany's worried sick. She told Grandma if you aren't back by Sunday, she's going out looking for you herself."

Beany. Beany wants me back. "What day—?"

"It's Saturday. Everybody's worried sick. Larkin's madder than a sweat bee."

"What?"

"Says he's gonna strangle you."

"Larkin?"

"Yeah."

"He's dead." I choke on the words.

"No he ain't—he's mad. Said you lit out. Didn't follow orders. You were supposed to come back here together. He searched under every rock in Rochester for days."

"He went over the falls!" The words are a pitiful croak.

"Uh, uh, not completely."

I try to push up on one elbow, but fall back, moaning. Grip my head with both hands. Fight my sick stomach. "How'd he not go over *completely*!" I ask when the wooziness passes.

"He got hung up on a tree. Part way down. Then some men came along and pulled him up. Threw him a rope or something."

"He's alive?" I rub my sore eyes gently. Larkin's alive?

"Yeah, and gonna go savage as a meat ax when you get back."

I sigh. "I'm not going back."

"Yeah, you are. Grandma said find you and we did. It was me thought of the cave."

I open one eye to see him grinning.

"Beany's a terror, worrying about you. Grandma's scared she'll stop eating."

Beany has the Railroad to keep her going. She doesn't need me. "I'm done with those people."

"What people?"

"*Our people. Your* people. Those Railroaders ain't mine. I don't belong."

"Yeah, you do. They couldn't have pulled this last one off without you!"

"Pulled it off? Didn't you hear, Talbot? I killed a baby!" I begin to shake violently.

"No."

"I let a baby drown. I let a baby fly out of my arms and shoot over a waterfall!" I roll up in a ball, the pain in my head so hot I expect my brain to melt. Would be happy if it did.

Talbot is silent for a moment. "They're not blaming you, Tessie."

I cover my face with my hands. "Well, I'm blaming me."

"Don't."

"Get out, Talbot!" Pain explodes through my upper body. "Keep Cooper out. I don't want to see him—or Beany—or anybody!" Vomit fills my mouth and I wretch violently, while Talbot looks the other way.

They take me back anyway. Cooper ignores my pleas, my curses, and hauls me out by my feet, saying he's sorry to treat me so roughly when I'm such a wreck, but figures I'm mean enough—and considering my tricks, dumb enough—to survive. They drive me to the Black Pole in a wagon, thwarting the early November wind with heavy blankets.

Plunked in a chair near the stove in the Buffalo kitchen, I stare up apprehensively, while Larkin, sporting a cavernous cut across his forehead and a violent bruise across half his face, bends down to glare into my eyes.

"I outa smash you good, girl."

But Mariana pushes him out of the way and out of the kitchen. She undresses me, eases me into a tub of warm water, and sluices the dirt and vomit off me with scented soap and soft cloths. Then, while the gypsy whirls about the kitchen mixing strong, smelly concoctions meant to break my fever and soothe my searing pain, Wixumlee and Beany dry me off like a baby, dress me in clean long johns, and fill me with hot soup.

Mariana has Larkin set a cot up near the stove and he checks on me every day. When he walks into the kitchen I cower, but he only stands beside the cot, fists on hips, and asks, "How you doin', Tess?" We never talk about the trial we suffered. Maybe, for Larkin, it's pure adventure. Maybe he enjoys teasing death.

Nobody mentions the dead baby. But I'll never forget him. The dream won't let me.

It comes every night and often in daydreams. With pictures, smells and sounds. The fishy river. The crash of water on rocks. The icy spray. Larkin's order—"Hang on to that baby!" The mama keening as mournfully as a seagull caught in a fishing snare.

I hold myself responsible for the baby's death. And now I'm sure Ma losing my little brother was my fault, too. Did I say something to get Pa mad? Why did Pa hit Ma and make her lose her baby? I know it was my fault.

CHAPTER TWENTY-EIGHT

One week after they bring me back to Wixumlee's lair, The General sits down beside me in the dining room. It's my first dinner outside the kitchen. Beany is on her second helping of pork chops but turns worried eyes on Wixumlee.

"Tess won't eat."

"I see that. What's wrong with you, girl? If Mariana doesn't stand over you with a spoon, you don't eat. You gotta gain back that weight you lost."

"I can see her ribs when she dresses," Beany says.

I take a small bite of fried potato, taste onions and gag. Onions always make me think of August.

"Oh, for the love of —." Wixumlee grabs a napkin and swipes away the potato spit. "You used to be a good eater. Now you pick worse than Beany."

"I don't pick no more." Beany washes down her pork with a swallow of milk and reaches for another slice of rye bread. "I'm building up my strength for the next rescue. You and me are going together, Tessie."

I cringe. No, Beany. I'm not going. I drop a bite of meat into my mouth, hoping to get Wixumlee off my back.

"That's better. Keep it up. I need you strong, Tess. You're a bigboned gal. Now put some meat on those bones."

As soon as Wixumlee leaves, I drop my fork on the table and my head in my hands. A minute later I push back my chair.

"What's the matter, Tessie?" Beany's knife hovers over the butter bowl.

"Gotta get out of here."

"Where you going?"

"For a walk."

"You better ask Wixumlee."

I look into Beany's dark chocolate eyes. When Beany is older, she and Larkin will get married and have beautiful children.

"Paint some pictures tonight, Beany. Happy ones."

Today, Wixumlee bought Beany oil paints, canvas already stretched onto frames and a set of expensive brushes.

"Sure. I'll draw you, me and Lucy at *The Lily*." Her words trail off as I slink out of the dining room.

Lucy is one of the runaway mama's contacts in Ohio. It's Lucy's job to find food, clothes and shelter for a family of six. Now a family of five. She's prepared for two babies, but only one will show up. I pull on my warm coat and go outside.

"Where you going?" Larkin drawls. He and Quin, bundled against the wind, sit outside the Black Pole sharing a bucket of beer. Wixumlee allows it once in a while, and I've never seen either of them drunk.

"For a walk." I shove my hands in my pockets, afraid to move 'til he gives me permission.

Larkin pulls his long body off the chair. "Let's go."

"Uh, I — want to —." Then I realize this is when he's gonna make me pay for losing the baby and running off like a fraidy-cat. Well, maybe he'll sock my nose back in place. That would be one good thing to come of it.

"I'm not getting good reports on you, Tess."

I swallow the lump in my throat.

"Everybody tells me you're getting lazy."

I peek at his face. He doesn't look mad. But in his business, you don't have to be mad to smash somebody. And Larkin has plenty of reason to be mad at me.

I made the babies scream by not finding the bottle of sleep fast enough. I let my paddle slip off the log that punched the hole in the bottom of our canoe. I didn't obey him when he said, "Hang on to that baby!" And then I couldn't even find that baby under the water. And how hard was that? Just reach down and pull it up, that's all I had to do. But I didn't. I watched Larkin swim straight at the falls, swimming after the baby I was to weak to hang on to.

By some miracle Larkin didn't tumble completely off that waterfall, and now he's alive and ready to give me the beating I deserve.

Larkin sits down on a short stone wall that keeps Canal Street scum away from a pretty little garden, so out of place in this dirty, noisy harbor. Most of the flowers were killed by the autumn frost,

but the stalks of a few bushy plants—August called them mums—
sprawl busily across the garden paths.

"Sit down."

I sit. Pull my bottom lip between my teeth.

"Now why are you being such a ninny?"

I look at him again out of the corner of my eye. At the black
curls grazing his sliced forehead.

"Yeah, I'm talking to you, Tess Riley. What's this I hear from
Beany that you're not going on any more missions?"

I look away from him, across the water.

"Talk to me, dammit!"

'I—what—."

"I—what! What the hell's wrong with you?"

Confused and scared to death of him, all I can manage is a limp
shrug. He wants me along on a mission? Why would he ever want
to partner with me again?

"Dammit, look. Every rescue has problems. Some are little and
things work out just about how we planned anyway. Some are big—
like the ones we had last time." He pauses. I hold my breath.

"Now, you think that baby dying over the falls was your fault,
don't you?"

My chin hits my chest.

"Pick up your head! Don't you dare hide! Answer me! You
think it was your fault, don't you?"

I nod once.

"Well, it wasn't. It was a tragedy. And I feel awful about it. Sad
for the mama and the baby's pa. But it wasn't anybody's fault, and
above all it wasn't your fault."

I stare at the ground. How did Larkin get so mixed up, so confused?

"It was just a rescue where everything went wrong!" Larkin
jumps up and stands in front of me. I close my eyes. "No! No, everything *did not* go wrong."

He leans over and put his hands on my shoulders. "Look at me,
Tess!" He pulls me to my feet. "I said look at me."

My eyelids feel heavy as curtains, but I blink them open.

"We rescued two people. A mama and her baby. We united
them with their family."

When Larkin puts his arms around me, I flinch. He squeezes me
gently. "It wasn't perfect, Tess, but it was damn good." He pushes
me away, grips my shoulders and speaks firmly once again.

"The only thing you did wrong was take off." He wags a finger in my face. "Don't you ever do that again!"

That night in bed I try to figure out what to make of Larkin. What he said on the Slip is crazy talk. Telling me I did a good job. Like an innocent baby getting sucked over a waterfall was just a hangnail and not a knife wound. I know different. A hug from Larkin doesn't make me a good girl.

CHAPTER TWENTY-NINE

"I'm through coddling you, Tess. It's nine o'clock. Get out of bed and get to work, or I'll get Larkin up here to get your tail moving." Wixumlee knows—everyone knows—I'm scared of Larkin and they use that threat liberally. "You've got ten minutes." The bedroom door slams.

Not that Wixumlee ever coddles me. Well, maybe she did for a few days after Talbot found me sick and stinking in the cave. Most of the time I've known the woman, she's been pushy, demanding, insulting, mean and angry.

And everyone else is the same. Larkin's gone back to giving me the evil eye and called me chicken when I refused to learn to shoot a rifle. He badgered and threatened me 'til I dropped the weapon and rolled into a ball on the beach at Sandy Town. Cussing mightily, he hauled me back to the Black Pole and told Wixumlee I was a sissy and not worth shucks. I stood like a condemned prisoner in the middle of the kitchen floor, while Wixumlee tapped her long, painted fingernails on the kitchen table and considered my fate.

"This is your hero, Beany? This is the gal you tell me can whip her weight in wildcats?"

Charcoal pencil posed above her sketchbook, dark eyes steady, Beany did not defend me.

It took every bit of gumption I had to defy Larkin, but I did it because I want no part of patrolling Sandy Town with a rifle or guarding the slave wagon bound for Buffalo's harbor. That's what they want me to do, I know it. Everyday they tie me tighter to the rails of the Underground Railroad.

This morning, with Wixumlee gone, Beany sits on her bed and watches me dress.

"Listen, Tessie. I got a plan."

I pull on a sweater and refuse to look at her.

"I already told Wixumlee about it. She thinks it'll work."

I tie my brogans.

"We're gonna go right down into the deep South and bring slaves north. Not wait for them to escape and get north on their own. *We'll* go down and *get* them. Just like Harriet."

I'm angry and scared at the same time. What good will it do to tell Beany she's dangerously mistaken, when Wixumlee already told her the plan is good?

"We?" is all I manage to squeak.

"Yeah. You and me."

I fiddle with my belt buckle and fight the churning in my stomach.

"Beany, you don't want to do that."

"Yes, I do! Wixumlee said it's a good plan that has some ideas they never tried before."

Egging her on, that's what that wild woman is doing. Egging Beany on. Another warrior for her army.

"Why do you hang on every word she says? She's nothin' like your mama."

"'Course she's nothin' like my mama!"

Alarmed by Beany's shout, I watch the bedroom door for Wixumlee or Mariana to come storming through.

"My mama was weak. That's why she died."

"Don't say that."

"And she taught me to be weak. That's why I couldn't save her."

"You couldn't fight those slave catchers!"

"Because she never taught me to fight! She taught me to never talk back. Never look anyone in the eye. She was stupid!"

"Shut up, Beany!"

"She should have kept going north and not stop in a dumb, nothin' town like Seneca Falls."

"Wixumlee's filling your head with bunkum!" Damn! Did the woman hear that?

"She should have gone straight to Canada. But she didn't and now she's dead! Gone! Wixumlee's my mama now!"

Sobbing, Beany throws herself on the bed, burying herself in blankets. When I walk downstairs to the kitchen, Mariana's withering glare sends me to the print shop without breakfast.

The press was idle for weeks while I moped and recovered from my injuries, so I spend most of the day scrubbing out dried, caked ink. Wixumlee, Mariana and Beany walk past the shop twice, but don't come in. Larkin doesn't bring me work, but that doesn't mean they've forgotten me. They're planning a big rescue two weeks from now and I'm told I'll be part of it. Even after the nasty scene with the rifle, they won't leave me alone. Keep tying me to the Underground rails and pulling the ropes tighter and tighter.

I have two weeks to escape. To go someplace this slave business can't touch. A place without a Wixumlee or a Larkin—or even a Beany. Beany doesn't need me. She's healthy, lively and caught up with plans—and with people—I hate.

A few days ago, I found a new batch of drawings scattered about the bedroom. Pictures of a young, wild-eyed girl, long curls flying, fighting bare-handed against angry, white men with whips and chains.

Beany's lost her marbles, but that's not surprising, living in this horrible house, this Underground Railroad depot, with its mad leader and violent army. How can they expect me—confused, lonely and weak as an old woman—to be a part of that?

Maybe Coop will help me run away. I rarely see Cooper and know Wixumlee purposely keeps us apart. With Coop around I'd be stronger, but he's down in Sandy Town helping with the salvage operation, keeping the foofoos in line, repairing the shacks. He's pals now with Larkin and Quin. On the one night a week we eat supper together he ignores my complaints about being forced to work on the Underground Railroad.

"It's a good cause, Tess. I'm helping, too."

"You are?"

"Yeah. When the wagon load of drunks comes back to Sandy Town, I put the guys to bed and watch they don't beat up their women. Wixumlee knows I won't tolerate that. And twice," he whispers, "I helped Quin drive the runaways to the Buffalo harbor and put them on ships bound for Canada."

"You did?"

"Yeah! And I feel real good about it. Like I'm doing something important. Something to make up for not saving August."

I fiddle with my supper. "Coop, you still hanging around with Nicky Pappo?"

"See him now and then." Coop nods to Larkin, who drops into a chair at our table and unbuttons his coat.

"We got work tonight, Coop. An emergency." Larkin looks at me. "Take off, sis. I gotta talk to your brother."

Relieved, I disappear. An emergency means slaves are coming in unexpectedly. That means a plan must be hurried into place. Hurry means lots of room for mistakes. I don't want to be around when mistakes happen.

Outside I suck in cold air and count the hours 'til bedtime. I hate going to bed, knowing I'll be shaken awake by that merciless dream. I have the one about my baby brother now almost as often as I have the brown baby one. Both come in daydreams and night-mares. With all that searching, I should have found the kid under the murky Genesee by now, or swum out to snatch it from the falls. But no, each dream has me nailed to the river bottom, unable to move. The dream shouts what everybody else denies — Tess Riley is a coward.

"Hey, girly girl. When you gonna grow some hair?" Nicky Pappo strolls toward the tavern smoking a cigar.

"Scram, Nicky. Larkin's inside."

"Ooohhh — Larkin. I'm *scared*."

"You should be."

"I can't even cross the street because this is *Larkin's* side of the street."

"Shut pan. Why do you have to hang around? Just itching for trouble."

Pappo snorts. I look closer and see that Nicky has grown some fuzz on his baldy head. "They still open in there?"

"No. Place is closed. Get lost."

"I need food. And I need to talk to Cooper."

"Go someplace else!"

But Pappo doesn't go someplace else. He flings open the Black Pole's front door and struts in, coming face to face with Larkin at the table near the window.

Shouts!

A scuffle!

The tavern door opens with a bang and Larkin heaves Nicky outside then hangs on the doorframe laughing. "I told you to keep your scrawny carcass out of here. Go eat down with the pigs behind the slaughterhouse."

On his butt in the mud, Pappo spits out a wad of dirt. Glares at Larkin. I've seen that same glint in Larkin's eyes many times.

"You let him in here, Tess?"

Alarmed, I shake my head.

"Get in here, girl." I duck under Larkin's arm and leave Pappo in the street, wiggling a tooth.

That guy is so dang dumb! Why did he show up here today and rile Larkin? Seems he shows up whenever Wixumlee's planning—or in the middle of—an Underground operation.

Like tonight. Larkin comes in and whispers about an emergency—*wham!*—Nicky Pappo shows up at the Black Pole. Me and Larkin ride three runaway slaves up the Genesee, get tangled in a life and death struggle with the river—*bam!*—Nicky Pappo shows up the next morning at the bottom of the waterfall.

Did Pappo hire those soaplocked highwaymen to stop Lucy and me on the Rochester road, so he could snatch Wixumlee's mama?

Pappo's a white southerner with a nasty disposition and a meaner tongue. Slave catchers make good money. Maybe it's worth hanging around Cooper and the Black Pole and getting socked in the jaw if he can dig up information about runaway slaves.

I wonder if Larkin—if anyone—suspects Pappo's treachery, or do they just consider him a pest. Pests are worse. They look harmless, but they're deadly. I'm getting more worried about Pappo, but scared of what Larkin will do if I push my suspicions.

Larkin sends me to the kitchen to help Mariana pack a basket of food. Please, Lord, don't let him make me take it someplace.

Mariana drops sausages, chicken, bread, cheese and bottles of cider in the basket, covers it with an oilcloth and ties it up with string. "Larkin says take this to Sandy Town."

"No!"

"Hush, girl!"

"I can't go down there!"

"Do what you're told."

"Let Talbot take it."

"He's with his mama. She's not feeling well."

"It's dark."

Mariana jams her fists onto her hips. "You gonna defy Larkin?"

I stare at the basket.

"You know he's just looking for an excuse to swat you after all that nonsense about learning to shoot that gun."

I reach out and grip the basket handle.

"There's a smart girl. Now take it to the blue cottage."

"How can I tell a color in the dark?"

"It's the fourth house. Quin will be inside. Just give it to him and come right back home."

Home. That's a laugh. The Black Pole—home? I don't have a home. I don't have a family. Even Cooper abandoned me.

It's cold outside and a light snow falls. At least I'm wearing warm clothes. Wixumlee spares no cost in outfitting her gang. I have more pants and flannel shirts now than ever. New ones, not the church basement kind. And sturdy brogans without cracks or flapping soles. A crate of winter coats was delivered the other day and I took a red and black plaid jacket with a thick, fur collar. And gloves. I never owned a pair of gloves before. And a black knit hat that covers my ears.

I eat three meals a day and wander into the kitchen anytime for bread and butter, warm muffins or apple pie. I sleep in a clean bed and can throw on an extra blanket whenever I want. Just reach in the trunk and pull one out.

But I'm not happy. Have never been so miserable. The people who feed, clothe and shelter me don't love me. Or even like me.

Ma yelled at me and pushed brooms and mops into my hands, but she put her arms around me and kissed me even when I was big. I usually shrugged her off with a, "Quit it, Ma," but, secretly, deep inside, I liked it.

Wixumlee's only touch is a slap. Mariana, too. Since I've gotten healthy again, both women keep me in line by pushing, smacking or threatening to have Larkin do worse. Wixumlee only keeps me around 'cause Beany wants me—or wanted me. After our fight over August, I'm afraid my days are numbered.

I come to the end of Commercial Slip and head down the rutted road toward Sandy Town. Mariana's parting words were "don't dawdle." The runaways need this food before they board a boat. Boats leave on schedule. Those escaped slaves won't get another good meal 'til they hit the lake's north shore—Canada. They need this food I'm carrying right now.

All I have to do is give it to Quin in the blue house—the fourth house—turn around and walk *home*. That's easy.

But it isn't. The dozen cottages are tossed across the sandy beach like seashells spilled by the tide. I search among the scattered shanties and can't figure which one is Quin's. Which shack is *fourth*. Fourth from what? The road? Fourth from the water?

As for color, in the inky November night all the sand-washed shacks look the same washed-out grey.

I switch the heavy basket to my other hand. The beach is deserted. Lights burn inside all the huts, but not a soul stirs outside. Should I knock? If some foofoo answers, then what? I remember the black-mustached man slipping the knife from his shirtsleeve and waving it at Quin.

Lordy, I hate being out here alone, cold and confused. Anxious.

I count the houses again. That one could be the fourth house. Or that one could be the fourth. Neither one was blue.

Dang it, Mariana! I should have received perfect instructions. My heart skips inside my chest and the wind turns the sweat on my forehead icy. Calm down, Tess. Think.

I take a deep breath. Just count four houses. But in the moonlight the house that turns up number four is a pale yellow. I step off the road and walk a little closer. Well, the number three house looks sort of blue. Mariana said "blue house — the fourth one." Should I go with *blue* or *fourth*? Damn you, Mariana!

Runaways are waiting. The ship is leaving. Mariana said "blue" before she said "fourth." So the first instruction is pro'bly right. I take another deep breath, flick snowflakes from my lashes and walk toward the dusty blue shack. Knock on the door. Please let it be Quin. Please let it be Quin.

No. The man who opens the cottage door is a stranger and behind him Nicky Pappo sits at a table playing cards. When Pappo sees me, anger spreads across his face like a flame through oil. His lashless eyes hold me while I hold my breath.

Slave catchers! In Sandy Town! In the middle of Wixumlee's lair! The stranger stares at my basket then back at Pappo. Nicky clenches his fist as if to say, "Get her," but I fling the basket of food at the man and yank the door shut.

I race across the sand toward the road. There's yelling behind me and running. I hear Pappo's angry cries and think I hear Quin. Glancing back over my shoulder, I see Quin standing at the door to the fourth house, not the blue house! Heavy steps follow me, but I hear Pappo's voice call them back.

I gallop faster, slipping on snow-covered stones, gulping in cold lake air, wishing now I'd eaten better the last two weeks and had more energy. Panting, tearing down the road, I dash along Commercial Slip and lose myself in the alleys beside the canal.

Quin was in the fourth house, right next to Pappo and didn't know it. Didn't know that weasel was right there, following Quin's every move. And where were Coop and Larkin?

I'm pretty sure — in my quick scope of the cottage room — that I saw a third bounty hunter tucked into a corner. Three slave catchers and three saviors. If there's a fight, who'll take care of the slaves? Who'll guide them to the ship? Were they counting on me to fight if there was trouble?

Gasping for breath, I slide to the ground behind a narrow building, pull my knees up to my chin and sob. They should know better than that. They should know better than to count on Tess Riley.

CHAPTER THIRTY

Everyone in the room hates me. Even Beany. Maybe even Cooper. I sit on a chair in the middle of the kitchen, head down, arms hugging my chest, tears pouring down my chapped cheeks. My broken nose—stuffed and running—makes ugly honks when I sniff.

They surround me in an angry circle. Wixumlee. Mariana. Beany. Quin. Larkin. Cooper. The three men—exhausted, shirtless—dab at their cut eyes and scraped chests with warm, wet rags. Mariana nurses a knife wound on Quin's left shoulder.

Larkin found me after midnight, frozen in the alley, snow drifting around my legs. I didn't protest when he threw me over his shoulder, carried me to the Black Pole and dumped me in the chair. Now they all surround me, demanding answers.

"It wasn't my fault." I cringe at the sound of my pathetic whine. "I didn't know which house." Sobs shake my shoulders. "Mariana said—."

"Don't blame Mariana, you worthless lump. You can't do anything right." Wixumlee hurls words like sharp stones.

Mariana jerks her head around from stitching Quin. "You almost got your own brother killed!"

I look sheepishly at Cooper. Blood drips from his smashed nose onto his split lip. He looks hurt and confused.

"I didn't know which house! She said the blue house—the fourth one. It didn't work out!"

"Shut up!" Larkin steps toward me, and I cover my head with my arms, crouch to protect my middle.

"Don't touch her!" Cooper takes two steps and stands nose to nose with Larkin. Their fists clench and unclench.

"Now you boys back off. You've given enough and gotten enough beating tonight. I'm not gonna have you fight each other." Wixumlee puts a hand on each man's arm and sends them to opposite sides of the kitchen.

"The only one who didn't get a beating tonight is this one."

She pokes my bowed head with a sharp fingernail.

"Beany! I can't believe this is the same gal you told me fought like a wildcat on the towpath." Instead of the sadness I used to see in Beany's face, I see disgust.

"I didn't spoil your plan. It was Nicky Pappo! He's a slave catcher!"

Wixumlee waves her hand, dismissing me and my accusation. "Pappo! That little weasel."

"I saw him twice in Rochester. Right in the middle of rescues."

Wixumlee and Larkin snap to attention.

"I did. Maybe now you'll listen."

"Stop that smart mouth and tell me exactly when you saw him." Wixumlee folds her arms across her chest.

I sit up a little straighter. "First near the ticket booth when I picked up Lucy. I think he fixed it with those soaplocks to rob us on the Rochester road so he could snatch your mama!"

Wixumlee's eyes narrow. "And what other time?"

"At the bottom of a waterfall. After the baby—." A knife twists in my stomach. "He was sitting on a rock, watching me. Made me go with him, but I got away."

No one says a word. The kitchen is as silent as a morgue.

"He sent those logs down on Larkin and me, I know he did! To swamp the canoe. To kill those runaways."

"Why would he want to kill runaways?" Larkin leans over my chair. "If he's a man hunter like you say, he'd want to capture them, so he'd get the reward. Pappo's a little mouse with a big squeak. And you're a tiny mouse with no squeak at all."

From the corner of my eye I see Coop shift from foot to foot. "Leave her alone, Larkin. She feels bad enough." The big men lock eyes.

Wixumlee shakes her head. "You see what you're doing here, girl? You're turning these friends against each other. Boys, I already told you. I won't have you fighting."

She turns back to me. "Now, Tess, let's go over what happened tonight, just so you understand the consequences of your actions. Look at me, girl."

I blink at her with swollen, watery eyes.

"First you took the basket of food — the only food six escaped slaves would have gotten in more than twenty-four hours — to the wrong house. No, no, don't give me lip about *blue* and *fourth*. You should have figured it out."

I stare at the floor, already convicted.

"Second, you saw some Canal Street lowlife playing cards inside that house, so you threw the food at him."

"Not at Nicky. At the guy by the door. And there was a third guy in the corner."

Wixumlee's eyes narrow. "When you threw the food and slammed the door —."

"I slammed it to give myself a chance to run!"

"Larkin, take this girl outside and beat her."

Larkin moves. So does Cooper.

"Stop!" Wixumlee holds up her hands. Chuckles nastily. "Back to your corners, boys. I didn't mean that. I just want this foolish girl to stop interrupting me!" Her hot yellow eyes burn holes in my head. "You gonna shut pan now?"

Heart slamming, I slide wild eyes from Larkin to Wixumlee and nod.

"Good. So, you threw the food, slammed the door, and do you know what happened next?"

I shake my head slowly, but have a good idea.

"Well, there was one hell of a fight. And you know what else?"

I shake my head again.

"Nicky Pappo wasn't in it!"

"I saw him! Heard him yell!"

"No, girly, you saw slave catchers, three of them, but Nicky Pappo was not one of them."

I look desperately at Wixumlee. At Larkin. At Cooper. My brother returns a small, weak smile and shakes his head. No Pappo.

"Those slave catchers burst from that shack like a blast of dynamite and started ripping doors off cottages," Wixumlee says.

I watch Coop press a wet cloth over a deep cut near his bruised right eye.

"There were six bounty hunters all together," he mumbles. "The ones you saw and more in another cottage closer to the water. They had guns on the foosfoos living there to keep them quiet."

"Until you busted things up." Larkin balls his fist, studies his raw knuckles and punches the fist into his other hand anyway.

"They started going house to house, throwing the foofoos out of their beds, searching for runaways. They knew you were bringing that basket of food to runaway slaves. They busted into Quin's cottage. Quin had two women and a little girl in there. He had to fight three slave catchers himself…"

I peek at Quin, gingerly touching his shoulder where Mariana had cross-stitched an ugly design.

"…'til me and Cooper got there. 'Course, that meant we had to leave *our* runaways—two little boys, an old man and an old woman—practically unprotected." Larkin folds his arms across his broad, bare chest. "That left the papa alone to save his family."

"So now it was six man hunters against our four." Wixumlee paces the floor. "Slightly better odds, but my boys still got knocked into a cocked hat. All because you blew their cover."

"I—."

"Quiet!" Wixumlee raises her hand threateningly. "You know who saved the day?"

I shake my downcast head.

"The foofoos! The ones roughed up by the slaver catchers recognized Larkin and Quin from the tavern and Cooper from patrolling Sandy Town. Saw they were in a battle for their lives and joined the fight. Figured our boys were protecting their little shacks. That evened the odds to about fifteen to six." Wixumlee smiles wickedly. "And that's when we made short order of those slave catchers."

The kitchen falls silent.

"What happened to them?" Beany speaks for the first time.

"They're gone, baby doll. That's all. They're just gone." Wixumlee bends her face close to me. "But your Nicky Pappo wasn't one of them!"

The only good to come from the whole mess is that I'm sure they'll never send me on another mission. I've destroyed their confidence, their trust. My only fear is they might be done with me completely. May not keep me around at all.

For the next few days, whenever my eyes meet Beany's, she turns away. I'm doomed. Without Beany on my side, I'll be banished from the Black Pole, maybe even from Buffalo.

CHAPTER THIRTY-ONE

It's a week before Christmas in Black Rock and I still work for Wixumlee, even though, as I feared, Beany turns completely against me. She calls me useless and a coward and forces me out of the fancy upstairs bedroom onto a cot in a corner of the wash room off the kitchen. I still eat my meals at the tavern, but Beany never joins me. She eats with Larkin and Wixumlee at the large oak table in the dining room. Cooper's supposed to join them but some days he takes his meals in the kitchen with me, guilty, I guess.

I figure Coop had something to do with me not getting banished from the Black Pole. Wixumlee likes Cooper.

"He's smart and he can fight," she says.

That's all The General wants—at least from those who figure in her Underground Railroad schemes. Maybe she's rewarding Coop's heroic efforts at Sandy Town by letting me stay. Whatever the reason, I'm still setting type for the *GosSlip*, running errands for Mariana and keeping an eye on Savannah.

As I hoped, Wixumlee's untied me from the Railroad completely. I'm not ordered to do anything that involves the Underground. Not even fill a food basket, let alone drag it someplace.

In the weeks since my pathetic performance at Sandy Town, my life has become less complicated, less fearful. I still shrink at the sight of Larkin, but he ignores me. Hasn't noticed that my appearance has changed. I still wear blue denims, comfortable flannel shirts and bulky sweaters, but my hair is longer, nearly chin length all around. I keep it clean and my bangs cut. Mariana—to my surprise the only person besides Coop who pays me the least bit of attention—mixes up some sluice I pour over it to make it shine. I'm taking Mariana's advice to stand up straight and give up that clumsy two-part slouch that makes me look like I have springs for a belly.

I figure, if I keep clean, follow orders and mind my own business, I can continue my comfortable—if lonely—life at the Black Pole.

So, when Wixumlee flies into my wash room-bedroom early one morning, screaming that Beany's gone, I can't decide which I feel stronger—fear or anger. Not only has Beany—a girl with no experience living on her own—run off to Lord knows where, she's shined Wixumlee's evil eye on me once again. Waving a piece of crumpled paper, the wild woman demands to know where Beany is.

"I don't know." I stare up from my cot nervously. "Beany doesn't talk to me." I pull the blankets up to my chin.

"She just disappears? Think, girl! Where would she go?"

"I don't know!" Beany—wandering the countryside with slave catchers and bounty hunters roaming in packs!

"You think she went back to Seneca Falls? Or to see Harriet?"

I shrug. She's going to blame me for this. Always me!

"Answer me, fool!" The frantic woman whirls about the room waving her arms. "Answer me! Did she go east—back home?"

Mariana comes from the kitchen and stands in the doorway.

"I don't know! Why ask me?" Anger sears my belly. I hate getting blamed for something not my fault. "Cripes—maybe she went south. You're the one who told her that snatching slaves off plantations is a good idea!"

Wixumlee falls on me like a panther on a lamb, striking me with both fists 'til Mariana pulls her off. To my horror I see I struck back, one blow at least. Wixumlee shows a spot of red above her lip, although I pray for my sake the raging woman nicked herself.

She lunges for me again and Mariana—shorter than Wixumlee, but sturdy as a fence post—spins her around and slaps her face. My mouth drops open. I've never seen anyone argue with Wixumlee, let alone strike her. I huddle on the bed near the wall.

"Tess don't know where Beany is," Mariana shouts into Wixumlee's face. "And it's not her fault Beany's gone."

Instantly, Wixumlee crumbles, buries her face in her hands and bawls. I lick blood off my lips and stare at the crazed woman.

Mariana sits on the cot and puts both arms around Wixumlee. "Get dressed, Tess, and find the boys. I'd send Talbot, but he's with his mama. Savannah started screaming the minute she heard Beany disappeared."

Yeah, Beany disappeared. And whose fault is that? Not mine!

"Go! Don't sit there feeling sorry for yourself. Wixumlee can't help being frantic over her Beany."

Her Beany. Shaking with both rage and fear, I pull on my clothes. I should have escaped this lunatic household long ago. Taken Beany with me.

"I'll make you some coffee, honey," Mariana coos into Wixumlee's hair. "Tess will bring the boys. We'll organize. Make a plan." She sounds like Cooper. Make a plan. I know plans sometimes work and sometimes don't.

Mariana has a full breakfast ready when the big men burst into the kitchen, shouting questions. Wixumlee sits stiffly at the table, one hand wrapped around a stout coffee cup, her other hand fingering the note she waved at me in the wash room.

"Quiet now. Sit down." Mariana nods at me and I take a chair at the table farthest from Wixumlee.

The General shifts in her chair and sighs. "Boys, Beany took off. We don't know where. But we've got to find her fast. It's dangerous out there for any colored girl, but especially for Beany. She's a babe, a lamb."

Mariana pushes a platter of sausages and ham at Quin. "Fill your plates, boys. We can't think on empty bellies."

Cooper scoops scrambled eggs onto his plate and passes the bowl to Larkin, who passes it untouched to Quin.

"Hey there, Larkin. You put some food on your plate," Wixumlee scolds. "I know you're worried, but you heard Mariana. You can't think — or act — on an empty stomach."

"Did she leave a note?" Larkin eyes the paper twisted in Wixumlee's fingers. Glances at the raw spot above his boss' lip.

Wixumlee picks up the paper, smoothes out the wrinkles with her long thumbs. She doesn't want to read it, I can tell.

"What's it say?" Quin pushes eggs onto his fork with a piece of toast.

Wixumlee covers the paper with her hand. Looks swiftly around the table, her eyes settling briefly on me. "Okay, I'll read it, but all it says is she's a silly girl." Wixumlee's voice catches on the last few words. She smoothes out the paper again. "It says, 'I'm going to find my mama.' Now isn't that silly?" Tears slip down Wixumlee's cheeks.

So, the witch lied. She knows where Beany went, or says she

went. To find her mama. To find August's grave? So she's gone back to Seneca Falls. It says so right in the note. So why was the crone wasting time terrorizing me?

My pleasure watching Wixumlee squirm disappears when Larkin leans forward and stares down the table at me. And that's when I decide I hate him, too. He's just like Wixumlee! Making it my fault. Like I told Beany to run off.

Well, it's not my fault. And that note makes no sense to me anyway, considering how Beany feels about August. Not long ago, I had to defend August against Beany's attack. Beany called her mama stupid. Said she hated her. Said Wixumlee was her mama now.

Maybe that's what Wixumlee's bawling about. If Beany's going back to Seneca Falls to find August's grave, she isn't thinking of Wixumlee as her mama anymore. *Boohoo*. The General's feelings are hurt.

Wixumlee wipes her tears away. "Everybody eat. Come on." Her voice cracks. "Somebody pass me the toast."

I pass the plate, and when our eyes meet I see real fear, real pain bounce back at me, but I don't feel a twinge of sympathy. Wixumlee's treated Beany like a toy. First Beany was her clean-up project. Once the girl fattened up and dropped the ribbons and silk, she became Wixumlee's warrior, a colored Joan of Arc.

Wixumlee encouraged Beany's fighting spirit and her mad rescue plans.

Yeah, honey, sure, you go down there and snatch those slaves away from those mean old white massas. Good idea, sweetie.

Beany is just another of Wixumlee's tools and I hate the woman for it. Wixumlee's responsible for Beany's doomed flight. No one else.

"You know Beany best, Tess. Where do you think she went?" Larkin's face creases with concern.

I stab my fork at a chunk of ham. You're wrong, Larkin. I don't know Beany at all.

"You think she went home, Tessie?" Cooper squeezes his coffee cup with both hands. "Looking for where August's buried?"

The image of August inside the cold ground shocks me. I can't help repeating, "buried?"

"Buried!" Wixumlee slaps the tabletop. "Buried! You don't think they left the woman to rot in the sun!" Mariana pats Wixumlee's arm. The General's crazy as a loon. Brokenhearted one minute, raging the next.

She scares me, but I feel my temper rise. "Last time Beany and I talked about her mama, Beany called August stupid for getting killed." The clink of silverware stops. "Why would she go back looking for her grave?"

Wixumlee doesn't say a word, but Larkin shifts in his seat. "I can't believe she didn't tell you something." His eyes are hard, dark disks, accusing me.

"I'm the last person she'd tell. Beany doesn't like me anymore." It's painful to admit. When I was a brash, thirteen-year-old, tousling with boys on the towpath, I didn't care if anyone liked me, least of all mousy brown Beaner. Now Beany's rejection is a knife in my gut.

Cleo walks into the kitchen and sits beside the stove.

"How's Savannah, Mama?" Wixumlee asks. "She fall back to sleep?"

"Yeah, Talbot lay down with her after I make her drink that cup of Mariana's brew. He want to come downstairs though. He worry sick about your Beany. But I say no, he stay with his mama."

Wixumlee shakes her head. "We can't figure where that child went." She caresses Beany's paper note. "She has no worldly experience. What would draw her someplace?"

"Maybe she go see that little white girl, help me get here." Cleo accepts a small plate of eggs and toast from Mariana.

"Lucy? How could Beany expect to get from New York to Ohio?" Wixumlee presses her coffee cup to her forehead as if the warmth might help her think. "She has no reason to visit Lucy, none at all. That can't be it. If she went anywhere it's back east where her mama's buried, or…" she glances at me, "…maybe south."

"What?" Larkin jerks in his seat, splashing coffee onto the table.

Wixumlee sighs. "South." She sits up straighter. "You know, Larkin. You hear her talking at supper. She has this idea of going down into the deep South and rescuing slaves."

"I never took her seriously."

"She even told Tess about it."

All eyes fall on me.

"And I told her it was a dumb idea. Dumb and dangerous." I want to add, *but Wixumlee called it grand*, but don't dare.

"Well, if that's what she's doing—heading south—it won't be hard to find her." Quin, who's been sitting quietly, catches everyone's attention. "She's only been gone a few hours. We're sitting here jawing when we should be contacting our people in Pennsylvania. She can't be more than a couple hours from Black Rock—nowhere near the border. We'll put out the word for our people to start looking. We'll have her back in no time."

"That's true. She can't be far, whatever direction she took. Let's tell our people and get out on the road." Larkin bounces his fists on the table. "We're wasting time!"

Quin stuffs breakfast rolls into his shirt pockets. Wixumlee fumbles with her napkin, oddly helpless, and Quin takes charge.

"I'll send the Sandy Town boys south," he says. "Then I'll check with the ship captains. See if anyone spotted a stowaway—just in case she got it in her head to go to Canada. Wixumlee, you send telegrams to the Underground. With a few hundred eyes watching, we'll find her fast."

I should help but fear sticks me to my seat. New York's crawling with slave catchers, brutal, ruthless men I've lost to in the past. I've broken a long, ugly streak of bad luck by easing out of the excitement. Hunting for Beany means jumping right back in. As much as I love Beany, fear for her, I fear the fight to find her even more. Quin and Larkin think finding Beany will be easy. I know it will be just the opposite. And the quest gets off to a horrible start.

"Tess, come with me."

I stare open-mouthed at Larkin.

"I'll go with Cooper."

Larkin gets up from the table. "You're coming with me."

Before I can protest, Savannah runs screaming into the kitchen, waving her crazy eye patch, mouth as round and dark as her gaping head hole.

"Talbot's gone! My baby went after Beany!"

CHAPTER THIRTY-TWO

Larkin saddles a buckskin gelding and a reddish mare for me. He snarls when I say I've never been on a horse, tosses me into the saddle, and we gallop east away from Black Rock. I wrap my long legs around the mare's belly and grasp the saddle horn like a rudder. The air's cold, the wind brisk, and snow's starting to fall.

Larkin's convinced Beany went back to Seneca Falls. He won't listen to my fear about getting arrested for Constable Parker's broken head. Says if I don't stop whining he'll yank me off my horse and beat me with a stick.

I shut pan and watch Larkin fearfully 'cause I hear panic in his voice. I never saw Larkin panicked before and hate seeing it now. Not even when we were hanging on to tree roots a hundred feet above a rock-jumbled waterfall had Larkin shown anything but a cool head. Now, I see fear in his wrinkled brow, threatening tone and the way he kicks his horse.

I think back to the uproar in the kitchen and to Quin left behind to organize the search, made more difficult and frightening now with Talbot gone. Quin had to almost sit on Wixumlee, who fell into a fit worse than Savannah's when she heard her grandson was missing. Mariana and Cleo had their hands full pouring the gypsy's calming brew down mother and daughter's throats and hanging on to them so Quin and Coop could get out the door and round up the rest of the gang.

I wish I could have stayed with Cooper, but here I am bouncing on the back of a horse, following half-crazed Larkin, my body already a mass of aches and bruises. He pushes the horses at a gallop, stopping only at taverns and general stores to ask if anyone has seen a young, slim, shiny haired, colored girl with skin like polished oak or a black-toned boy a bit younger. Nobody has, but Larkin promises a reward to anyone who telegraphs useful information to the Black Pole tavern in Black Rock.

It takes two days of hard riding to reach Avon, a town I never wanted to see again. My butt is blistered by the time we stop to spend the night with an Underground conductor who has no news of Beany passing through. Why didn't we see her on the road?

Larkin has me up before dawn and on a fresh horse. Sitting brings tears to my eyes. We make good time on the hard-packed road, but I pay the price. My pants are blood-streaked when I fall off my beast in a Canandaigua stableyard. The Underground station master there has not one word to share about anyone seeing a colored girl or colored boy traveling together or alone.

Where are they? Are they traveling only at night like August did after Beany's pa was killed? Like runaway slaves journey — away from the highways? Are they catching rides on farm wagons? Stealing horses? The way Larkin and I are galloping, we prob'ly passed them by. Will danger pass them by?

I wonder if this station master and his wife, who feed us a supper of carrots and potatoes, have heard about the accident at the Rochester falls last October. I wonder when they look at me, if they know I'm the one who let the baby float to its death. The man says he'll keep after Railroaders in neighboring towns to continue watching for Beany and Talbot. I watch their eyes when they say goodnight, looking for accusation, then follow Larkin, worn and weary, to the stable for bed.

We're back on fresh horses before dawn. Larkin barely speaks as we gallop along the pike, and I wonder why he forced me to come with him. Not for companionship, that's for sure. Maybe he values my contacts in Seneca Falls, although it would be easy enough to track down Ma at the boarding house or Lucy — if she's home for Christmas — on Washington Street.

I suffer another day and a half of hard riding through Geneva and Waterloo and am convinced I'll die in the saddle. Larkin finally reins in his horse at a tavern near the crossroad heading into Seneca Falls. My knees buckle when I slip off my mount, and I clutch the stirrup to stop from sliding to the ground. The panting mare turns her head to watch me shake the blood back into my feet.

Larkin pays a shabby boy to water and wipe down the horses, then buys sandwiches and mugs of hot cider inside the tavern. I ease painfully onto a bench and am so tired I can barely lift the meat and bread to my mouth.

We had several changes of horses, but these last beasts are exhausted, and I think it's cruel to make them gallop any longer. Cruel to them and me. My cheeks are cracked from the biting wind, my muscles sore. I wish we could rest in the warm tavern and continue to Seneca Falls in the morning, but Larkin swallows his sandwich, drains his drink and marches outside. I follow reluctantly.

"Man at the bar says he saw a colored girl hop off the back of a wagon this morning. Says she looked cold and hungry." He takes his reins from the water boy. "He told her to come inside, but she ran into the bushes. Could be Beany."

"Did he see Talbot?"

"No." Larkin jumps into the saddle and rushes his mount into a gallop. I lead my mare to a tree stump and climb up, wincing when I touch the hard, cold saddle. I keep the mare at a gentle lope. This is familiar territory. I know how to get to Seneca Falls, so why rush? I'm starting to tolerate the ride when Larkin races back, swats my mare's rump with his hat and sends her off at top speed.

Ma opens the door to the back porch and shrieks, "Thank you, Jesus!" I'm glad seeing a tall, broad-shouldered, colored man standing behind me doesn't concern her. She pulls us into the kitchen and throws her arms around me, squeezing so hard my eyes tear. "Oh, Lordy, Lordy. Thank you, thank you, Lord."

"Okay, Ma, okay."

Larkin stares like he can't believe somebody's hugging me.

"Ma, okay, already. Look—this is Larkin."

He nods. "Ma'am."

"Oh, you're frozen, poor boy. Come in. Are you hungry?"

Larkin shakes his head and tramps indoors.

"Where's Cooper? Is he with you?" Ma looks expectantly at Larkin, as if he might turn into her son at any second. "Where's your brother, Tess?"

"Uh, in Black Rock." I think. Who knows where Wixumlee sent him.

"Tess, your hair's longer. It looks nice." Ma pats down my slippery mane. Larkin glances at my hair as if surprised to see I have any at all.

"Ma, we're looking for Beany. Is she here?"

She rubs her forehead. "Well, I thought she was with you. I sent you that box of her things months ago.

"Yeah, we got it. But is Beany here now — in the house?"

"No. No, is she lost?"

"She took off, ma'am." Larkin rubs his hands together for warmth. "Almost a week ago. We think — I think — she headed back here to Seneca Falls."

"We thought maybe she wants to see where August's buried." August in the cold ground. Covered with dirt. I choke on the rock-hard lump in my throat.

"Oh, dear." Ma sits down heavily at the table. "Take off your coats. Here, Larkin, sit down." She pushes at a chair. The heat coming off the wood stove steams my wool coat and feels good on my frozen neck and shoulders.

"Oh, that poor child." Ma covers her face with her hands. "To lose her mother. So tragic. Poor, poor August."

"Maybe she went to Lucy's house." Larkin stretches his long legs toward the stove. "We can check there."

"Oh, you should know —." Ma shakes her head. "Oh, I can't bring myself to say it."

"What?" Larkin and I both ask.

Ma's eyes tear. "Slave catchers are in Seneca Falls."

A razor sharp chill rips through me, followed by a tightening in my throat. It feels like somebody is squeezing my neck with both hands. My heart pounds so hard I wobble in my chair. I can't take a breath. I open my mouth slightly as if to scream, but freeze, mouth gaping, eyes unblinking.

"Tess! Tess!" Ma shakes my shoulder. "She's not breathing!"

Larkin jumps up and slaps me between my shoulder blades. My head snaps and a loud noise — something between a cough and a gasp — bursts from my lungs. I wheeze, sucking in air with the strength of a furling sail. Sweat drips down my burning forehead onto my bent nose. I grip one icy hand with the other and bring them to my mouth.

"Tess, oh, my poor, poor girl." Ma wraps her arms around me. "Don't be afraid. They won't hurt you. I know you fought them on the towpath. Lucy told me."

"Where are they, ma'am?" Larkin's voice is urgent.

"Right in town." She looks hard at the tan-skinned man standing in her kitchen. "You're not safe here, Larkin."

Biting down on my fingers, face buried in Ma's shoulder, I watch a riot of violence flash behind my closed eyes. Huge horses, saliva ringing their mouths, drag a wagon almost into the canal. My knife glints in the morning light, slices Big Slaver's cheek, bounces off across the towpath. I'm back. In Seneca Falls. The murderous towpath just outside Ma's door.

"Don't worry about me, Miz Riley." Larkin reaches out and pulls my hands away from my mouth. "Tess!" He shakes my hands. "Come on now. You're okay!"

I see myself doubled up in the dirt, watching Big Slaver kick August in the stomach. Hear Beany call, "Mama's running!" See Beany kneeling over August's thin body. Her hand pressing down on the jagged red hole in August's chest. Hear Coop's captain say *she has a chance* but see the lie in his eyes.

Suddenly I'm crashing through the kitchen doorway, slipping across the icy backyard, heading straight for the canal, emptied now for the winter. At the edge of the ditch, I'm knocked to the ground. Turning in panic, I see One Eye leering down at me. I kick and try to crawl away, but he turns me over and slaps my face hard.

"Stop it, Tess! Wake up!" Larkin pulls me off the ground, grips me around my waist and hauls me back to the kitchen. Ma is on the back porch, wringing her hands, wailing.

"What's wrong with her? Oh, Lordy. What's wrong with my girl?"

Larkin sits me in a chair near the stove. "Do you have a blanket, ma'am?"

Ma rustles in the broom closet. "We should put her to bed."

"No. I'm sorry. I need Tess to help me find Beany. And a boy named Talbot. He ran off, too. With slave catchers in town, we have to work fast."

There's a bump at the door and Ma groans. I raise my head slightly and see Pa propped in the doorway. How much did he hear?

A stream of vomit shoots up from my stomach. The mere sight of the man directly responsible for August's death causes yellow bile to spew forth like lava from a volcano. Right away Larkin knows he's the man who murdered Beany's mama. He leaps like a panther, grips Pa by the throat, throws him to the floor, and bangs his head against the hardwood once, twice.

Ma throws a towel over the stink on the floor, picks a rag from the sink and wipes my face and mouth.

"He's not supposed to be here," she says coldly, barely glancing at Pa laying powerless beneath Larkin. "Mister Manning told him right after August—. Mister Manning threw him out. Said keep away from this house—and me." I hate the pain in Ma's voice.

She rinses the rag in the sink and wipes my sweater. "But he comes around when he knows Mister Manning's out of town. Asks for liquor money."

Larkin leans on Pa's shoulders. "Where are the slave catchers? Tell me now."

"I don't—."

Larkin reaches beneath his pant leg, pulls out a slim knife, and stands the point on Pa's chest. "I'll cut you like you cut August."

"I didn't!"

"You did!" Larkin pressed the point far enough into Pa's chest to make him squirm. "And you know exactly where those man-hunting scum are."

Pa gasps and his foul liquor smell nearly overpowers my rancid vomit. I keep my eyes on him. Watch his bleary gaze move from Larkin to Ma.

"Moira—help me. Help your husband."

I leap from the chair and fall down on the floor next to Larkin. "Kill him."

"Tessie. I'm your papa."

Larkin flicks the knife and a pencil-thin red line appears across Pa's neck. He dips his finger in the blood and holds it up for Pa to see. "Last chance."

Pa squirms. "At the hotel! They're at the hotel."

"How many?"

"Three."

"Who?"

"Plantation owner and two bounty hunters."

"They come for someone in particular?"

"A black wench named Molly. Run off from her owner visiting Rochester."

"Rochester?" Larkin looks doubtful. "That's a long way from here. Why would she come this way?"

Pa moans. "I don't know! How would I know?"

"You seem to know a lot. Too much."

"Don't tell them I told you," Pa whines. "They'll kill me."

Larkin's laugh is cruel. "Looks like you're a dead man all around." He lifts Pa to his feet and shoves him out the door. "Beat it." The drunk hurries off, not looking back.

I stare at Larkin in disbelief. "You let him go? You should have killed him!"

"He's your pa. I'm not gonna kill him."

"He'll hurt us." I bury my face in my hands. "He'll tell. He'll turn you in. You shouldn't let him go!" This is a big, big mistake.

Larkin squats on his heels beside me. "I got the information I want."

"You had a chance to get rid of him."

"I won't kill a man in cold blood." He stands and takes a mug of hot coffee from Ma.

I sit stone still on the floor. Larkin doesn't know Pa like I do. The man will be back. He always comes back and he always brings worse trouble. He's the devil. Lucifer. The demon drunk who sold out August for a bottle of booze.

And now he's seen Larkin—another trophy for the slave-catching scum. Larkin's skin is light and he's able to move about less noticed than a black boy like Talbot, but slave catchers suspect anyone with even a little color. A little bit of color is good enough for them. Good enough to throw a man in chains and haul him south. But if they stop Larkin, he'll fight. He won't care that the Fugitive Slave Law says he can't. And if Larkin fights, I'll be drawn into it.

We leave our horses in Ma's barn and walk up Fall Street to the hotel. I'm alarmed by every approaching footstep, but Larkin is bold. His long strides drive him up the street, past store windows decorated with tinsel, ribbons and snowflakes.

I tug on his coat sleeve. "Larkin, what if they catch you?" I can't say *slave catchers*. I can't picture Larkin a slave.

His pulls up his collar against the wind. "Nobody's catching me."

"There's three of them."

"I'm here to find Beany and Talbot, not get stolen."

I'm shivering hard from the wind. "What if they mistake Beany for this Molly."

He nods and sets his lips. "Good chance that'll happen. One colored girl's as good as the next to slave catchers."

I want to hang on to Larkin's arm, but dig my hands into my pockets instead. "No one's seen Talbot. And we don't really know if that girl jumping off the wagon outside town was Beany. It could have been this gal Molly."

"Yep, could have been." He brushes snow off the curls above his eyes. "First thing to do is check out those slave catchers at the hotel, then we'll go to Lucy's house."

"But—if they see you—and stop you."

"Nobody's gonna stop me. Slave catchers ain't gonna get me. We're going to find Beany and Talbot. You and me. Together." The ever-confident Larkin pushes open the hotel's heavy front door and waves me inside. I take a deep breath and cross the threshold into the warm, pine-scented lobby.

We're greeted by loud voices. Men arguing near the front desk. A high, shrill voice stabs into the quarrel. Me and Larkin slide behind a thick pillar, not hiding, but not flaunting our entrance.

"I know her. That's Miz Stanton," I whisper. "Are those the—?" I point at two scruffy men in filthy pants. Wide-brimmed hats hide half their faces. They shuffle their feet behind a third man, finely dressed in black suit and top hat. He's angry and jabs his finger into the chest of an older man standing beside Elizabeth Cady Stanton. She looks ready to sock the guy. Both men are red in the face and so worked up I see flakes of spit fly like ice chips from their lips.

"You are an abomination!" Miz Stanton's companion shouts.

Larkin studies the group. "Who's that?"

"I don't know the man, but Miz Stanton ran that women's convention in town a few years back and Frederick Douglass came. Her husband's an abolitionist but he didn't do squat for August when she got caught."

"Mind your own business, you meddlesome northerner!" Top Hat's drawl flips around the lobby like an angry eel.

"You have no right to flaunt your evil in this town!" Miz Stanton's companion shouts.

"The law's on my side!"

"Hunting people like they're animals! Chaining them! Beating them!"

I grab Larkin's arm. "They caught somebody!"

Larkin stares at the loud slave owner, soaking him in.

"What should we—?"

"Shhhhh." Larkin tilts his head, touches his ear. "Just listen."

"Release him," Miz Stanton insists. "He's just a boy."

My heart surges and I squeeze Larkin's arm. They caught Talbot.

"You say he's not *yours*—to use your ungodly word," Miz Stanton hisses. "So, even using your logic you have no reason—no right—to hold him."

"We ain't lettin' a nigger kid go, lady," one slave catcher says, scratching his stubble. "Prob'ly got separated from his mammy — maybe his whole family — while on the run. We're gonna catch ourselves a whole slew of niggers now, soon's we make him talk." I feel the muscles in Larkin's arm bulge and stiffen.

"You admit he's not the one you're *hunting*," Miz Stanton's companion says. "And you have no proof he's a runaway slave! The boy is most likely free."

"Ain't no such thing as a free nigger."

"And if there is, there shouldn't be," drawls the second slaver, a pot-bellied slob sporting a scraggly beard that lays on his chest like dried hay.

"Enough! I'm not debating my personal property with strangers." The slave owner twirls his top hat and sets it on his head at a jaunty angle. "I have a dinner engagement. Do not follow me into the dining room or I'll have you arrested. Merry Christmas."

He spins on his heel, leaving Miz Stanton and her companion fuming. The hired hunters slink toward the door. Larkin moves around the thick pilar as they approach, turning me with him.

"No, I haven't seen him or heard anyone talking about him or anyone else." Lucy Manning sits on the edge of her chair, hugging her sides.

I finger the roast beef sandwich in front of me. "They must have found him outside town and brought him in quietly."

"Not like last time." Lucy's voice trails off. Not like August.

Larkin swallows the last of his lunch. "Thanks. It was good."

We sit at the table in Lucy's kitchen, watched by the cook, who hovers uncertainly after laying out sandwiches and fruit. Lucy's parents and little brother are out of town visiting relatives and not expected back for two days. Lucy stayed home to catch up on her college reading. Her brother Jeremy is expected to arrive soon from Yale for the holidays.

"Someone has to visit the jail and find out exactly who's locked up." Larkin looks from me to Lucy. "And it can't be me."

Lucy and I exchange glances. The last time we paid a visit to the town lockup, there was a jailbreak. Constable Parker got his head cracked and now spends his days in a chair, drooling — or so Lucy says.

"Who's the new constable?" I pick at my sandwich crust.

"A man named Cline. He's not bad. Well, he's nothing like Parker." Lucy sips hot tea. "Tess, the man with Elizabeth Stanton you said was arguing with that slave owner — ."

"You know him?"

"From your description, I think he's her cousin, Gerrit Smith. I read in the paper he's coming to visit. He's an abolitionist."

I grimace, but Larkin snaps to attention. "Gerrit Smith? He's active up in Peterboro. Smith pro'bly got a telegram to watch for Beany and Talbot." Larkin leans across the table. "I bet Smith heard a black boy was brought to the jail and figured it was Talbot. And from the way he and Miz Stanton argued with the slave catchers at the hotel, it sounds like they've been to the jail and know what the boy looks like."

Elizabeth Cady Stanton passes slices of apple pie around the table. "He's about twelve or thirteen years old. Not too tall. A nice looking boy, but he has scars on his head and arms. Owner abuse, I suppose."

"Dog bites." Larkin cuts into his pie.

I stare at mine, ashamed to look up.

"It's Talbot all right," he says. "But Beany wasn't in the cell with him?"

"No one else. Only the boy." Gerrit Smith warms his hands near the stove. "They picked him up in Waterloo, walking along the canal. Roughed him up, trying to get him to give up the people he traveled with."

"He wasn't traveling with anybody." I poke at my pie. "But even if he was, Talbot would never talk." Snitches are punished most severely.

"How did we miss him on the Geneva road?" Larkin chews thoughtfully. "He played a hunch heading east. Or maybe Beany told him something before she took off. But we still don't know if Beany is anywhere near Seneca Falls. I could be all wrong. She could have gone in the opposite direction." The thought makes his shoulders sag.

"Since we know nothing about the girl Beany's whereabouts, we should concentrate on freeing your friend Talbot." Smith turns his back to the stove. "It's quite late and snowing heavily. I doubt they'll move him tonight. Let's get a good night's sleep."

He looks directly at Larkin. "I am active in the abolitionist cause, young man, and I am at your disposal."

Larkin studies the bearded white gentleman then nods. "I trust you."

CHAPTER THIRTY-THREE

"They're gone. Jail's empty. They took him." Lucy shouts the news from her front porch as we ride up after spending the night with Ma. She'd taken me and Larkin to see August's grave and my belly is sick with loss. Now this new agony.

Miz Stanton huddles in a wooly coat beside Lucy. "Gerrit stopped at the jail early this morning," she says. "Constable Cline said the slave catchers came for Talbot before dawn. They just pulled him out of the cell when Cline opened it, and he had to force them to give the boy his coat." Her voice cracks with held-back tears.

High up on his prancing horse, Larkin curses. "Which direction did they take?" The chill in his voice bodes disaster.

I remember that the slaver catchers who attacked Sandy Town disappeared without a trace. "They're gone. They're just gone," was how Wixumlee put it. I know the men who snatched Talbot will be gone, too, when Larkin finds them. He won't kill them coldly. He'll fight them first to get Talbot, but then he'll make them gone.

Lucy buttons a heavy sweater across her chest. "Cline said the slave catchers rode west toward Geneva. Someone tipped them off about a colored girl camped on Seneca Lake and they went after her. The two slave catchers, the plantation owner and Talbot."

"Cousin Gerrit is telegraphing Railroad people all along the Geneva routes to watch for Beany and this girl Molly," Miz Stanton reports. "He also sent the message with riders to the more remote areas."

"So, we don't know if it's Beany or Molly camped on the lake." I wrap a green and red scarf, a Christmas gift from Ma, tighter around my neck. The temperature dropped last night, and the ground is covered with inches of new snow that the biting wind blows busily into drifts.

Larkin spins his horse around. "Doesn't matter who it is. Beany or Molly. We're going after them."

"Wait!" Lucy runs down the porch steps. Larkin reins in his straining steed. "What should we tell Mister Smith?"

"Tell him to stay here. We'll need a place to hide once we get Talbot and the girl—whichever girl it is." Larkin's horse paws the snow.

I had the dream again last night, asleep in my old loft. The speeding river, the banging logs, the thundering water, the silver mist, the floating baby, the wailing mama. And here I am riding straight into another fight.

"Tell him to watch the telegraph office. We'll send word soon as we have them. Let's go, Tess." Larkin kicks his horse and gallops down Washington Street. I turn my mare slowly, clutch my sick stomach, blink woefully at Lucy and Miz Stanton, and follow.

My face is ice-coated, fingers numb inside my gloves, but Larkin won't stop. We ride at a fast lope past Waterloo toward Geneva. When the horses slip on the feathery snow that collects on the hard-packed road, the unexpected jolts shoot extra shivers of alarm up my frozen back.

"Larkin, please—gonna fall off," I wail through the stiff folds of my Christmas scarf. We ride another couple miles in the screaming wind, before he pulls his horse up at a tavern on the eastern fringe of Geneva and dismounts.

"Quick stop. We're almost to the lake." He drops some coins into my stiff glove. "Get us something hot." He takes my reins and leads the horses into the shelter of a lean-to.

Inside the tavern I buy coffee and stare longingly at a cinnamon bun. Larkin stomps inside, shaking snow from his hair, and joins me at a small table. Several men glance our way and mumble among themselves. Larkin is almost done with his coffee when one limps over to our table.

"You a colored man?" he whispers.

Larkin sets his mug down, places a fist on either side of it, and glares steadily at his questioner.

The man sits on the edge of a chair, staring at Larkin like he can't decide whether to talk or not. Finally he whispers, "This town's got troublemakers."

"I'm looking for them."

The limpy man sighs with relief. "They were in here a half hour ago, draggin' a colored boy. The kid's froze solid. Looks like he's been walkin'."

Larkin's fists tap the tabletop steadily. "Those are the ones I want. Where'd they go?"

"Down to the lake. Said they're huntin'."

Larkin slides a coin across the table. "Thanks."

The man slides the coin back and draws a double RR with his finger on the tabletop. "We're all lookin'."

Larkin nudges my arm. "Get the horses." When I sit tight in my seat, he slaps my hand. "Go! I'll be right out."

Glancing over my shoulder as I head out the door, I see the limpy man whisper into Larkin's ear.

Larkin kicks at some coals laying in the middle of a ring of stones. I stand near the water, tears freezing the tightly wrapped scarf to my face.

"They got her, Tess. They got Beany."

"Ain't no proof it's Beany," I croak into the moist wool. "Could be that gal Molly."

"Then they got Molly!"

I turn my back to the lake. It looks frozen in the middle, but gray water sloshes near the shoreline.

"Look." I point a shaky finger at scuffle marks in the snow. Then to broken branches where someone ran through the dry bramble.

The snow around the small campfire is flattened in a wide swath. Shoe prints squeeze the snow into ice. A man's large boot prints head through the woods, away from the Geneva road. I don't even know this gal Molly, but I imagine her looking like Beany. I see Beany's large, chocolate candy eyes wide with fear, looking over her shoulder as she runs.

"Well, there's a chance one of Gerrit Smith's men found her. Has her hid somewhere." Larkin slaps one hand with the reins.

I collapse in the snow. "No. Slavers got her. Got her and Talbot both." I bend over and sob.

Larkin leans down and swats the side of my head. "Stop blubbering!" He grips my shoulders and jerks me upright, but I hang from his hands like a rag doll.

"Listen." He shakes me. "Pick your head up, dammit!" I can barely see through ice-clogged lashes. "We'll split up."

"No!" I grip his shoulders. "Don't leave me alone." I drop my head against his chest and cry, brokenhearted. Slave catchers caught Beany.

Larkin shrugs off my hands. "Listen to me. I'll follow these tracks into the woods. You go into town."

I shake my head. "No, Larkin, please." If he leaves me and I'm alone, someone will hurt me.

"Do you want to find Beany and Talbot?"

I hold my breath.

"And this gal Molly?"

The searing, cowardly part of me says no, let them go. They ran away, let them pay the price. And damn Beany! Damn her for doing this to me! Making me gallop my butt raw from Black Rock to Seneca Falls, maybe on a wild goose chase.

I stare into Larkin's rock hard face and wonder if he'd beat the snot out of Beany for running off. Ha! Not a chance. But I see in his eyes he's ready to slap courage into me right now.

Courage. Where is it? I straighten up a bit. What should I do? Save their lives? Stay a coward? The old Tess, the grasping, hidden Tess, the bruiser and the brawler says yes we must find them! We must rescue them!

When Larkin lays a hand on my shoulder, I flinch. "Go into town. Stop in the taverns, the shops. Have something to eat. Listen to the talk. Learn something!"

He shakes my shoulder, but not roughly. "Listen. I'll meet you in that rum hole we stopped at earlier. Bring me some news! If I'm not there, wait for me."

Without looking back, Larkin leads his horse across the trampled bramble path into the woods.

I turn to face the town. Geneva squats on the north shore of Seneca Lake like a toad in a mud hole. My thighs are sore from riding, so I walk the mare slowly away from the shoreline toward large, heavy buildings that march down both sides of the business district. Trouble lurks here, waiting to pounce, I know it. I'm alone. Larkin's left me.

As much as I hate to admit it, Wixumlee's right. It's my fault Beany ran away. How stupid of me to stop paying attention to the girl. I never should have let Beany get the upper hand. I should have challenged her whenever she blabbed those crazy rescue plans. I let my responsibility toward Beany slide. Got pampered by clean clothes, a warm coat—gloves! So Beany was led astray, as much by me as Wixumlee.

I walk the mare at a snail's pace, my heart thumping harder with each step. The only way to make it up to Beany is to find her.

Bring me some news Larkin ordered.

I stop in front of a narrow, windowless pub. Not the tavern where the limpy man whispered to Larkin and drew the double RR. A different pub. A groggery. The best place besides the towpath to find information.

I wrap the mare's reins around a hitching post, pull open the heavy brown door and step inside. The pub is dark, and I hang by the door until the inside takes shape. A stained oak bar. Small tables. Men. It's quiet inside. No one at the bar turns to stare. I glance from the bar to a table in front of me.

Sitting on a bench, his back to the door is Pa. Opposite him— glaring at me—is Nicky Pappo. My stomach lurches and bile rises in my throat.

I knew it! What greater proof Pappo's a man-hunter than to catch him sharing a table with my old man—the most evil, vengeful, murderous, proven slave catcher in western New York. If only Larkin was here to see. Or Quin. Or even Cooper. They would believe Cooper.

Eyes still on me, Pappo whispers something to Pa, but the old drunk doesn't turn around. He pulls down his shirt front and shows the cut from Larkin's knife. He's turning Larkin in! Telling Pappo Larkin is searching for Beany and Talbot! Pappo fills Pa's glass from the bottle on the table between them. Pushes the whole bottle within Pa's reach. Then Pappo stands up slowly, his eyes linked with mine. Unblinking.

I spin, punch the heavy door open with both hands and run.

Hunched in the limpy man's tavern where I'm supposed to meet Larkin and bring him some news, I tell myself I did not ruin the mission. I didn't! I stumbled on Pappo and he's wondering why—guessing why—I'm not in Black Rock. But so what? Pappo had already cornered Pa and was pumping him about runaways when I walked in. Pa had already traded Beany and Talbot—and prob'ly Molly—for a bottle of booze before I got there. Like he'd traded August.

But I could have been braver. I didn't have to *run*.

Seneca Falls is my hometown, and I can come back any time I want.

I rub my forehead with both hands. You ran, Tess, you ran.

Dang! I should have ignored the way Pappo's glare sliced through me like a blade. I should have grinned, bought Pa another drink, chatted them up and strutted out cocky and confident. Like the old days.

Instead, I ran like a mouse from a cat, telling Pappo as plainly as if I'd squealed it from the rooftop that I suspected him of treachery.

Stop! Dammit, Tess, it ain't your fault! Who knows how long Pa and Pappo sat in that pub, trading secrets. That old drunk spilled the news about Larkin looking for Beany and Talbot before you got there. Believe it.

I burrow deeper into the corner and watch the door for Larkin. Ten minutes pass, then twenty. I run the scene over and over in my head. Opening the door. Seeing Pa's skinny back and dirty hair. Will Larkin accept this proof that Pappo's a slave catcher? Or at least an anti-abolitionist spy?

I bet Pappo was looking for this runaway Molly, even before Pa told him about Beany. I bet he gets regular telegrams from plantation owners wanting him to hunt down escaped slaves. This wasn't some chance meeting in a gin joint between Pa and Pappo, oh no. Pa's a regular contact, I'm sure. And Pappo's in that slave ring with those two man hunters who snatched Talbot. That's why they're all in Geneva at the same time.

Pappo wants to catch Beany to get back at Wixumlee for treating him like pig drool. Pappo's sending Beany south. And won't he enjoy Wixumlee's agony when he lets her know Beany and Talbot are lost forever.

The tavern owner scowls at me, so I dig in my pocket for a coin to buy a cup of soup. Just as I sit back down, a gust of wind chills the room and Larkin's bulk fills the doorway. White crystals sparkle on his black hair and mustache. His eyes dig me out of the darkness and he jerks his head for me to come. Reluctantly, I slide from the bench and walk outside.

Larkin stands between his horse and mine.

"You want to tell me why I found your horse covered with snow, tied in front of a doggery?"

I swallow hard. "You didn't find Talbot?"

"I'm asking the questions!"

I drop my head.

"Look at me. What the heck happened?"

I take a deep breath. "I saw him, Larkin! Wixumlee wouldn't believe I saw him at Sandy Town, but I saw him this afternoon with my Pa!"

"Who?"

"Nicky Pappo! He's a slave catcher. He's looking for—."

"Sweet Jesus." Larkin stares across the road toward the partially frozen lake, then back at me.

"He's looking—."

"Shut up!"

"It's true!"

Larkin grabs my collar and shakes me. "Quiet!" His voice drops low. "Listen." He pulls me and the horses into the lean-to. "I saw a girl—doesn't look like Beany—must be Molly—near a fishing shack on the west side of the lake. She's chained outside. Her and Talbot."

I stare at him then press my face into the mare's neck. "But you—you didn't rescue them."

"Alone? Am I dim-witted? I came back for you."

My body convulses and I grasp the mare's saddle horn for support. Larkin wants me to fight—hand to hand with slave catchers. I gather the mare's reins.

"So, it was Molly's campfire we saw on shore," I say. "The slavers spotted her, she ran through the woods, and they caught her."

As much as I want to rescue Talbot, I'm still thinking that when we mount up and Larkin takes off toward the shack, I can bolt in the opposite direction. Gallop away and never be seen again. Larkin won't follow—not now. It could work. I could be free.

He watches me closely. Can he read my mind?

"I don't know what happened around that campfire. Might not have anything to do with Molly. Or Beany." Larkin's gaze holds me. "Maybe Molly was holed up in that shack getting warm, those hunters had the same idea and stumbled on her by chance."

"Or Nicky Pappo told them where to look!"

He scowls. "Shut pan with that Pappo crap. Mount up."

CHAPTER THIRTY-FOUR

From the outside, the fishing shack looks a lot like the trapper's shed on the Genesee River near Avon — not fit for human habitation. We tie our horses near a stand of pines and creep across the snowy ground to within a hundred feet of where Talbot and Molly are chained. The sky throws icy flakes and the wind gusting off the lake is wicked enough to whip cream. Talbot has given Molly his coat and she stands behind him protectively with her back to the lake in a pitiful attempt to block the wind. What's left of a cotton dress flaps around her skinny, bare legs as she shifts from one rag-wrapped foot to the other.

It's late afternoon, nearly dark. Most folks are heading home from work to a tasty supper — looking forward to sitting around a hot fire, telling stories — tempted to bundle down early into warm, dry beds. But not in my corner of the world. Here on the west shore of Seneca Lake, the only people mildy comfortable are slave catchers tucked inside a fishing shack, out of the wind.

"The odds are good." Larkin brushes snow off his lashes. "There's two of them and —."

"There's three of them! You forgot the owner."

"He went back to Rochester. The guy with the limp told me in the tavern."

"Well, you still shouldn't count me as one full —."

"I *am* counting you and you better not disappoint me!" Larkin holds my gaze. "If we can get Talbot loose —."

"He's chained! You can break a chain?"

Without taking his eyes off me, Larkin pulls a hammer from his coat pocket and raises it to within an inch of my nose. Even though Coop broke August's jail chain with a hammer, I say, "That doesn't look strong enough to —."

"Shut pan! Are you looking for a smash?" Threats. Always threats.

I peer down the snowy slope at the shivering boy and girl huddled against the wind. It's their own fault they're in trouble. Nobody kicked that gal Molly off her plantation. She chose to run and knew the risks. And Talbot should have been smarter than to take off after Beany. And Larkin—Larkin to the rescue! I don't want any more trouble. Yet I'm threatened, bullied into being the big, brave rescuer I don't want to be—know I can't be. I can't save Talbot. I can't save anybody.

Looking sideways at the hammer, I ask, "Any other weapons?"

Larkin pulls a short-nosed gun from his coat pocket. Pulls his pant leg tight around his calf to show the outline of a knife. I remember the fancy dagger I flicked with the canal boys. The shiny blade that cut Big Slaver's cheek before bouncing away on the towpath.

"What do you have?" Larkin asks.

"Nothin'."

"Don't you have a knife or something?"

"No."

"Cripes!" He puts the gun in my hand.

"No!"

"Quiet! I'm going down to break that chain. You watch the door. Anybody comes out—shoot him."

I start to cry. Larkin slaps my head, his disgust obvious. "You act like you've never been in a fight."

"I don't know how to shoot." I gulp sobs.

"Point it and shoot it."

"You take it."

Larkin grabs my collar and shakes me. "When we get home I'm gonna clobber you! Right now I don't have time. But later—you are gonna get it!"

I almost laugh. I'm going into battle with an idiot! We are about to die. Nobody will ever clobber anybody.

But I take the gun and point it at the shack, while Larkin slips down the slope. When Talbot sees him, the boy's face lights up. Larkin raises a finger to his lips, takes off his coat and wraps it around Talbot's quaking shoulders. He says something to Molly then starts clanging away at the chain with his hammer.

Ting! Ting! Ting! I hear the tinny chink of steel on steel. Those slavers must hear it, too. Any minute they'll bust out of the shack and I'll have to shoot this dang gun. I grip the cold pistol with my bare right hand and pull a glove onto my left with my teeth. I wrap Ma's Christmas scarf around my face, and my hot breath melts the snow settling on it. Smelly, wet wool.

Bam! The door to the fishing shack whips open, hitting the wall. Startled, I drop the gun. Snatching for it in the snow, I look back in panic at the shack. A man hangs in the doorway. I look again. Pa steps out into the wind, head cocked to listen. Odds now — three to two.

I find the gun, brush it off with my gloved hand and point it. Larkin is still pounding the chain. Ears full of wind and hammering, he didn't hear the door open. If anyone comes out — shoot, that's what he said. Well, someone did come out. Pa!

Shoot, Tess. Improve the odds. *Shoot!*

I watch Pa move toward the side of the shack where Larkin hammers the chain. I squeeze the trigger. *Zing!* A splinter of wood flies off the siding and Pa jumps. Alerted, Larkin reaches for his knife. In a panic, Pa spins back toward the doorway, hands covering his head.

"Shoot!" Larkin screams into the wind. I can't hear him, but I see the word form on his lips. Furious, he seems to double in size. Taller, wider, stronger, wilder, he looms protectively over the chained prisoners. "Shoot!"

Suddenly, the two slave hunters, guns drawn, crowd the doorway. Pa pushes past them into the shack.

One slave catcher turns toward where Talbot and Molly cower near Larkin. I take aim. *Zing!* He grabs his shoulder, stumbles around the corner, comes face to face with Larkin, and slips to the ground.

Following the sound of the gunshot, the second slave catcher looks toward where I crouch but ducks back inside the shack.

If the shack has a back door, that slaver and Pa can be sneaking up on Larkin from behind. This gun has four bullets left. I wish I could put them exactly where I want them — but I'd refused to learn to shoot. Made a fool of myself crumbling up on the sand when Larkin put a rifle in my hands.

Zing! Chink! Metal explodes. *Zing! Chink!* Larkin shoots off the chains holding Talbot and Molly with the dead slaver's gun, and soon they're running toward our horses. I move to follow but stop. Larkin isn't running with them. He must be waiting for the second slave catcher — and Pa.

I pull the scratchy scarf away from my face. I want to follow Talbot, but an equally powerful urge says stay with Larkin. Suddenly, the sound of a rifle blast ricochets across the lake and back. I see Pa running crazily alongside the shed, chased by a cyclone of snow. Crashing along the ground, locked in combat are Larkin and the second slave catcher. Pa points the rifle at the twisting, snarling men, aiming here—then there—trying to get the bead on Larkin.

I stare at the cold pistol in my hand. I point the gun. *Just squeeze the trigger, Tess.* Pa raises his rifle belly high.

Shoot, Tess!

There's a blast of gunfire, a shocking silence, and the slave catcher shakes himself out of Larkin's grasp.

The big man falls onto his back, spread eagle, and Pa raises the rifle over his head in celebration. The slave catcher kicks at Larkin, who lies motionless. Pa says something, waves the rifle in my direction then points after Talbot and Molly. They make their decision and charge after their escaping prisoners. I slide down the slope, fall on the ground beside Larkin, and watch white snow turn red in a wide arc beneath him.

"Larkin." I feel for breath beneath his nose. Touch him gently. "Larkin?"

He opens his eyes. They're washed with pain. "Go after them, Tessie."

I burst into tears. "No! You're hurt."

He paws weakly at my coat. "Go get Talbot and Molly."

"I'll stay with you." Blood seeps out of a ragged hole in Larkin's shirt. "You're hurt bad."

"Help's coming. But you gotta go after Talbot—and—." Larkin's eyes close and his head tips to one side.

"Larkin!" I brush snow off his face. Glance at Pa's boot prints chasing after the wide misshapen forms that were Molly's rag-covered feet. I lift Larkin's head. "Open your eyes!"

When he does, the pain in them makes me wince. "Stuff snow inside my shirt. Right on the bullet hole. Then go after them."

"No."

"Do it! Pack me with snow and go get them!" His head falls back.

I scoop handfuls of cold white snow onto the red hole in Larkin's creamy brown skin.

"That's good, girl. Now—do your job."

My heart breaks at the sound of his ragged breath. His eyes fade.

"Larkin?"

"Dammit, Tess! Do what I tell you!"

I stand and try to study the tracks left by the pursuers and the pursued, but I'm crying too hard to see clearly. Wiping my nose on my sleeve, I look down once more. Larkin's eyes burn into mine, but only briefly. I gulp my tears, turn and follow the tracks toward the shoreline.

Whimpering like a lost child, I stumble through a stand of scratchy pines. An icy wind blows off Seneca Lake and snatches at the ends of my Christmas scarf. I hear shouts where we tied the horses and fumble in my pocket for the cold pistol with its last four bullets. I draw the gun out, and it hangs limp in my hand, shiny and unwanted.

There's another shout, then I see them—Talbot holding on to the gelding's saddle, trying to mount, and Pa snatching at his legs, trying to pull him down. But where's the other slave catcher? Larkin's horse dances to the side, dragging Talbot with him. My mare tugs on the reins tying her to a tree and whinnies.

Larkin said *go get them*. Breathing shallowly, I jog slowly toward the horses, looking around for Molly, and from the corner of my eye see a small, dark shape huddled on the ground a short way off to my right. I squint. *Is* that the ground? No. Not the ground. That's the lake. The water. Something—somebody—is out on the water. On the ice! Molly? I can't make out a head or legs, just a small, round mound.

If it is Molly, why are she and Talbot separated? Why is he with the horse and she's on the ice? What idiot would take off across a half-frozen lake? I recall the cold Genesee River rising up my legs to my chest. No! Oh, no! I'm not going out on that sloppy ice after that crazy girl!

"Get down, boy!" Pa shouts. I look away from the lake and see him slap at the horse and rider. The big gelding screams and rises on its hind legs, Talbot in the saddle clinging to its neck.

The frightened animal flicks its hooves. I hear Pa's surprised yelp and watch him melt onto the ground. Talbot whirls the horse like a cavalryman and gallops toward town. My mare yanks free and follows.

I hang onto the trunk of a leafless maple, waiting for Pa to get up. Seconds pass. A minute. There's no sign of the slave catcher, so I creep up to Pa's body. And here he is, motionless, on his back, eyes wide open, a wedge-shaped gouge in his forehead exposing the bone. I stuff the gun slowly into my pocket then—for some reason—can't stop myself from making Ma's cross over the man who terrorized my childhood and sent me down a trail of brutality and revenge. Or from sucking in one long sob.

"Hey, girlie. Come on, now. Come back here."

Startled, I rush from Pa's body to the shelter of trees and look back at the lake. The slave catcher stands near the frosty shoreline, but he's not calling to me.

"Come back, darlin'. That ice gonna break out from under you."

He's calling Molly. I strain to see across the blackness and pick out the girl laying flat on her belly on the cold, rough ice. She crawls farther away from the shoreline, looking back once, twice, to see if the slave catcher follows her. Sweet Jesus, why would she go out there? With a whole country of solid ground to run in, she crawls out onto a half-frozen lake!

Well, I'm not going after her. I'll wait for those Railroaders from the tavern. Larkin said somebody's coming. He must have planned for reinforcements before we headed for the fishing shack. He was whispering to that limpy man, wasn't he? If he'd told me the plan earlier—instead of when he's shot flat and blood red—I'd know what to do now. But once again, I'm the last to know. Nobody ever tells me nothin'. Always send me in blind.

The slave catcher tests the ice with his boot. He's not dumb enough to go out there, is he? He won't follow that gal Molly. I take a step away from the trees. He bounces lightly on the ice, rubs his chin and bounces again on both feet.

"You just wait there for me, girly." He drops down to his knees then his belly.

Sweet Jesus! Don't go after that crazy girl.

"I'm coming, sweetheart. I'll bring you back here where it's safe." Then he wriggles like a lizard onto the ice.

Damn! I'm not crawling out there! I'm not getting caught in a death struggle with a murderous man hunter in the middle of a frozen lake.

Talbot, where'd you go? Please come back and bring somebody with you. I listen hard for horses, wagons, men on foot, but the air is eerily silent.

"Go 'way!" Molly waves a fist toward shore. "Leave me alone!"

Her voice, thin and frail, draws me farther from the trees, but not to the water. I'm not brave. I'm not Larkin. Larkin would have clobbered that guy by now and had the kid back. But Larkin is laying flat in the snow, bleeding to death.

With mounting dread, I watch the slave catcher crawl to within fifty feet of Molly. I bend over, slap my hands over my ears and try to keep Larkin's order — *go get them* — out of my head.

Go get them, Tess.

No! I won't! I'll wait for Talbot. Talbot went for help. He'll come back with lots of gun-toting Railroaders before that slaver grabs Molly back to shore. I bite down on my chapped knuckles. But what if that hunter *does* drag her back to shore? What will I do then — all alone in the almost dark?

I close my eyes and see August stretched out between Beany and Big Slaver, both yanking, both demanding, both ripping her of strength and sanity. I couldn't help August. I can't help Molly. She needs Larkin.

Larkin! Larkin's dying in the snow. With failing breath Larkin gave me one last order. *Go get them.*

He doesn't know it's now *go get her.*

"Wait for me darlin'." The slave catcher's call is sweet with deceit.

I stand up straight and touch the gun in my pocket through my coat. Four bullets left. That's a lot. What if — what if I sneak up behind him on the ice — he's looking at Molly, not behind him — and plug him four times.

Bang! Bang! Bang! Bang!

That'll be easy. Won't it?

"Come on, girly. Come back to me now."

"Go! Go 'way!" Molly tosses the words over her shoulder and keeps crawling.

I wrap my hand around the hard steel in my pocket. I couldn't help August. Four bullets left. I take a deep breath. I didn't help August. Take another breath. Pat the gun. August.

I pull the gun from my pocket.

Knees shaking, I tiptoe across the wet gravelly sand to the shoreline. Now I see that the ice doesn't meet the sand. About three feet of icy, gray water separates the two. I'll have to slosh through bone-numbing water just to reach the ice.

Larkin said *go get them*.

When I step into the lake my sturdy brogans protect my feet for a few seconds before the water—so cold it burns—sends a fire-like iciness up my legs. I shiver but sweat runs down my forehead into my eyes. Sweet Jesus, I'm freezing and sweating at the same time. Just like I did in that cave after I ran from Rochester after the baby went—.

The frigid water soaks my pants, but I stalk through the clinging cold until I step onto the ice. Shaking, I take a ragged breath.

"Come on, baby girl. Wait for me, sweetheart. Wait for papa."

The slave catcher's ugly wheedling tone—so much like Pa's—full of lies and treachery—sends fiery anger sweeping through me. Instantly, I'm burning hot.

"Let me help you, darlin'."

A maddening heat spreads from head to toe and pictures of August's stabbed chest, the lost baby, and Larkin's bloody wound flood my brain.

"Papa's comin' for you, girly."

Three innocents lost violently because people like Pa and this man hunter are allowed to have their way.

"You wait for me now. Don't go out too far."

Strengthening my grip on the pistol, I drop down, spread out flat, and crawl across the ice.

Determined.

Committed.

August—the baby—Larkin—the horror of their loss fuels my quest. But it's not revenge I seek, but justice. I lost them all. I won't lose Molly.

The slave hunter concentrates on his prey and I gain ground quickly. I'm thirty feet from him when Molly glances over her shoulder, stiffens, and stops.

No! Don't watch me. Don't tip him off.

"Yeah, wait up there, girly," the slaver croons, unaware I'm behind him. I raise my hand to my lips and shake my head. Shut up, kid. I'm your friend.

"Go! Get out!" Molly sounds more fearful now than before.

"Almost gotcha!" The slave catcher giggles like a boy reaching for a tadpole.

Suddenly Molly rises up on her knees, faces me and screams. The slave catcher flips around and glares, first at me, then behind me. A new terror grips my heart. Is someone stalking *me*? The pistol slips in my suddenly sweaty palm. I look behind.

Beany! It's Beany! Scampering along like a sled dog on hands and knees! And crawling fast behind her—reaching out to grab her—Nicky Pappo!

Bad odds! Bad odds! Puke rises in my throat and burns as I swallow it back down.

I aim the gun—*Bam!*—and shoot that slave catcher where he sits.

"Get down, Beany!" I point the pistol at Pappo. I lean right, then left, trying to aim.

"Tess!" Beany shakes her head and keeps crawling.

"Lay down!" I scream.

"Put that gun down!" Pappo yells. He's almost reached Beany.

I slide far to one side into a frigid puddle. The ice is soft here. Aiming at Pappo, I pull the trigger. Nicky yelps and slaps his shoulder but keeps crawling.

I scramble to my knees, aim and shoot again. With an eerie creak, the ice opens up. I shoot one last time and slip underwater.

Within seconds I'm up again, raging, knowing before I look that my last shot missed. Now I'm in the water thrashing, and Beany and Molly are up on the ice alone with the last slave catcher—Nicky Pappo.

"Tessie!" Beany slides to the rim of the broken ice and reaches out.

I slap her hand away and try to get my own grip on the icy slab, but my frozen fingertips slip.

"Help—Molly." My face is stiff with ice. My teeth rattle. "R-Run." The empty gun is frozen to my hand.

Pappo's pale face appears next to Beany's. When he reaches out and grabs my hair, I swing the gun, catching him on the ear.

"Ow! Dammit!" Pappo grabs his head and cusses, but doesn't let me go. I lurch backward, pushing off the ice with my hands, and pull Pappo over the top of me into the lake. A mouthful of icy water lands in my stomach like a sharp rock.

"Run." I can barely breathe the word. "You—Molly—run." Beany, tears freezing on her cheeks, stretches her arms across the water.

"No, Tessie! Don't."

I push away again, grab Pappo around the neck, and sink with him below the surface. When we rise, I feel my head bump against solid ice above me. Pappo struggles to unclamp my arms. The bullet that winged his shoulder gives me advantage. He's bleeding. In pain. Panicked.

He isn't prepared to die.

But I have made my choice.

CHAPTER THIRTY-FIVE

Hell is spending my entire death with Nicky Pappo. Feeling my arms frozen around his neck and watching bubbles blow past my face as he breathes my name. I'm dead. It's over. Leave me alone, Nicky.

I'm so, so cold. Yes, a cold, wet eternity is my punishment for being a coward. For not saving August. For losing Lucy's money. For letting Talbot get chewed by dogs. For peeing my pants. For letting a baby float over the falls. For picking the wrong house — blue or number four. For getting Quin stabbed and the rest of the gang — including my own brother Cooper — bruised and bloodied. For losing Larkin.

I hear Nicky's voice, taunting me.

On the other hand, it's kind of funny that Hell is cold and wet. Ma should know Hell isn't hot and dry. Not that Ma has to worry.

"Tess." Pappo's face floats above mine, shimmering in a haze of ice cold pain.

Shut up, Nicky! Leave me alone. I'm dead. You're just mad 'cause you're dead, too.

I entered my icy Hell, hanging like a side of beef around Nicky Pappo's neck, pulling him down with me, down under the freezing water. I was glad when the ice closed above us. Happy, because I knew I could hold on to him long enough for Beany and Molly to crawl off the frozen lake. Long enough to wipe one more slave catcher off the earth.

"Tess."

Larkin? What's he doing down here in my cold, wet Hell? Larkin's good. A bully but a good man. He doesn't belong in Hell. Larkin was shot dead by a mean drunk and should be in Heaven.

Ugh. Pa. He's down here somewhere. I have to spend my whole death with him, too.

Hey! Put me down! Who's this? The Devil's cronies come to drag me off. Drop me in a box. Throw hot coals over me. What happened to cold and wet? Guess I'll burn in Hell after all.

"Tessie." Chocolate candy eyes. Watery. Sad. Melted pudding. "Tessie."

Beany's in Hell, too? Did that dopey kid jump in after me? Dang! This is not fair. Even if she drowned herself trying to save me, Beany belongs in Heaven—with August and Larkin. Does everybody who dies on the same day go to the same place? Pretty soon those ugly slave catchers will show up.

Cripes, things get messed up even in death.

CHAPTER THIRTY-SIX

Hell is sniffing cooked cabbage for the rest of my death.

"Wake up, Tess."

Nicky! Get your face out of here! Go be dead somewhere else.

"Here's some warm soup, honey." Mariana? The whole dang bunch of them died and went to Hell.

What's that shrieking? Hell's hearing some crazy woman getting her toes smashed with a hammer.

"Come on, honey. Somebody take Savannah, please. Go back upstairs, darlin'. Is that girl waking up?" Wixumlee. The Devil.

I squeeze my eyes tight, afraid to see Wixumlee with hooves and a spiked tail, waving a pitchfork, commanding Hell like she did Earth. Something—somebody—grips my dead hand. Don't open your eyes. Wixumlee's caught you for good now.

But I do open them, against my will, and see a hard, bare stomach. I look up and here's Larkin, a big, white bandage wrapped around his ribs, holding my hand. Okay. Larkin can be dead with me in Hell.

I start to smile, but then the most frightening, most sickening sight pops into my vision. Nicky Pappo, white bandage on his shoulder, another covering his ear, leans over me and grins.

"She's awake!" Pappo drops his face close to mine, and I feel his warm breath on my face. He doesn't *look* dead.

Larkin smoothes back my hair. "Hey, Tessie, welcome back." His smile is warm enough to melt granite.

Larkin and Nicky—side by side—grinning like naughty brothers.

My head goes blank.

CHAPTER THIRTY-SEVEN

"You guys have the same dumb smile." I figure neither one will smack me, laying here weak as a kitten in the Black Rock kitchen. "You look—."

"We're cousins," Larkin says throwing an arm around Nicky.

Maybe I really am dead!

"Yeah, his old man and my old man were brothers." Nicky nods.

Cousins? Larkin and Nicky Pappo? One's black. One's white.

"And Quin's my uncle," Larkin says proudly.

It only gets worse.

"How'd you—?" I shift in the fancy chaise longe Wixumlee brought down from her own bedroom. Beany sits closeby, watchful, in a small chair. Talbot hangs over the back, smiling. Quin winks at me and takes a big bite out of a ham sandwich. Savannah stirs something on the stove but turns one sad then one happy eye on me, as if unsure of her mood.

"Oh, it's a long story," Wixumlee says, waving her hands impatiently. "The same old story with a new twist."

When I gawk at the polka dot cousins, Nicky exclaims, "My Pa was a white, antislavery minister in Mississippi. Mama died when I was a baby."

Larkin chimes in. "Those brothers should have been named Good and Evil. The bad brother took advantage of a slave—Quin's sister. She had me and died."

"Like I said," Wixumlee grouses, "an old story with a new twist."

When Quin decided to run from the plantation, he took Larkin and came to Nicky's pa for help. They all fled Mississippi and ended up in a Louisville tavern run by Mariana, who introduced them to

Wixumlee, a young dancer at a fancy hotel. When she wasn't prancing onstage, Wixumlee pushed runaway slaves north to freedom. After several moves, the renegade band settled in Black Rock, New York, on the lip of the Erie Canal and a short shipride across Lake Erie to Canada.

Perfect.

"So, you both grew up in the Underground Railroad." I sip from a cup of steaming broth Mariana holds to my lips.

"Yeah, before it even had a name." Larkin sticks a fork handle inside his bandage to scratch his belly. "Nicky brings us information."

"He's my most trusted spy." Wixumlee beams. "A bit crazy sometimes, but always reliable."

I have my doubts. "If you're such a great spy, why did I keep seeing you?"

Pappo turns red and drops his head.

Larkin busts out laughing. "'Cause Nicky's sweet on you!"

Now my face burns. Sweet? Sweet Jesus! I've been wondering if some guy would ever go sweet on me and it turns out to be bald, quirky Nicky Pappo!

"He was keeping an eye on you, Tess." A smile skims Wixumlee's lips but she mumbles, "Lord knows somebody had to." She pokes Nicky's head. "But I was furious! He was jeopardizing our operation. If you could spot him, so could the enemy. But he wouldn't listen to me. Didn't like me sending you on those rescue missions. Said you weren't trained, weren't prepared."

"She wasn't!" Nicky scowls at Wixumlee.

"She was learning!" The General shouts back. "Is it my fault she's slower than a snail?"

"Uh, why didn't you just tell me he was a good guy?"

Everyone falls silent.

"Because I didn't trust you." Wixumlee's eyes flash. "Maybe I still don't."

Groans all around.

"I was determined to keep Nicky's identity secret."

"But it shouldn't have been secret from me!"

"Especially since you were asking her to work for you," Nicky grumbles.

"You mean *telling* me to work for her." I'd lost much of my fear of Wixumlee somewhere beneath the ice.

Wixumlee's glower bounces between me and Nicky. "I only know how to give orders. That's what works." She falls silent, but I still need answers.

"Why didn't you kick me out?"

"Good question! I had my fill after that mess-up with Mama on the Rochester road, but Nicky threw a conniption fit!" She throws up her hands.

"She was as damaged as Beany," Nicky tells her. "She needed help, too."

"I didn't have time to tutor a sissy," she shouts. "Still don't."

"You're impatient," Beany says, touching Wixumlee's sleeve. "You loved me. I wish you had been nicer to Tessie."

Wixumlee's shoulders wiggle with agitation.

"Nicky even started growing his hair, 'cause he thought you'd like him better." Larkin yanks Pappo's curling stub.

I scramble to change the subject. "So, when you guys fought—that was all play?"

"All part of the act." Larkin grins. "Every time we tangled, Nicky slipped me information about runaways heading our way or slave catchers in town.

"Your *GosSlip* job—Nicky set that up," Wixumlee says stiffly.

"Did you know this, Cooper?" I look past Larkin to where my brother sits, massaging a sprained ankle—a souvenir of his struggle to pull me and Pappo off Seneca Lake.

"Not from the beginning." He glances accusingly at Wixumlee.

"I didn't trust you either!" she shouts at him. She jumps up and jams her fists onto her hips. "I'll be honest—."

Quin laughs. "Well, that'll be a first."

"You shush." She swats at him.

I look around, seeing them for the first time. These folks aren't just tied together by a tavern and a Railroad. They're a family.

"I was afraid you two—and especially Tess—would try to get Beany back before she was ready. I wasn't trying to *steal* her," Wixumlee declares. "I just knew she needed time to heal and she wouldn't heal eating scraps in a stable."

Beany jumps up and wraps her arms around Wixumlee to soothe her but comes back to me.

"I'm sorry I was mean to you, Tessie. And for all those bad things I said about my Mama. I don't hate her. I could never hate her. She loved me so much." Beany's eyes fill with tears. "I was just mad—really mad."

I smile weakly, remembering when Beany pushed me out of her bedroom. "But why'd you run off, Beany?"

She shrugs. "I don't know. Just dumb, I guess. I started out going to find where Mama's buried. Then I was gonna find Harriet and go south on her next big rescue. But before I got to Seneca Falls, I found Molly camped beside the lake."

"Molly!" I lurch in my chair. "What happened to Molly?"

"She's fine." Wixumlee waves her hand. "We put her on a boat to Canada. Tell Tess the rest, Beany."

"I wanted to take Molly with me—I was sure Harriet could help her—but she didn't trust anybody. She wanted to stay in that shack, while I went to your ma's house for food and clothes."

"But Ma said she didn't see you!"

"She didn't," Wixumlee says, wagging her finger at the girl. "Nicky caught Beany on the Geneva road to Seneca Falls and stashed her at that Underground tavern.

I glance at Pappo, who smiles.

Beany clasps my hand in both of hers. "I'm sorry it turned out so bad, Tessie. I'm sorry you and Nicky almost drowned. Larkin got shot. Cooper hurt his leg."

"We didn't just almost drown." Pappo sheds his shyness and points a finger at me. "Tess *tried* to drown me. She pulled me under the ice!"

"I thought you were a slave catcher!"

"I'm trying to pry your arms off my neck, and you're hanging on, hell bent on murdering me! When we bumped our heads under that ice, I thought we were gonners." Nicky stares at me accusingly. "You tried to *kill* me."

"I tried to kill a *slave catcher!*"

"And you would have died yourself, Tess." Wixumlee picks up my hand gently. "You were willing to give your life so Beany and Molly could escape."

I look down at our joined hands. The room is silent.

"See, I told you Tess would come around. Just needed a good reason." Nicky smiles at me, and I see his grin really is a lot like Larkin's.

Larkin punches Nicky's arm. "Yeah, she had a good reason—getting rid of you!"

Nicky points to the bandage on his shoulder, then to his head. "She shot me, pistol-whipped me, and tried to drown me. I'm just damn lucky Coop came and pulled us out."

Wixumlee had sent my brother to Geneva after Nicky telegraphed he'd found Beany. By this time, Coop knew Nicky was a good guy. When Beany snuck off again to help Molly, Nicky took off after her. When Talbot galloped up saying Larkin was shot, Coop formed an abolitionist posse and set out for the lake.

"When I got there, Beany was standing at the shoreline, straining to see out on the water," Nicky says.

"I could see Tessie way out on the ice and I went crazy." Beany grips my hand.

"She crawled out there so fast all I could do was race after her," Nicky growls. "I was burning mad!"

When the Underground posse arrived at the lake, they saw Beany and Molly on the ice, screaming and pointing at the water. While Coop and Talbot crawled to their aid, Beany managed to snag Nicky's coat.

With pure luck, Nicky and I had floated out from beneath the ice, frozen in a death grip, which made it easier to pull us out. Coop twisted his ankle dragging us to shore, where Gerrit Smith and a band of Railroaders waited with a wagon, blankets and heated bricks to thaw us out.

They found Larkin and hauled us all back to the Geneva tavern, where a doctor and roomful of praying Railroad women revived us enough to weather the long wagon ride back to Black Rock. Nicky — apparently a hard man to kill — recovered quickly, but everyone worried I wouldn't make it.

"We didn't think you'd ever wake up." Mariana fusses with the clean sweater she's pulled over my head. "And when you seemed awake, you mumbled the strangest things."

"I thought I died and went to Hell."

Mariana scowls. "No wonder we almost lost you! You gave up!"

"Well, I was *mixed* up. I didn't know if I was alive or dead. I kept seeing Nicky's face hanging over me."

"That's because Nicky never left your side. Neither did Larkin." Coop smiles at me. "They were scared sick you were gonna die, Tessie."

Larkin and Nicky nod like eager puppies.

"I knew you'd make it," Coop boasts. "I figured if you got up the courage to go out on that ice, the old Tess Riley was back!"

"The old Tess is back!" Beany raises her arms in victory and dances in a circle with Talbot. Everyone hoots and hollers as if they'd just won a high stakes horse race. Quin grabs Wixumlee and dances her around the kitchen. Savannah drops her stirring spoon and twirls in some kind of wild toe dance.

I stare at them thinking maybe I have died and Hell is just a confusing place where everybody changes personalities. Everybody except Wixumlee. She knits her brow and swats at Quin but he won't let her go.

"Well, now that I'm back, are you gonna let me in on stuff? Tell me what's going on. The *truth*. So I don't make dumb mistakes— like try to drown your number one spy. I gotta know who's on our side."

Our side. *Our people*. Will I finally be one of *our people*?

Everyone looks at Wixumlee. Quin's snake-inked arms wrap around her shoulders and after a tense second or two, he shakes her. "Stop being stubborn. You know you like the girl."

Wixumlee grimaces but mumbles, "Well, okay. Tess is in. No more secrets."

"Wixumlee, you are so naughty," Quin scolds. "You just like to be coaxed." And he plants a big kiss smack in the middle of her mouth.

Everybody cheers and stamps their feet. The men fake punches at each other's bellies then remember their wounds and slap hands instead.

"Oh. And Larkin?" I meet the big man's eyes. "You don't ever talk about pounding me again."

He drops his jaw in shock. "Ah, Tessie, I'd never pound you."

"Well, you threaten often enough." I pout.

He wags his head. "Yeah, yeah, I say it, lots of times, but I'd never do it."

"Why not?"

Larkin throws up his hands, disbelieving. "Cripes, Tessie, you're a girl."

The old wiggly smile plays on his lips. He runs his hand gently down my shiny, dark hair and winks at Nicky, who glares at him with lashless eyes.